THE END OF THE ROAD

THE END OF THE ROAD

ANDREW WELSH-HUGGINS

THE MYSTERIOUS PRESS
NEW YORK

THE END OF THE ROAD

Mysterious Press
An Imprint of Penzler Publishers
58 Warren Street
New York, N.Y. 10007

First Mysterious Press edition

Interior design by Maria Fernandez

Library of Congress Cataloging-in-Publication Data is available.

ISBN: 978-1-61316-382-5
eBook ISBN: 978-1-61316-386-3

10 9 8 7 6 5 4 3 2 1

Printed in the United States of America
Distributed by W. W. Norton & Company

For William McCulloh

Teacher, mentor, friend

"Nobody's fool, that stranger," wise Penelope said,
"he sees how things could go. Surely no men on earth
can match that gang for reckless, deadly schemes."

— *The Odyssey*, Robert Fagles translation

Hello Ohio, the back roads
I know Ohio, like the back of my hand
Alone Ohio, where the river bends
And it's strange to see your story end

— "Ohio," Over the Rhine

1

When the bullet tore through Myles's left shoulder, nicking the brachial artery and spinning him around in a cloud of blood like a kite caught in a sudden wind shear, Penny was just over three miles away at the costume shop, arguing with a girl wearing too much mascara about the store's return policy and thinking about how much she'd rather be home.

When the second bullet punctured Myles's chest and careened through his right lung, sending him to the ground as his mouth bloomed red and the pain sheared his brain in two, Penny was doing her best to hold her tongue, because she really needed this job, not that the girl was helping with so much attitude. Attitude and lies—like Penny believed for one second the girl had put the cowgirl costume on once and taken it off again when she saw it didn't fit, and not pranced around some party in it half the night.

When Myles, to Pryor's surprise, rolled to his right and pumped off three shots of his own—*pop-pop-pop*—shattering the side window behind the driver's seat of the van and forcing Pryor to squeeze his good eye shut as tiny, gravel-sized shards of glass sprayed his face, Penny stopped midsentence, *this close* to tearing the girl a new one, because of a sudden, inexplicable feeling that something wasn't right.

She paused for a full five seconds, wrestling with her thoughts, before dismissing the worry as nothing more than a continuation of the dread she'd felt since picking Myles up at the prison the day before, followed by Pryor's frightening midnight visit several hours later. Who wouldn't think dark thoughts given all that? It was a miracle she was able to do her job when it came right down to it.

And so it was that when the van raced through the stop sign, barreling down the street because of the shattered window and because of Archie's insistence that there'd been a cop right behind them—a claim Pryor doubted as soon as it left Archie's mouth—Penny was taking a deep breath and offering the girl store credit as a compromise. As a result, she had no way of knowing that the last thing Myles heard before the darkness swallowed him was the screech of tires and the sound of a child's voice yelling and his own wet, ragged breathing, each gasp slower than the last.

2

Pryor asked again, even though he knew the answer wouldn't change. "Sure that was a cop?"

"I'm sure." Archie's voice sullen and low.

"Sure?"

"*Sure*," Archie said.

Pryor had his doubts.

They were parked down the street from Michigan's apartment listening to the sound of sirens fill the air. No way in hell they could go anywhere close to Pryor's or Archie's at this point. He thought briefly about Mae and her place, if you could even call the squalid squat where she stayed a room, and then remembered he'd already taken care of that headache and she was out of the picture. Someone else's problem now. So it was Michigan in the end, and it worked out in a way because he had the cardboard and the tape they needed to cover the shattered window which beat having to go buy supplies some place, which would have added yet another complication to the mix. That was all Pryor needed, because he had to think carefully about what should happen next. Very carefully.

Baby—Myles—had thrown him for a loop. He had to give him that. What kind of idiot goes jogging with a target on his back like the one

Pryor put there the night before, warning him on the porch of Penny's mother's? But there he'd been, catching Pryor and them unawares as Archie drove the van around the corner at the bottom of Eureka, and before Pryor realized what was happening Myles produced a gun from somewhere and a sharp *crack* spider-webbed the windshield right where he was sitting. Leaning out the window, returning fire, Pryor thought: *It wasn't supposed to go like this. I was the one supposed to get a drop on* him. None of that would have mattered though, because his aim was true and Myles went down like a dog, red blossoming on his chest and in his mouth. And it would have been all right and he would have finished him then and there if Myles hadn't surprised them again, firing back after he was down and bleeding out, and if Archie hadn't suddenly yelled, "Cop!" and gunned it up the street before Pryor took the kill shot.

Except Pryor really wasn't sure the car behind them had been a cruiser. Which made him wonder what the fuck Archie was up to.

It also made him wonder again what Myles was thinking, running around like that. And whether he had counted too carefully on Archie and Michigan keeping their mouths shut if his plan had worked and he'd taken Myles out.

"Where to now?" Michigan said, interrupting his thoughts.

"I'm thinking."

"There goes another cop," Archie said.

Pryor looked up and saw the third cruiser in a row streak past up on Broad. When it was gone, he turned and saw that both Archie and Michigan were staring at him. The look in their eyes made him feel like a mother hen. Always taking care of them. Always the one they went to for direction. Mother fucking hen. No. Not a chicken, he thought. He was a, what, that guy with the stick with sheep. A shepherd. That's what. A shepherd with a bunch of sheep. Seems like all he had to deal with anymore. Mae too—until last night. At least that was done with. At least that problem was out of the way.

And just like that, he made his decision.

"We'll go on out there, I guess."

"Out where?"

"To the farm."

"Now?"

"Now," Pryor said.

"We have everything we need?"

Everything but Baby, Pryor thought bitterly. Pissed at him for not cooperating, and now pissed at him for not dying properly.

Though part of that was on Archie.

Because he wasn't sure that had been a cop behind them.

"Yes," Pryor said. "I've got everything I need. It won't be long now."

"Hope you're right," Archie said, starting the engine as yet another cruiser roared east along Broad.

"Me too," Pryor said.

3

He'd been out running. That's what Mama told her as they drove like hell to the hospital, the manager's cries of protest at her untimely departure still echoing in her ears. Good riddance. The guy was a perv and a creep, anyway, always staring at her chest when they were alone in the store. Mack was safely back at the house with Ma-Maw watching him. Early evening, light fading, but not quite dark yet. A time of day that was supposed to be safe. Not two blocks from the house when it happened.

Running. After what Pryor had said to him. The way he'd threatened Myles last night, not even out for one full day. What the fuck?

He was in surgery at Grant for what felt like hours. They arrived at eight thirty and nobody would tell them anything. They were in the waiting room, Mama, red-eyed and shaky, Penny drawn up within herself, looking at nothing and everything, when the detectives came by. A Black guy and a white lady. They made Penny stand up and took her around the corner to a different waiting room, smaller and empty except for some old magazines and a plastic plant in the corner. The lady took her and Myles's names.

"He just got out?" the Black detective said.

"Yeah."

"Today?"

"Yesterday." Avoiding eye contact so he wouldn't see how scared she was.

"Any idea who would do this?"

Penny shook her head.

"Certain about that?"

"Yeah."

"He's out a day and someone shoots him," the Black detective said. He was big and beefy, like he'd played football and not just in high school. She wondered idly if he knew Archie. Head shaved with a goatee and freckles running up and down his cheeks.

"So?"

"So maybe it's connected?"

"Connected to what?"

"To whatever he went in for."

Penny shrugged. Kept her face a mask, trying to reveal nothing. Maybe one good thing she'd learned at work, around those costumes all day long.

"They found a gun."

"What?"

The lady detective. "They found a gun by Myles."

"Okay." Her stomach contracted.

"Does he own a gun?"

"No, obviously."

"Do you?"

"No."

"Any idea why he'd have one?"

"Who says he had one?"

"I just said they found one, next to him." The lady's face unnaturally brown, like she tanned or vacationed a lot. Penny saw hints of black roots in her too-blond hair.

"He just got out of prison," Penny said. "He's a felon now. He's not going to have a gun. He was jogging, wasn't he?"

"It appears so."

Her heart beating fast, thinking about what the detective was saying. Thinking about what Myles said that morning, at breakfast, as they reviewed the implication of Pryor's visit the night before. *It's him or me, sounds like.*

"What was he in for?"

"What?"

The detective repeated her question.

Penny paused. She guessed she'd have to tell them. They'd figure it out, sooner or later. Cops always did.

"Armed robbery."

Now she really had their attention.

"He was the driver," she said, quickly. "He didn't go inside the bank. That's on camera."

"What bank?"

Again, the hesitation. Why the fuck had he gone running? Unless—

"The bank, miss?"

"Chase Bank," she said. "Eakin Road."

"When?"

"Four years ago."

Now it was the detectives' turn to pause.

"Didn't somebody die in that?" the lady said.

Penny nodded, miserable.

"A customer," the detective said. "Had a heart attack, right?"

Penny nodded again. Fought to keep the mask on.

"Pryor pulled that job," the Black detective said.

Another nod. Not trusting herself to speak.

"But he didn't go to prison."

She shook her head again.

"Why not?"

The lady detective said, "Hung jury."

"Hung?" her partner said.

"I remember now. Pryor had an alibi of some kind, right?" The lady, to Penny.

"I guess."

"Even though this guy testified against him." Penny realized she was talking about Myles.

"Yeah."

"Lucky bastard," the lady said, and Penny knew she meant Pryor.

"Whatever."

She could see it in their eyes, the pieces falling into place like a sped-up film of someone putting a jigsaw puzzle together.

"Pryor must have been angry about that," the Black detective said. "About Myles testifying against him, I mean."

She didn't answer.

"You seen him around, since Myles got back? Heard from him?"

Another head shake, more vigorous this time.

"You're absolutely certain about that?"

Pryor on the porch the night before, grinning, blinking his eye.

"Well lookey who's home."

"Beat it," Myles told him, standing protectively in front of Penny, as she tried not to launch herself at Pryor and scratch his eye out, especially given the way he was looking at her, barely dressed in the bathrobe she hastily put on when the knocking woke them up.

"Listen, Baby. Got another job for you," Pryor said.

"Get lost."

"It's a big one, Baby. Big pay-off. Set you up for a long time."

"Stop calling him that," Penny said

"Calling him what?"

"Baby."

"Stop calling him by his name?"

"It's not his name. And this ain't no fucking movie."

"You're pretty when you're pissed, Penny."

She felt Myles tense beside her. She placed a warning hand on his back. They couldn't afford to give Pryor the satisfaction of losing it. Not now.

"Fuck off," Myles said.

"Well, problem with that is, you sort of owe me. What you did to me. My bung hole's still sore from where you screwed me over."

"I took a deal. That's life."

"Fuck life, Baby. I got a proposition."

"I said—"

"Drive for me again. You're the best I ever had. Do the job, we call it even."

"I told you, I'm done with that shit."

"Done?"

"I'm not going back."

"Back? You haven't even left yet. Just because you're out doesn't mean you're out."

"I'm not driving," Myles said. "I'm not doing another job. I'm not doing anything for you. What's over is over."

"So, you're a nobody, then."

"What?"

"From now on, you're a nobody, Baby. And you know what happens to nobodies."

"Penny?"

The Black detective.

"Yeah?" She blinked, coming to, staring at the waiting room's drab walls.

"I asked if you're sure you haven't seen Pryor around?"

"I'm sure."

"Any idea why he was out running like that?"

"Who?"

"Myles."

"No idea."

"Maybe he was looking for someone? Like Pryor, perhaps?"

"I don't know," Penny said, wondering if that were true. "He started running in prison. In the yard. He probably just wanted some exercise. Stretch his legs on actual streets."

The tanned lady said, "So no idea who might have done this? If, say, Pryor was involved? Or why Myles had a gun?"

"I told you no."

Fuck fuck fuck.

It went on like that for a good ten minutes. She knew they could tell she was lying. Not that that was any big surprise. You'd have to be an idiot not to figure out what was going on, especially with Pryor's name popping into the middle of things like a turd under a Christmas tree. But Penny wasn't telling them anything else. Not yet. She knew what Pryor was capable of. She'd seen it. Myles had nailed him to the wall that day in court, laid it all out. And yet somehow Pryor walked free. And it wasn't the first time he'd beaten the system, or left bodies in his wake. Darren Garretty, hello, just for starters. And of course, Cousin Ed. And most dangerous of all, Pryor had a long memory. Very, very long.

Obviously.

In the end, they gave her their cards and told her to call them if she thought of anything. Clearly frustrated. The Black detective reminded her about obstruction charges. Said they were on her side but only up to a point.

"You change your mind, you call us."

"I don't know what happened," Penny said.

"I hope he's okay," the lady detective said.

"Thanks," Penny said, walking back to rejoin Mama.

Around midnight, a doctor finally emerged and called Penny's name. A dark-skinned guy with a British accent. He said Myles was stable but unconscious and only time would tell.

"He's very strong. Healthy heart. Someone else, that many shots . . . I don't know."

Penny thanked him. She didn't know what else to say. Mama surprised him by reaching out and hugging him. After a moment, he hugged her back.

They gave her five minutes. He was lying in a bed with tubes snaking out his gut and wires everywhere attached to machines that were flashing lights like some kind of bomb about to go off in a spy movie. He looked almost half machine himself. He was pale, yet his chest rose and fell regularly, thanks to the ventilator covering his face. Of course. He couldn't breathe on his own. Penny took his hand and called his name, but he didn't respond. She sat there until a nurse came and told her she had to leave. She leaned over and kissed Myles on the forehead and left the room and went down the hall and back to Mama.

And began thinking about a plan.

4

There were two ways to drive into Darbytown from Columbus. You could take the last exit off I-70 in Madison County, turn right onto the Madison-Union Road, then turn left on old 31, cross into Darby County a mile later, and drive into town from the east. That's the way Pryor preferred. A week ago at dusk, coming that direction, he clipped a groundhog that crept too far onto the berm on the right side of the road just as he drove by. The van shuddered a bit as he jerked the wheel over onto the gravel, but he hadn't minded after seeing the animal in his rearview mirror convulse in paralyzing quivers as it crawled a few feet before going still. Satisfying, like. Blue van with a gray door that Pryor found on a side street on the South End. Good enough for what they needed it for.

That way into Darbytown was good for that kind of thing. For groundhogs. The other way took longer and involved wider roads that fewer animals crossed, at least when it was light out. You stayed on 70 into Darby County, took the exit for Route 31, turned right, then right again, and rolled into town. It was the way they took tonight.

Thanks to the stunt pulled by Myles—by Baby—that forced them to leave town tonight instead of tomorrow, they were a day ahead of schedule. But it shouldn't really matter in the end, Pryor thought. He texted Robby as they left Columbus and told him there'd been a change of plans. Robby hadn't been too happy about it, but that wasn't Pryor's problem. Michigan behind the wheel, slowing at Pryor's order as they came into town proper and the street changed names to Main. A joke comparing Michigan's skills behind the wheel to those of Baby, but what were you going to do? They drove into the town square under a canopy of maple branches arcing over the street, limbs intermingled like warriors locked in a death grip. Pryor told Michigan to do a once-around, follow the yield signs to the left, and slow again as they passed the bank so everyone could have a good look. Darby Farmers National Bank. Weathered granite exterior with a pair of stone pillars like petrified tree trunks guarding the door. Lots of windows, but the lobby itself not visible from the street.

They pulled into the restaurant parking lot two minutes later. Pryor made Michigan park the van at the far end. It probably didn't matter. Lot pretty full, even for a Thursday night in September, just like Robby predicted, meaning they wouldn't stick out much either way. Except for the cardboard over the van's window, but some things just couldn't be helped. According to Robby, the restaurant did nothing but shovel people in and shovel food inside them and shovel them back out morning, noon and night, no matter the day of the week or the month of the year. Amish-style cooking. People couldn't get enough of it.

Robby showed up a couple minutes later. He parked three spaces away and exited his car slowly, looking around. Pryor whistled for him, short but loud, and Robby's head jerked up at the sound. Everyone knew Pryor's whistle.

"Okay," he said, walking up to the van, sweat beading on his upper lip.

"Okay, what?" Pryor said.

"I'm ready. I can drive you out there. Show you where it is."

"We're not ready."

"Okay," Robby said, uncertainly.

"We're hungry. You said this place has good food."

"I guess."

"Amish style."

"Yeah."

"What's that mean, anyway?"

"I'm not sure."

"What do you mean, you're not sure?" Training his eye on Robby, holding his gaze until he looked away. Which didn't take long. "It must mean something."

"Home cooking, I guess. Like, you know, filling?"

"Sounds good. Go buy us three dinners. Chicken dinners."

"Now?"

"Now."

"I thought you wanted—"

"We'll get to that."

"I'm not sure I've got enough money."

Pryor stared. "You remember our deal?"

"Yeah."

"You remember what I said about cooperating?"

"Yeah, but—"

Pryor handed him his phone. Showed him the headline he'd punched up. It had popped fifteen minutes ago.

POLICE RESPOND TO HILLTOP SHOOTING

Pryor waited while Robby read the short article. When he was finished, Pryor said, "We have a deal, right?"

"Yeah."

"Three chicken dinners."

After Robby trudged away, they sat with the van running and the windows rolled up, the air conditioning blasting until Michigan complained he was cold. Pryor ignored him.

"Why'd Robby get to go in there?" Archie said.

"Don't be an idiot."

"What?"

"Like you wouldn't stand out a hundred yards in every direction."

"Because I'm Black."

"Because you're so well dressed. Give me a break."

There's a cop, Archie had said. Pulled the van away before Pryor could finish the job. Not that he had any doubts Myles would survive the bullets he put in him. But still. Had there been a cop? He really wasn't sure. And that was his reward for letting Archie drive them through the neighborhood instead of Michigan. Michigan drove for shit but at least he did what you told him to.

"You could have sent me," Michigan said.

"Shut up."

Truth was, it was debatable which of the two would stick out more. Archie, a Black guy in a rural county without a single other Black living there as far as Pryor could tell, unless you counted some of the darker Mexicans working in the *azteca* kitchen farther up the street. Or Michigan, who had somehow thought it a good idea to have a blue dagger tattooed over the left side of his face, starting above the eye, down to the lid, and then tapering to a point below the eye. The notion, Pryor knew, was to model himself as some kind of warrior, like the guy in that movie about the Scottish hero. But the result was ludicrous, as if he'd been run over by a bike tire coated in blue house paint. That and his blond hair turned heads almost everywhere they went. It ruled Michigan out as a guy who could handle anything inside, from casing a place to doing the actual stick-up. One look at the security cameras and the cops would just roll their eyes and type in the BOLO. Jimmy O'Brien, aka "Michigan." O'Brien is not even a Scottish name—even Pryor knew that much. Once upon a time, it would have mattered to Pryor. It would have been one more thing to factor into his plan. But that was before Baby turned him down—before he signed his own death sentence by refusing to rejoin Pryor. The two of them together—they could have accomplished something. Because Baby was the best Pryor ever used.

Now he was stuck with just Archie and Michigan, each uselessly conspicuous in his own way.

But not for much longer. Not for what he had planned for them.

"You see the cop?"

Pryor started. Robby, back again, standing at the van window.

"What?"

"The sheriff's deputy. Came in right after us."

"Deputy?"

"Yeah."

"Where?"

"Over there." Robby jerked his head behind him. Robby: tall and pudgy with long dark hair that always looked like it needed washing.

"Get in."

Robby did as he was instructed. Inside, he handed each man a plastic bag. The smell of roasted chicken filled the interior.

"Guy see you?" Pryor said.

"Don't think so."

"What was he doing?"

"Nothing. Just drove in, took a look around, drove off again."

"He didn't make you?"

"Don't see how he could have."

Pryor didn't say anything. He reached into the bag and pulled out a white Styrofoam container of food. He opened it, picked up a chicken breast, and took a bite. Shit. Robby was right. Amish style. It was good. Warm and juicy and salty. He glanced behind him and noticed Archie and Michigan were watching Robby instead of opening their own meals.

"So, you ready?" Robby said.

"Do I look ready?" Pryor said, spooning himself a glob of mashed potatoes.

They sat for a few minutes in silence, eating their chicken dinners. Pryor would say this about the Amish. They were weird birds, with the horses and the buggies and the old-timey clothes and the houses gutted of plumbing and electricity, and all those kids wearing miniature versions of their parents' outfits like creepy life-sized dolls. But they sure as hell could cook chicken. When he was finished eating, he closed the white box his meal had come in—not very Amish-y, come to think of it—and tossed it onto the passenger seat floor.

"All right," he said to Robby. "Now we're ready."

5

Penny thought about leaving as soon as they arrived home from the hospital. Strike while the iron was hot—wasn't that the expression? But she changed her mind after coming inside with Mama and accepting hugs from Ma-Maw and Clyde and peeking in on Mack. He went to sleep just fine, they assured her. But she couldn't leave without saying goodbye to him, a proper goodbye, even though she couldn't explain where she was going. And the more she thought about it, there were things she was going to need she couldn't just acquire in the middle of the night. A reliable car, for starters: the Aurora stalled twice at lights just on the fifteen-minute drive home from Grant. And a working phone—her piece of shit flip phone wasn't going to cut it. And of course, the most important item. Three things she didn't have. But she knew where she could get them. Hoped she could get them.

If only she'd known what Myles was up to. If only he'd told her—trusted her—so she could help. Which she would have done so gladly.

Pryor, licking his lips as he moved his eye down her exposed leg last night before she covered it with the robe.

And startling her that day in the costume shop, two weeks before Myles was due for release, asking about him. About her. Whistling at her the way he did, the sound so loud, eye trained on her chest. Asking innocently about Donald Trump masks when the manager walked up, asking if everything was all right.

No, the trip would have to wait until morning. Which was probably a good thing, because she had to figure out exactly how she was going to do this. Not the why—she'd known that even before seeing Mama's anguished face as she entered the costume shop with the news. She'd known from the moment she sat down beside Myles that morning and he offered the only realistic solution to their problem, whether he was serious about it or not.

We could kill him.

Well, she considered. She guessed he'd been serious about it after all. Serious—and so hopelessly naive.

No, it was not the why, or the what, or any of that. It was the how she had to think about. For that she needed just a little more time.

◆

Penny slept better than she'd expected. Awake by seven, her skin sticky in the humidity, Mack sprawled beside her like a starfish. She rubbed her eyes, kissed their son lightly on the cheek, and gathered her things. Her plan had formed overnight, crowding out her dreams, and although she couldn't quite see to the end of the road, she knew where to start. The beginning of the journey had become as clear as the air after a late-summer thunderstorm passes through.

She stuffed a shirt and socks and some underwear into a blue drawstring nylon bag with "Columbus Metropolitan Library" printed on it that she found in the basement. Left over from some summer program when she and Brandi—Brooke now—were kids. She added a bottle of water and a half-empty wax-paper bag of cereal pulled from the box. She found two slices of pizza in the refrigerator leftover from Myles's welcome home party two days earlier. She had one for breakfast and stuffed the other in a plastic bag and threw it in with the other things. She found the knitting she left on the chair the night before, exhausted as she came home from the hospital, and stuffed that in there too, long needles right on top.

She'd almost thought it was going to work out—Myles being home and all—as first the party wound down, and then she put Mack to bed, and eventually they retired to her room.

Sitting beside Myles and taking his hand. Him looking at her, his eyes wide, taking in her face. Reaching over and putting his free hand around her neck and leaning in and kissing her. She wasn't sure how to respond right away, it had been so long. Then something stirred in her, the remnants of an old fire, and she kissed him back. Slowly, in an awkward dance of whispers and giggles and cautions not to wake Mack, they fell back onto the bed and tugged heatedly at each other's clothes and soon were grappling naked beneath the sheets. Fucking like teenagers. There would be time for something slower down the road, over the next few days, but not tonight. It had been a long three years, and now she had Myles back, for good.

"Penny?"

Mama, standing in the kitchen doorway, shapeless in an oversized Ohio State T-shirt and white sweatpants, a red crease on her left cheek from where she slept funny. Penny hadn't heard her come down.

"I need to go away for a couple of days," Penny said.

"Go where?"

"There's something I need to do."

"Do?"

"I need you to watch Mack. Watch him carefully, you understand? You be with him all the time. You and Ma-Maw and Clyde. All right?"

"I don't understand."

"I'm sorry, Mama." Penny walked to her and held her. Not even fifty, her mother felt soft and frail, the way Ma-Maw felt when you hugged her and how much older was she? The years had aged Mama. Penny had aged her, she thought, fighting back regret like sudden nausea. That year she ran the streets with Myles after high school—

"What about Myles?"

"I'm going to the hospital to see him now. I'll tell him."

"Is he awake?"

"I doubt it."

"Then how?"

"How what?"

"How will you tell him?"

"I'll take care of it," Penny said.

She left her bag by the front door and walked back upstairs. She sat beside Mack and rubbed his back, his tiny shoulder blades like stunted wings, until he stirred.

"Hi, little guy."

"Mmm."

"Mommy has to run an errand. I'll be gone for a little bit. But I'll be back."

"Daddy."

"He's at the hospital. He's just fine."

He reached out and grabbed her around the neck. "I don't want you to go."

"I won't be long. Gramma's here. And Clyde and Ma-Maw are coming by soon. You mind them. And be a big boy."

"Can I see Daddy?"

"In a little bit. As soon as I get back."

"Will you bring me something?"

"Like what?"

"A toy."

"I'll see what I can do. You be good, okay?"

"Okay, Mommy," he said, laying his head back down on the bed. She stroked his damp hair until she heard his breathing even out again. She heard a clicking sound and turned and saw Gus come into the room. She held out a hand and the dog approached. She scratched him and patted the bed. The dog hesitated a moment, and then jumped up and lay down beside Mack.

"Good dog," Penny said, and stood up and left the room.

"Don't go," her mother said, meeting her at the bottom of the stairs. Her face puffy, eyes red and shiny, like she'd stuck her head into a bag full of bees.

"Myles had a gun," Penny said.

"What?"

She repeated what the detectives told her. "Do you know where he got it?"

"No."

"Did anyone come by?"

She shook her head. "He just went running. That's all I know. And then—"

"Okay." There was no use pushing it. All the people at the party. It could have been anyone.

"Remember what I said. Watch Mack all the time. You understand?"

"What about Brandi?"

"What about her?"

"Shouldn't I call her? Tell her about Myles. She could help."

"Don't call Brandi."

"Why not?"

"Just because."

"She might be able to—"

"Please?"

Her mom blinked her shiny eyes and nodded.

"I'll be back as soon as I can. Don't let Mack out of your sight." She hugged Mama a second time and then was through the door and outside. She started the Aurora, saw it had barely a quarter tank of gas, which was just enough, and headed east on Broad, toward the hospital.

6

Opioid receptors.

"Opioid receptors," J. P. mouthed, moving his lips as he drew out the syllables.

Then, reading aloud: "Opioid receptors."

He looked around shyly, unused to hearing the sound of his voice by himself like that. Sasha raised herself from the couch, turned in a circle once, twice, licked herself, then plopped down and went back to sleep with a sigh.

J. P. didn't know why he struggled with the phrase. It wasn't that hard a concept. The pills, the Oxys, the Percocets, the Vicodins, and of course the heroin, all did the same thing, more or less. Rewired your brain, was the way the book put it. Cooked the brain, more like it. He understood that part. It was the technical aspect he stumbled over. The chemicals in the drugs blocked receptors—not quite sure what those were, but he'd get to that—that were found in people's heads. That explained the dazed looks, the flat affect, whenever he and the paramedics walked into the houses, into the basements and rec rooms and bedrooms—heck, even the town library, more than once—and found the overdoses laying there like discarded mannequins. The way they saw the girl last week, turning blue, eyes fluttering, breathing shallow like someone had just told her some really bad news, yet hardly anyone in the room seemed to care. Only the little brother, couldn't have been more than thirteen or fourteen, who'd stumbled downstairs after he heard something and found his sister and had had the good sense to take her phone and dial 911.

Not that it made any difference in the end.

Outside, the sound of a car door shutting. Sasha off the couch like a shot, a blur of white fur and ribbons. A minute later, the jingle of keys in the bungalow's back door, and then June was home in a swirl of papers and purse and pink flowery vinyl lunch bag and the smell of her perfume. "Hello?" she said, her voice carefree, but entering the dining room she stopped, the expression on her face someplace between bemusement and annoyance.

"You're all dressed. Didn't you get my text?"

"Well, yeah, but—"

"But what? Listen, Deputy, this baby's not going to make itself."

"I'm sorry." He glanced guiltily at the textbooks. "I got distracted."

"I'll give you distracted, J. P. In about six-zero seconds." She shot him a smile not at all like the one she saved for church. "C'mere, Sasha," she said, setting her things on the kitchen table before turning and scooping up the pom.

"Distracted, my foot," she sang out as she beelined for the stairs.

J. P. blushed, following the progress of his wife's backside until she disappeared around the corner, and then lifted his phone to reexamine the text in question. Two hearts on either side of a peach, sent minutes before, so just as she was leaving school. No question what she had in mind. And he did, too, for sure. At this rate, he could embrace the work you apparently put in to have a baby. It's just—the exam, his first, only a week off. The class harder than he anticipated. *Drugs and the Criminal Justice System.* He'd make it through, but the material was tough. "Tough as week-old tenderloin," as his father used to say.

Just one more paragraph, J. P. promised. He adjusted himself—radio, cuffs, mag case, Taser, flashlight, SIG—and went back to the textbook, back to opioid receptors and breathing rates and skin color and muscle spasticity. Another word he had to say out loud. But he never had the chance. He heard the upstairs toilet flush and the faucet run and then June's voice from the top of the stairs, loud and insistent.

"What the heck? Don't you have to leave soon?"

"Sorry, sorry," he said, pushing the book aside.

"Sorry is right if you don't get up here."

He stood and undid his utility belt and set it on the chair, the gun thunking lightly on the wood, and then beat feet for the upstairs bedroom. There, he found the blankets pushed down to the foot of the bed and June sprawled on her side on the bottom sheet, not one stitch of clothing on, shooting him that smile again.

"Now we're making progress."

"Roger that," J. P. said, kicking off his shoes and fumbling at his belt.

"I packed your dinner. You saw it?"

"Yes," he said, pulling off his brown uniform trousers with the black stripe down the leg.

"Two sandwiches, and chips, but also carrots, all that Vitamin A," she said. "The better to see me with."

"I can see you just fine," J. P. said, sliding his boxers off and moving onto the buttons of his dress shirt.

"You like what you see?"

"Yes, ma'am."

"Then why don't you show me?" she said, in that affected drawl of hers he only heard at one particular time, always between the two of them.

"Well now. Looks like someone's finally on duty," she said as he finished undressing and climbed into bed, the frame creaking a bit at his girth, and into her arms. J. P. kissed her and she kissed him and that went on for a minute or so and then he paused, and she said, "What's wrong?"

"Trespasser," he said, reaching over and palming Sasha. He dropped the pom gently onto the floor where she landed with an indignant yip.

"Silly Sasha," June said, and the matinee resumed and the next thing J. P. knew he was on top and inside her, and they rocked up and down for a while making all kind of noise, and then June's breathing deepened and she gasped in that singsong way that always signaled it was about to happen, and then it did happen and she breathed out that sound like she was hitting a high note during the final hymn. And then a short minute later it happened to him too and he made the same *ooh* noise he always made only this time really loud. For him.

"I love you, Deputy," June said after a few moments.

"I love you too," J. P. said, audibly enough for her to hear it, because they'd talked about that.

But also because he meant it.

"Pillows," she said after a minute, and he raised himself and carefully positioned them beneath her rear end. "Helps the little spermies slide home," she informed him the first time she made the request, and who was he to question it?

"Anything?" June said a minute later as she maneuvered his head onto her stomach.

"Sounds like gas," he said. "Is that a good sign?"

"Maybe there's a whole choir in there."

"Gonna need a bigger car in that case."

He shifted himself and lay beside her, thinking about opioid receptors.

"J. P.?"

"Yes?"

"Promise me we'll still do this after we have kids. And even when I'm old and fat. Fatter, anyway. That we won't be like just any old couple."

"You're not fat."

"I'm serious. You promise?"

"Oh, if you insist."

"I mean it, J. P." She turned to him. "The other day, at the Dutch House after church? Jan Rittmaier told us she and Hank only do it once a year, on his birthday. Can you imagine?"

"Wow," J. P. said, his mind reeling at the revelation about his one-time, long-ago girlfriend. Not at the thought of the Rittmaiers only doing it annually. That pair, he was surprised it was so frequent. But at the notion that Jan confided something that intimate to June and the other girls from Bible study. He tried to imagine telling one of his few male friends something similar, and decided quickly not in ten thousand years. Correction. Ten thousand and one.

June took his left hand and intertwined his fingers with hers. He looked at her engagement ring next to the gold band. His grandmother's ring—his father's mother—because that's all he could manage when he proposed. A quarter carat. So small.

"I love my ring," she said, following his gaze. "And I love you so much."

"I love you too," he repeated.

"I'm so proud of you."

"Thank you," he said, forcing the words out.

After another minute, she hoisted herself off the bed and headed for the bathroom. When she returned they traded places and then he dressed and went downstairs and fastened his utility belt back around his thick waist. He closed the textbook and carried it over to the bookshelf and slid it between his book on public speaking and the book on marksmanship June gave him the previous Christmas, their first since the wedding.

"Church tonight," June said, coming downstairs in the sweats she wore after school while she planned for the next day. "We'll probably go to Dutch House later. Do you want anything?"

"Maybe not."

"You sure?"

"Yes," he said, not sure.

"That was nice," she said, kissing him on the cheek. "Even if you didn't read my text."

"I read it."

"Then follow the instructions, next time. Wake me up when you get in?"

"Yes."

"Your cowlick," she said. She used her fingers to smooth out his hair.

"It's fine."

"Not quite. There. Now it's perfect."

"Thanks."

"That was nice," June repeated.

"Very nice," he said.

"Glad you agree, Deputy. Now go make the bad guys behave."

7

J. P. drove into the employee lot behind the sheriff's office and parked quickly. He left his car in a hurry and strode up the walk to the brick building, watching himself approach in the glass double doors like someone with a gun to his back, forcing him forward. Not happy with the sight of his reflection but nothing he could do about that right now. He went inside and smelled green beans and instant mashed potatoes and what passed for Salisbury steak in warming pans drifting down from the jail, dinner already prepared. The cheapest meals possible, under Sheriff Waters. Not like when J. P.'s father was around, when he knew better than to run a jail crowded with a bunch of hungry prisoners always on the edge of revolt.

J. P. glanced up at the camera in the corner and waited for Joyce to click the interior door open. Was it his imagination or had she waited an extra couple seconds to hit the button? Taken her time because what were the consequences? He pulled impatiently on the door as he heard the buzz and went inside.

The others were already in roll call, if that's what you called sitting at the conference table while Vick slouched by the door with his clipboard, reading off assignments.

"Holy shit," Marks said, looking at J. P. as he took his position against the wall. He never sat. They had never sat when his father was here. "Are you *late*?"

"Sorry."

"God in heaven," Marks said. "Might be a first. The mighty J. P., late for duty. Everything okay?"

"Okay," J. P. said, keeping his eyes on Vick. But Vick was watching Marks as if he were the only person in the room.

Marks stood up, which was a sight, because he was a big guy the way mountains are big. But not mountains of rock, J. P. thought. Mountains of garbage.

"Deputy," Marks said, approaching J. P. "Something seems amiss with your uniform."

"Not hardly."

"Deputy," Marks said, looming over him. "Do I detect the smell of perfume on your dress shirt?" He leaned in, made a big production of sniffing. The guys at the table laughed. Vick grinned but didn't say anything.

"Yeah, right," J. P. said.

"Deputy," Marks continued. "Were you up to something before work? Is that why you're late?"

"I—"

"Deputy, have you been busy with the Mrs.?"

J. P. felt his face go red.

Marks reached down and put his hand on J. P.'s baton, wiggling it back and forth until J. P.'s utility belt squeaked and dug uncomfortably into his waist.

"Have you been giving the missus the *stick*, Deputy?" Marks said, to a chorus of guffaws. Even Vick joined in.

"I would appreciate you not—"

"Not what?"

"I would appreciate you not talking about—"

"Didn't think you had it in you, Deputy," Marks interrupted, giving the baton a final tug and leering at him. "But I guess *she* had it in *her*, huh?"

That earned the biggest laugh of all. J. P., his face burning, pushed Marks's hand away, straightened his belt and stood at attention. He trained his gaze on the picture, as he often did. Across the room, above the lockers, the framed photo of his father. The one of him standing beside his sheriff's office SUV. Darby 1, his handle went. First Officer, Darby County Sheriff's Office. The picture the day he took office. A picture that, afterward, hung in the lobby for all the world to see until one day Sheriff Waters moved it back here. And that was that.

"Okay. Fun's over," Vick said, tapping a pen on the clipboard. Though he didn't seem like he meant it.

He read off the assignments. Marks running radar on Route 31 going out of town, the easiest spot in the county for making your quota. Dalton serving warrants. Jenks going with Children's Services on an alleged abuse checkup. Livingston on patrol on the north side of Darbytown.

"Got another call from old man Hartzell," Vick said, looking at J. P. "Check it out."

J. P. looked over at Marks, who was grinning at him. A grin J. P. wished he could do something about, the way you did something about a rash.

"I checked it out yesterday."

"What?" Vick said, a little sharply.

"I said I checked it out yesterday. And two days before that. It's nothing."

"He says someone's watching his house."

"You can't watch his house," J. P said. "It sits back from the road behind a clump of trees. You might be able to see the barn from the road, but that's it."

"Now you're a geographer? Check it out."

"I already—"

"*Check it out*," Vick said. But eyes on Marks as he spoke.

So J. P. nodded and said he would check it out. Again.

Even though he knew Dalton was going straight to his girlfriend's house, which wasn't right for a bunch of reasons starting with the fact she was Dalton's wife's cousin. And even though he knew that sending Livingston on patrol was code for him to position his cruiser at the far end of the Metro Park parking lot while he did paperwork for half the shift. And even though he knew Marks was going to sit on the side of the road and let a bunch of people in good-looking cars blow by at seventy-five or eighty and wouldn't do squat, but would wait until he saw a Black or brown guy in a beater going two miles over and then it would be full-on sirens and God help the driver if he showed Marks even a little bit of attitude. Jenks was okay, but look out if there was trouble at the house Children Services was going to. If they actually had to remove a child.

And then there was Clayton Hartzell, J. P. thought, easing down the farmhouse drive twenty minutes later. Clayton and his sister, Priscilla. J. P. didn't mean to be ungracious, but it was hard to see who would want to spy on their property other than a real estate developer, especially one with access to a decent demolition crew. Not that a sale was likely anytime soon. Clayton had made his wishes on that front known long ago. They'd carry them both out feet first before he sold. J. P. was pretty sure the farmhouse hadn't been painted since Clayton and Priscilla's father built the place back in the thirties. Which might have been more recently than the barn sitting across the gravel turnaround. A giant structure that could have been red at one point in its existence but now was gray as a winter sky before rain and listing to the right like a barge in a perpetual state of capsize. It housed horses long ago, but the last was put down when J. P. was in high school, or so he was told. Told by the vet in Darbytown, who more or less accused Clayton of starving them.

J. P. parked and climbed the stairs to the farmhouse porch and knocked on the door, feeling his stomach tighten. He relaxed a little when Priscilla appeared at the door. But only a little.

"Took you long enough."

"I just came on," he said, apologetically.

"Clayton called two hours ago."

"I'm sorry about that."

"I bet you are." Spitting image of her brother, both thin and beginning to stoop, their shriveled faces like tightly squeezed fists.

"Is Clayton—"

"Barn," she said, and shut the door.

J. P. sighed, turned, and walked down the porch steps. He looked up the drive toward the road, hearing a car slow as it passed the entrance to the farm. Not exactly suspicious, considering that the road took a sharp left just past the farmhouse drive and taking it too fast was a mistake. He made for the barn. He was almost at the door when it rolled open with a clatter and Clayton emerged, scowling.

"Took you long enough."

"You thought you saw something," J. P. said, patiently.

Hartzell narrowed his eyes at him. "What's that supposed to mean? *Thought*? Like I'm seeing ghosts?" He rolled the door shut and shot the outer bolt.

"It doesn't mean anything. Just a question."

"A dumb-ass question."

Still patient, J. P. said, "Can you give me a description of the vehicle?" He hated words like *vehicle*, words no one ever said in real life. But everybody was so accustomed to true crime shows and movies that he found the jargon calmed people, like a doctor handing out antibiotics for a viral infection when all the patient needed was to lie down for a while.

"Blue van. Parked right up there." Clayton pointed at the road. "Heard it stop and I walked up and saw it. Just sitting there, almost two minutes."

"When was this?"

"Early this afternoon. I called right afterward. Two hours ago, in case you lost your watch."

"Get a look at them?"

Clayton shook his head.

"Driver? Man or woman?"

"Too far."

"The other day," J. P. said. He made a show of trying to remember. "I believe you said gray van?"

"So?"

"So, ah, two different vehicles, maybe?"

"Maybe not. Blue. Gray. What's the difference?"

"Guess the difference is people watching your house in one or two vehicles."

"How the hell should I know? Why I called you."

"And still no idea who it might be?"

"Not a clue. Like I told you yesterday. And the other time."

"Mind if I take a look around?"

"Around where?"

"Here. The farm. The barn."

"Why?"

"See if I can see anything. Maybe something unusual. Something that might help us figure out who it is."

"Yes," Clayton said.

"Thanks."

"Yes, I mind. There's nothing unusual down here," he said, jerking his head at the farmhouse, then the barn. "It's up there I'm worried about." He pointed toward the road again.

J. P. nodded. What else could he do? He looked at the fields stretching out behind the barn and off on either side. Acres of corn, stalks towering at seven or eight feet after a hot, wet summer. Just starting to brown. Planted not by Clayton, who these days J. P. wasn't sure was up to growing much beyond hemorrhoids. Priscilla was the green thumb in the family, with her big garden and all. Everyone knew that. No, these fields were planted by a farmer two miles down the road who rented the property. The corn made a decent protective cover, come to think of it, if you had any reason to spy on such a piss-poor property. Spy not from the road above, as Clayton maintained, but the other direction, from the south.

J. P said, "You ever see anybody out there?"

"Where?"

"In the fields. Early in the morning? Late at night?"

"No. Why?"

J. P. considered his response. Glanced at Clayton, who was glaring at him. It seemed unlikely, what he was thinking. But who really knew? Last summer the Union County sheriff dug up a thousand marijuana plants from fields not a whole lot bigger than Clayton's, after the state patrol did a fly-over. Farmer swore he hadn't known a thing. Probably true.

"No reason," J. P. said. "I'll write the report up, try to drive past a couple times a night. You see anything suspicious, call me direct, all right?" He handed him his card.

"Like it'll do any good."

"Only one way to find out," J. P. said, walking back to his cruiser.

8

They made Robby lead them out to the farmhouse. It wasn't necessary, of course. Pryor had figured out where it was right after Robby first told him about it, explaining there might be money inside the house. Money he could use to pay up. The money caught Pryor's attention, but only for a little while. It had him thinking about something else. Nothing Robby needed to know about. Just like he didn't need to know they already knew where they were going since Pryor had been there twice already, checking out the house and the barn. He wanted the notion that Robby was helping them out as clear as a freshly inked tattoo on the dumb shit's forehead. That he was an accomplice to whatever they were up to. That he was in it all the way up to his pudgy little-boy chin.

The property was deep in the country, a part of the world Pryor had been in rarely, if at all. He viewed fields through grills on the windows of a long, white passenger van years ago, going to and from prison in his one and only stint inside. He looked at them again through fences when he was out in the yard with the other inmates. But he hadn't bothered with the country much since. Too boring, with nothing to see. Like a seriously built girl with all her clothes on. What was the point? Now he stared at the fields in amazement as the van's headlights illuminated them; the tall stalks of corn in endless rows, like hundreds of spears bedecked with green feathers and stabbed in perfect symmetry into the ground; the curving road as Michigan drove them farther from town and farther into the country; the stand of trees where the road turned and then the turn down the driveway; an odd feeling as for the first time he took in the gray farmhouse up close, with its sagging porch and dilapidated railing, and the gray barn with the last of its red paint flaking off like burned skin. It was a place he needed, to make this plan work. A place to be sure everything was ready. But just for a moment, the barn struck him as something else, something he hadn't thought about until that moment: a place you couldn't leave once you went inside.

◆

Pryor might have missed the bank altogether, if it hadn't been for Mae. Life was funny like that. She's the one who told him about what the guy said, about the Amish doing everything in cash. A lot of cash. The banker guy, small with a little belly and a bald spot and a little silver fish symbol on his lapel, driving a nice SUV with that plastic decal of a mom and dad and three stick figure kids and a dog on the back. "My kids are honor students at Darbytown Elementary," the bumper sticker said.

The banker who after he was inside the motel room started panting as he told Mae he wanted to put it in all three of her holes and who said, fine, he'd pay extra, when she balked. The fish thing on the lapel something to do with church, as Mae explained it. Not that Pryor cared about that. He'd lost track of the number of devout Christians that Mae fucked over the years—Mae and the others that Pryor ran. Some of them preachers driving straight from church. And Columbus had a lot of churches. No, he was more interested in the bank, and the Amish, and the cash deposits.

He took a drive out there the following Saturday, him and Archie and Michigan, not so far, thirty-five minutes on the highway, and scoped it out. It was even better than he imagined. Plenty of parking, easy in and out, and how much security would a place like that have? Only problem, and it was a big one, was the sheriff's office two blocks down. That put a freeze on it, right there and then. He didn't think about it for six months. Not until he ran into Robby and they got to talking—Robby was real chatty when Pryor had a gun hovering near his right temple—and Robby mentioned something about an aunt and uncle and a farmhouse and hidden cash. Pryor liked the sound of the cash. But he liked the sound of the farmhouse and the barn full of straw even better. Because it gave him an idea. One that might just be worth thinking about further.

◆

Pryor made Michigan stop in front of the farmhouse, a couple feet up from an old pickup truck. Robby continued on up the road, no doubt happy as hell to be clear of them. The engine off, Pryor reached into the glove compartment. He pulled out the 9mm he used on the last guy who tried to put one over on Mae, shoving her halfway out of the car when she was finished, his wallet still in his pants, which were still around his ankles. "Blow and run," they called it. Pryor palmed the weapon for a moment as he recalled the memory of the guy soiling himself on the seat of his Toyota, so new it still carried temporary tags from the dealer, when he appeared at the driver's side window and suggested the john might have forgotten to give Mae something for her troubles.

It was the sight of the eye that always did it. Not the gun. The eye.

"What a dump," Michigan said.

"Shut up," Pryor said.

"I'm just saying. You think there's money in there?" Pointing dismissively at the farmhouse, the roof sagging like a weak smile and missing several shingles. Plants growing out of one of the side gutters.

"We'll see," Pryor said, but in truth, he shared Michigan's skepticism. Not that it was about the money.

"You're sure no one comes here?"

Archie, in the back seat.

"Sure I'm sure," Pryor snapped.

But what he thought was: am I? He only had Robby's word for it, and who knew how good that was. Really good, according to Michigan, who'd vouched for the kid, but that hardly settled the matter. Michigan reliable like Mae was sober. Pryor realized in that instant how much he missed Baby. The guy was steady under fire and didn't ask so many damn questions. It was a shame, when it came right down to it, shooting him like that. Not that he'd had any choice. But it would have made moments like this so much easier having him around. So much better than dealing with Michigan and Archie.

"I'll be right back," Pryor said, opening the door. He breathed in the warm country air, shutting his eyes and relishing a smell he normally associated with prison yards, or cemeteries. He opened his eyes, shoved the gun in his waistband, pulled his shirt out, and flopped the bottom edge over the weapon. He took the porch steps two at a time, stopped at the door, and knocked loudly. *Bam-bam-bam.*

When no one answered he glanced toward the van and saw that both Michigan and Archie were staring at the barn. At the barn, and not at him. But what was Pryor supposed to do about it exactly? Throw a tantrum that they weren't paying attention to him?

"What?"

Pryor turned and stared at the woman standing in the doorway, her shadow long under the porchlight—a single, fly-specked bulb, not even covered with a globe or shade. She was thin as a rake propped against a garage wall, wearing a shapeless patterned dress gray with age with a face like a dried-up apple someone stuck on the end of a stick. She was holding a shotgun in her arms, the double barrel leveled at his chest. She seemed about to say something else, but then stopped, her gaze fixed on his eye. He could see the transformation in her own eyes, as he'd seen so many times before, from the expression of someone used to not taking crap from anyone to someone thrown off balance purely by his face. The shotgun lowered a notch. Now they were making progress, Pryor thought, pulling out his own gun so fast it looked like a magic trick. Now they were back on course.

9

J. P. suspected old-man Hartzell had lost it for good. Who calls in reports of suspicious people, then balks at letting you look around? He grinned, thinking about what June, normally so clean mouthed, said of the couple one time. "*Bat shit crazy*," she said, moving her pointer finger in a circle at the side of her head. Then he thought about being with her that afternoon, and smiled. And then remembered Marks's taunting at roll call and his mood turned dark.

He swung past Clayton and Priscilla's place two more times that night anyway. Crazy or not, Hartzell might stop calling if he saw J. P. taking him seriously. The first time, around six, he made a point of turning down the drive and coming all the way down to the farmhouse. He paused, activated his siren so it gave off a couple of "whoops," and waited until the door opened. When Clayton came out on the porch J. P. waved but stayed in the cruiser. Just as well, given the scowl Hartzell rewarded him with. He drove around the gravel circle and then back onto the road. Mission accomplished.

Two hours later, after clearing a car-deer on the edge of town, J. P. swung through the parking lot of the Dutch House Inn. He thought about going inside, grabbing himself a piece of pie, but decided against it on second thought. He knew he needed to watch his weight—or at least knew June needed to watch it. Anyway, they were both trying to shed a few. And it's not like anybody inside needed to see an overweight cop picking up dessert. He signaled his location to Joyce, looked around, paused to let a guy walk past him carrying three dinners in plastic bags, and headed back toward the Hartzells'.

This time, he parked just a few feet down off the road. Still nothing to be seen. Below him, the farmyard visible from an outside light on the barn at the corner of the roof. A light on in the farmhouse, but probably not for long, he guessed. The Hartzells didn't have a TV and he knew neither of them liked to waste electricity. Slowly, keeping an eye out behind, he backed up and went on his way. It was a big county, and there was a lot more to do that night.

◆

J. P. considered a third stop at the farmhouse, around eleven, but instead turned a hundred yards early and followed a county road along the back of the property, past the fields, coming to a halt where a farm lane cut up the middle of the corn. He shined his utility belt flashlight onto the path, slowly moving the beam to the left and the right, then shifted it into the stalks of corn themselves. But it was useless, like using a match to peer into a forest. The car-mounted light would have been much more effective, but Marks had the only cruiser with one installed and somehow Vick never managed to order more. J. P. heard a rustle, deep in the field, and he whipped the light in that direction. Nothing. Raccoon or possum, most likely. He thought about stepping out of the cruiser, walking up the lane, surveying the property from the rear, coming up onto the barn and the house from behind, but decided against it. He was already closing in on the end of his shift, and in the unlikely event something happened, God knew how long it would take backup to arrive.

Instead, he reversed and went back east, following the main road around a series of curves until he emerged onto the highway two miles down. He went right and drove back into town. On the outskirts he passed the tractor company and the used car place and the Dutch House Inn, two stories and almost a block long, and regretted not going inside earlier. He thought for a second: would June and the others still be there, after church? No, too late. Nine thirty is their limit, tops, and now it was pushing eleven fifteen. He glanced in his rearview mirror as he approached the light and saw a couple walk out the restaurant's front door. He drove into downtown, around the square, and past all the dark businesses. He gave an extra-long look at the bank like they were supposed to—supposed to under his father, anyway. Then, on the spur of the moment he continued on back out of town. He pulled into the restaurant parking lot a minute later. He peered around in a way he hoped indicated he was just checking the place out, as you would, on duty and all, and walked up to the door.

Locked. He sighed, peeked inside, didn't see anyone, tried it a second time, and turned to go. He was back at the cruiser when he heard someone call his name.

"Everything okay?"

"Sure," he called back.

Tina. Still stuffed into the long gingham dress with white lace at the sleeves and collar that she had to wear for a uniform, all the girls had to wear, the ribbony white sash barely forming a waistline. Her prematurely thinning black hair tucked up inside a Dutch House Inn bonnet. They were third or fourth cousins on his mother's side. Tina a little bit older than him but sometimes seeming much younger, almost like a little sister.

"Sorry," he said with a wave. "Was just checking if you were still open."

"Did you need something, J. P.?"

He hesitated. "You don't have any pies left, do you?"

Five minutes later he was back in his cruiser with a boxed-up shoofly inside a white Dutch House Inn plastic bag. Ten minutes after that, he was on station, filling Vick in on Clayton and Priscilla. Marks came in five minutes later, a grin on his face.

"What's so funny?" Vick said.

"Busted this Mexican family, must have been seven kids in the car. No seatbelts, nothing. Guy driving could barely speak English. All he had was some kind of Mexican ID card, like that's worth shit. I wrote him a ticket, but I kept saying, '*Migra, Migra,*' like on TV. You should have seen his face. I thought he was going to shit his pants."

"What's *migra*?"

"Immigration. The feds. *De-por-tation*. What we ought to do with all these people."

"You didn't actually call the feds," Vick said, uneasily.

"Hell, no," Marks said. "I'm not stupid. I was just trying to get my point across."

J. P. said, "What point was that?"

Marks whipped around to stare at him. "That they don't belong here and they ought to take their little brown asses back to their own country."

"Just so long as you didn't call the feds," Vick said.

"How do you know they weren't here legally?" J. P. said.

The room went a little quiet at that.

"Jesus H. Christ—you a beaner lover on top of everything else?" Marks said. When J. P. didn't reply, Marks added: "Or is it because the school's full of 'em and you don't want to upset June?"

"I didn't say—"

"'Cause I know you don't want to do anything to make the missus mad." Marks winked at Vick, who responded with a grunt. "Not with them pillows to rest your head on."

"I would appreciate you not—"

"Appreciate what, Deputy?"

J. P. didn't say anything. Not that he didn't want to. He wanted to say a lot of things to Marks. He also knew Marks knew that, and was just waiting for him to lose it, to mess up. He took another look at the picture of his father on the wall above the lockers on the other side of the room, nodded at Marks and Vick, retrieved his lunchbox from his locker, and went home.

Once inside, he took the pie out of its box, set it on the kitchen counter, and cut himself a slice. He ate it standing up, not even bothering to take off his utility belt. After the day he had. Like that was any excuse, he thought, examining the empty plate guiltily after he inhaled the dessert. He thought about hiding the rest of it from June, realized how silly that sounded, and set it in the fridge where she'd see it when she woke up the next morning. His way of fessing up, letting her know she was right; he should have had her bring him something home. She was sound asleep, snoring lightly, when he walked into the bedroom a few minutes later. Sasha at her feet at the end of the bed. He undressed in the dark, slipped into a pair of shorts, and tucked himself beneath the blankets.

"Mmm?" June said.

"Night," he said, taking her hand.

Even after she squeezed his hand in return and rolled over, he lay awake for a long time, staring at the ceiling, eyeing a crack in the dim gray light that he'd noticed for the first time last week. In another day or two June would bring it to his attention and ask him to fix it and he would, almost immediately, the first chance he had on his next day off. She would say that's one of the things she liked about him, that he didn't like to procrastinate. And he would think, not for the first time: you don't know how wrong you are. Because not procrastinating involved not wasting time. Whereas all he wanted was the one thing he knew was out of his reach: more time. Just a little more time to waste.

10

Pryor didn't stint washing his hands afterward, rubbing them over and over again, standing at the spigot behind the barn using the bar of soap he found in the farmhouse's upstairs bathroom. *Jesus*, he said to himself as he rolled the soap around. *All that shit in there. All that shit—except for any cash.* Yet he wasn't surprised, to tell the truth. You did what he did, hung out the places he hung out, you heard a lot of rumors. You figured out soon enough that three-quarters of them were bullshit and the rest half truths. Every once in a while something would pan out, like that time he heard about the cache of guns in the house off East Livingston and when he finally investigated it wasn't just guns, it was a fucking arsenal. It was enough for a small army. Which was what he expected in terms of defense, but once again he'd been pleasantly surprised. There was just no accounting for how dumb some people were.

So: no cash. He was sure about that. Because it wasn't like he didn't look. He knew how to search for that sort of prize. And how to make people tell him things. And he'd been thorough. Very thorough. But the most he came across were a big jar of pennies and a smaller jar of loose change in an upstairs bedroom. Between the two it might add up to fifty bucks. He didn't bother with it. But as he kept reminding himself, it wasn't about the cash. There were other things at play.

Pryor kept washing his hands, rolling the soap over and over, until he heard the sound of the van being driven inside the barn and the door rolling shut and Michigan killing the engine. Satisfied, he dried his hands on his shirt, pushed open the door at the back of the barn, and went inside.

11

"You sure you're going to be all right?" June said, looking across the table at J. P. the next morning.

"Yes."

"Sure you're sure?"

"I read an article once," J. P. said, taking a bite of toast. "It said people can live for almost a month without food, as long as they keep drinking water. And even then. Some of these earthquake victims? They go days without anything at all. Sometimes little babies. And you're only going for two days."

"Hardy har har," June said, stealing a spoonful of his eggs. Then she went over the list one more time, starting with that day's lunch and that evening's dinner, which she'd already prepared, and moving onto Saturday and a complicated supper that involved chunks of ham and beans and pineapple and mayonnaise. J. P. nodded gravely, careful to indicate he was listening. No need to vex her, especially after the way they started their day that morning, back at it again—June happily relentless in their quest to have a baby.

In any case, unspoken between them was the fact they both knew a better than even chance existed that he'd eat two of every three meals at the Dutch House Inn while she was gone. But they each also knew he'd be spending the weekend hours he wasn't on duty on a ladder, scraping and painting the utility room, and would earn whatever meal he ended up with. And June liked to keep things organized, and J. P. liked that about her.

"You going to miss me?" she said.

"Yes."

"I know that. But are you going to *miss* me?"

"Didn't I make that clear a few minutes ago?"

"That you did, Deputy. I'll give you that."

They were eating their toast and eggs at the little table in the kitchen, phones in their hands, checking headlines and updates and statuses. Light just beginning to creep through the curtains. Already the September days were growing shorter and shorter. J. P. could tell June was pleased he didn't go back to sleep afterward, that he joined her for breakfast even though he hadn't slept nearly enough, his shift ending as late as it did. But he wanted to see her off before school, since she was driving to her parents' house straight afterward. A ninetieth birthday party the next day, Saturday, for a great aunt, way over in Licking County on the other side of Columbus, something her folks would understand him missing even though her brother was coming in and it hadn't been that long since he'd rotated back stateside for good. Certainly not an outing J. P. could have requested a day off for anyway. Not with Vick doing the rosters and Marks watching him do them.

"One of my girls asked me about this yesterday in class," June said. She raised her phone, showing him the screen.

"About what?"

"This guy robbed a bank. Killed a police officer."

J. P. put his own phone down. "Here?"

June studied the screen. "Des Moines. That's Iowa, right?"

"I think so. How she'd know about it?"

"Saw it on TV. I don't know why parents let their kids look at things like that. I'm not going to, that's for sure."

"What'd she ask?"

"Why someone would do that. Rob a bank. Kill a police officer."

"It's a good question. What'd you say?"

"I said I didn't know. But that there are bad people in the world that sometimes do things we can't understand."

"Good answer." Something his father might have said, he realized.

"John says some people are just inherently evil. Putting aside how they were raised and all that."

"He should know."

"What do you think?"

"About what?"

"About evil people?"

J. P. looked at his wife. His stomach suddenly felt funny, seeing the way she was staring at him. Didn't take a rocket scientist to know what she was really thinking on the subject of bank robbers and dead police officers and evil people.

"I like to think most people are good. But there's always a few that just can't get with the program. That's been my experience. Not sure I could tell you if they're evil to boot."

"I bet John would agree with that."

"Mmm," J. P. said. He liked June's brother. Liked him a lot. He was what his father would have called salt of the earth. But he also found his service record a little intimidating, truth be told—three tours in all in Afghanistan, plus a couple places after that he couldn't talk about. So many medals. So many encounters with people who were probably inherently evil. Not that John ever did or said a single thing to draw attention. It just was what it was. Intimidating, but in a different way than Marks's time over there tended to make him feel. Because any discomfort with John was on him, J. P. Whereas Marks was not afraid to tell you how tough it had been and then gauge your reaction closely, like a man who takes pleasure in delivering bad news about someone else's sick relative.

"You'll be careful while I'm gone?"

"No need to," he said, patting her hand.

"Why not?" The slightest look of alarm in her eyes.

"I've got Sasha to protect me. What else would I need?"

"Now I'm really worried."

After breakfast, J. P. carried the dishes to the sink to rinse them. June brought her cup and dumped out the coffee and for a moment they stood there and hugged, a good long hug, the kind he liked, and then kissed. They kissed so long that J. P. thought it might go someplace beside the kitchen, that some more rearranging of pillows afterward might be in order. But June broke away with a sigh.

"I'm going to be late. But I want you to keep thinking about that. The whole weekend."

"I'll try."

"You better do more than try."

He stood at the door and waved while she pulled away. After the taillights disappeared up the street he walked back upstairs, lay down on the bed and shut his eyes. He needed to study some more, before his shift began, and he wanted to try scraping some more paint. And he was hoping to stop by Feller's to put in some target practice on the range. But first he needed to sleep a little longer. Lying there, it was easy to make good on his promise to June, to think about her.

But before long, he also found himself thinking about Vick. And Marks. And Priscilla and Clayton Hartzell and the blue-gray van supposedly scoping out their place. After another minute he opened his eyes, his mind racing, knowing sleep would elude him for now, like a man who glimpses a figure in the mist down a wooded path and tries in vain to reach him, to see who it is, only to watch the figure recede each time he approaches just a little bit closer. J. P. walked downstairs and into the garage and changed into his old clothes and hunted up a scraper and went back inside, into the utility room he was repainting and went to work. It felt good to get a head start on the day.

12

Myles was still unconscious when Penny stepped into his room. They gave her fifteen minutes this time, and told her not to touch any of the equipment. She could tell the nurses at the ICU station didn't think much of her, with her worn clothes and shadows under her eyes and bulgy nylon string bag, and maybe they had a point. Penny didn't think much of herself either, right at the moment.

Sitting beside Myles, she squeezed her eyes shut and kept them that way until little flashes of colors danced across her interior vision. She tried to think how she'd reached this point, to this moment in time, sitting in the hospital like this. Myles fighting for his life beside her. This was not what they planned. In his last year inside, they'd come to an agreement about how things would be. Could be. Myles was more than ready to give up his wandering. To come home in a physical sense but also mentally too. The arrest had started him down that path, but as she reminded him, it was his decision to testify that changed everything. A decision she had to admit she was skeptical of at first. Because no one likes a snitch. And because of who he'd be snitching against.

There were other ways to do this, she knew. Speaking of snitching. She could go to those detectives, the ones who gave her their cards. The white lady with the too-tanned face and the roots that were showing, and the Black guy who reminded her of Archie. Tell them of Pryor's threats. She didn't doubt they'd pursue it. But then they'd want to know about the gun Myles had. And him just out of prison.

No, the problem wasn't the detectives, the police. The authorities. It was, as always, the person whom she'd be fingering. They tried once—Myles had tried, in that courtroom—and here's what they had to show for it. Myles, tubes snaking out of him as he breathed on a machine in a darkened hospital room. What if they did catch Pryor, arrest him, charge him? What if he went away for a long time? Prison walls were leaky. That's what Myles always told her. He said he couldn't believe how many cell phones he saw around, brought in somehow—shoved into visitors' underwear, tossed over walls, smuggled by kitchen workers, even sometimes by the COs. Pryor might be inside, might be inside for a couple decades, but he'd still be controlling things. Controlling Archie and Michigan and all of them. And how were Myles and Penny supposed to live with that hanging over them?

"It's the only way," she whispered. She flinched. She hadn't realized she spoke aloud. She held her breath to see if Myles heard, if her voice registered on him in some way. But he slept on, oblivious, wan and thin, ventilator doing its cold, mechanical work. Looking more like his father than himself, as though he'd aged twenty years in two days. And maybe he had. Penny reached out and ran her fingers across his right hand, careful not to disturb the pulse monitor attached to his forefinger. She stood. She realized that more than anything, even more than seeing Myles open his eyes and smile, she'd been hoping for a response to her statement. *The only way.* Because she desperately wanted it to be true. Needed it to be. Because if she was being honest with herself, she was more than a little scared. She was downright—

"No," she said, standing up. "Enough's enough."

It really was the only way, she thought, leaving the room and heading to the parking garage. She held her head up higher. Yes. She was certain of it now.

◆

Traffic was light on the highway, most of the commuters coming the other way, toward town, which was a good thing since she could barely push the Aurora to sixty. All she needed was one of those tractor trailers riding up her rear end when she couldn't go any faster. After she turned off at the Dublin exit she pulled into a gas station and asked directions; it wasn't as if Brandi had invited her up very often. Randy? That was another story. The kid behind the counter couldn't keep his eyes off Penny's chest while he tried to explain where the street was that she wanted. She thought, *I'm tired of guys who aren't Myles looking at me that way.*

She parked on the street in front of Brandi's house ten minutes later, after a wrong turn and stopping to ask a lady walking her dog directions. The lady looked at her and her car and told her what she needed to know with the voice of someone on the receiving end of a wrong-number call. Penny walked up the little curvy walkway to the door past flower beds and grass so stiff and green and weed-free it resembled a lawn in a computer game. She rang the bell, hearing the ridiculous, deep gong, like something in a castle. She glanced around while she waited. A neighborhood of big houses and big trees and big backyards and big cars. Black mulch rose in cultivated heaps across the front of almost every home like enormous piles of chocolate shavings. Driveways glistened with fresh tar jobs. She pressed the bell again. *Gong.*

She heard the thud of footsteps. The door opened. To her surprise, Randy stood there, wearing red workout shorts and a loose-fitting Buckeyes jersey. Bottle of beer in his right hand.

"Penny?"

"Is Brandi here?"

He eyed her curiously. "You mean Brooke? She's at a kids' thing. At the library. With Madyson."

"Why are you here?"

"Day off," he said, suppressing a burp.

"When's she coming back?"

He looked at her without saying anything, but not like that kid in the gas station, who gawked with typical teenage clumsiness. Randy's expression was like someone who's just finished a big meal and realized with a hint of surprise he's already hungry again. He took a drink of his beer. He wiped his mouth with his left hand.

"Not for a while," he said, eyes trained on Penny's chest. "She just left."

13

They slept late, later than Pryor planned on, but then, where was the fire? He looked at his phone. A little past ten A.M. Just under twenty-four hours to go. Well, less than that, given what had to happen between now and then.

He rose quietly, careful not to make any noise. Crept to where Archie and Michigan were sleeping, wrapped in the blankets Pryor lifted from Walmart right after boosting the van. Dead asleep, which was no surprise given how many beers he'd handed them the night before, watching them drink while he took swigs from his bottle of Jack. The two of them were overly curious about the farmhouse, about the lady who answered the door. Archie especially. But Pryor made it clear he was the only one going in or out.

He thought about doing it right now. Saving himself some time. First Michigan, then Archie—he wanted just a couple words with him first—one bullet each. A shame to waste ammunition like that, but you couldn't have everything. He went so far as to return to his own bunched-up blanket and retrieve his gun, the one he hid in his waistband before knocking on the door the night before. Beside it, the woman's shot gun. An antique, something from way back, 1950s or 1960s, but functional and beautiful nonetheless. It would be more than easy.

The problem, he thought, standing there, was the timing. Moving the gun from one hand to the other, like a man trying to make up his mind whether to steal a painting or just deface it. He hadn't expected to be here, be inside this cave of a structure, for this long. The original plan to come out here tonight, leaving less chance of detection. Archie and Michigan fully believing he needed them for tomorrow's job. Never occurring to them that the barn, at least where they were concerned, was less a hideout than a tomb.

On the surface, he didn't doubt what Robby told him, that his aunt and uncle were hermits who saw no one and went nowhere. Pryor's time inside the farmhouse confirmed that to his satisfaction. But you never knew. On the outside chance something happened, someone did show up, it wouldn't hurt to have Archie and Michigan around. Archie asked too many goddamned questions and Michigan was certifiably stupid and crazy, but both could hold their own in a gunfight. It wouldn't be the best outcome, not by far. But it would be better to have them around a little bit longer—or, who knew, a lot longer, depending on how the day went—than to be caught short-handed. A lot depended on what he could figure out about the cop that Archie did or didn't see the night before as they idled beside Baby's body.

"What are you doing?"

Archie, awake and propped up on his left side, eyeing Pryor.

"Nothing."

"Why do you have a gun?"

"Just checking," Pryor said.

"Checking what?"

"Checking how it feels."

"Okay." Sitting up now, still looking at Pryor. "And?"

"And what?"

"How does it feel?"

"Good," Pryor said, aiming it at Archie.

"Hey, woah now." He raised his hands in protest.

"Relax," Pryor said, setting the gun down. "I'm just kidding around."

14

"Maybe if you told me what you needed from Brooke I could help you," Randy said.

They were sitting on blond-pine stools in the kitchen around a center island as long and wide as two picnic tables end to end, the island containing a sink and six-burner gas stove and a wide wooden chopping board. Randy was having another beer. Penny was drinking water.

"Like I said. I just need to borrow her car."

"For what?"

"To run an errand."

"What kind of errand."

"Just something."

"What's wrong with your car?"

It's a fucking piece of shit, as you well know, asshole.

"It's not running so good," Penny said. "So you think she'll be back soon?"

"Think it's gonna be a while, like I said. Maddie's got a 'play date' afterwards." Grinning at his air quotes.

"Why's that funny?"

"No reason," Randy said, but it was clear what he was thinking: women's work.

◆

Penny knew perfectly well how it happened. She saw the whole thing unfold, from the sidelines. It was just hard to believe it happened at all. That Brandi actually pulled it off.

Brandi, her sister, a year and a half younger, out of high school with exactly zero prospects but with the body and looks that slutty cowgirl costumes were designed for. Broke, answering a Craigslist ad for a dancing job one morning. Two days later she was the newest member of the Candy Kiss Crew, ten girls who rode around in a van decorated with oversized red lipstick kisses and who performed at stag parties and fraternity bashes and the kind of office Christmas celebrations where the girls wore skimpy Santa suits and the guests were men whose wives were out drinking wine with girlfriends that night. Early on, Penny was still giving Brandi rides to some of the gigs. This one time she sneaked into a big house on a golf course in Grove City and watched them perform in front of a bunch of guys, and it was dancing the way eating barbecue with your bare hands is fine dining. But she'd give Brandi this: the money was good, and the dates that inevitably followed the performances did not involve dinner at Waffle House.

One night a couple of summers ago the Candy Kiss Crew were in a banquet hall north of the Polaris mall where a roomful of young First Ohio Bank executives were celebrating somebody's promotion when Randy walked up to Brandi. He told her how much he enjoyed her dancing and asked if she had always been that musically oriented and she must have done yoga and ballet, right? And before Penny and Mama and Ma-Maw and anybody else knew exactly what was happening, Brandi was sporting a hunk of glittering rock on her left hand the size of hail that takes out windshields, and eyes, and talking about patterns for towels and brushed steel refrigerators and copper countertops. Suddenly she wasn't Brandi anymore, either, she was Brooke, because, as she explained, on one of the few times she came back to their side of town and their house, "Brandi and Randy? Too cute, you know? Besides, I kind of need a more suburban-y name." So she pretended Brooke was a middle name she preferred and not long after that she was living in the big house in Dublin with Randy the First Ohio Bank executive and the mulch and the back yard and the garage and her own Honda Pilot to match Randy's and a golden Labrador named Cooper. A year after that, along came a fat baby girl named Madyson. And Brandi/Brooke hadn't been back home just by herself, without Randy and baby in tow, in a long, long time.

◆

Penny looked across the island at Randy looking at her. She thought of her niece, two years old and walking. Thought of Mack when he was that age. His hands on everything as he dashed from room to room. Not like Myles as a boy, who'd been quieter, from what she could gather. More reserved. The wildness didn't come until later.

"So, what can I do for you, Penny?"

"Thing is," she said. She thought of Pryor, standing at Mama's doorway. Staring at Myles with his eye, the way he did, knowing the reaction it generated. Calling him Baby, from that stupid movie, which he knew Penny hated. *So you're a nobody, then.*

"Yeah?" Randy licked his lips with his red tongue and took a long pull of beer. His eyes were shiny and she wondered how soon after Brandi and Madyson left the house he opened his first bottle.

"You still have your gun?"

"My gun?"

"Yeah. The Glock."

He examined her with new interest. "Maybe. Why?"

"I need to borrow that too. Along with Brandi's car."

"You need to borrow my gun?"

"You heard me."

"Borrow *Brooke*'s car and my gun."

"Yeah."

"You've got my attention now, Penny. Except the problem is, Brooke's not here at the moment."

"I can see that."

He tapped the bottle of beer on the island top. *Knock-knock-knock.* "And why the gun?"

"For protection."

"Protection from what?"

"You still have it or not?"

He put his beer down on the island, though his eyes never left her face. "Yeah. You wanna see it?"

"No. I want to borrow it. And some ammunition."

"I don't know. Maybe you should see it first."

"Yes or no's fine."

"I keep it in the bedroom. Next to my side of the bed."

"That's nice."

"I know what you're thinking. Wouldn't it be safer locked up? But it's like a condom. If it's not there when you need it, what's the point?"

"Uh huh."

"So you want to see it or what?"

"I'd just like to borrow it. If it's okay. Just for a day or two."

"For protection."

"That's right."

"Like a condom."

"Yeah, sure."

"You know, life's kind of funny," Randy said, leaning back a little on his stool.

Penny didn't say anything, just watched him.

"Brooke and me, we hit it off at first, you know? Really *gelled*, if you know what I mean." He made his hands into fists and pushed them together with a bony click like a man about to fight. Or in Randy's case, pay someone to mow the lawn.

"Okay."

"But you know how it is? It's like, everything's great, and the house and everything, you know? But then you have a baby, and it's like, wow." He laughed, and not in a nice way. "What a change."

"What do you mean?" she said, knowing exactly what he meant.

"We're family, Penny, or I wouldn't even be telling you this," Randy said, and as he spoke his right eye crossed. Penny remembered something Brandi told her once, right when the two of them started going out, when she and her sister were still talking. How Randy's right eye always crossed whenever he told "a little white lie" and how cute it was.

She was pretty sure Randy didn't know that Brandi knew that about his eye.

"But, no secrets, right?" Randy went on. "I mean, that's what family's for. So it's like, the physical stuff, you know? I mean, we were good together. But the baby." He laughed again. "Like a cold shower except wearing diapers and sucking on a binky, you know what I mean."

"Sure."

"Guy gets lonely."

"I bet."

"You must have been lonely," he said, staring at her. "Myles away like that."

"Maybe."

"Where is he, anyway?"

She hesitated. She realized Randy didn't know what happened to Myles. Why would he? Brandi was busy with her own thing, and the sisters rarely talked anymore. It was like different worlds with them. Or worse, maybe Brandi did know, and still hadn't bothered to be in touch.

Penny said, "He's resting."

"He's resting, and you're here asking for my gun and Brandi's car?"

"To borrow," she said. His unconscious slip from Brooke back to Brandi not unnoticed.

"Maybe you're still a little lonely."

"I'm okay."

"You sure? 'Cause I'd like to show you the gun. But I'm pretty lonely myself. It's been a long time, you know what I mean."

"I'm sorry about that."

"The thing is, if I stay lonely, I might not be able to show you the gun."

Penny didn't say anything. She lowered her eyes to keep the anger from showing. The fuck was it with men? She knew what she had to do, but she didn't want to. Really didn't want to. Not with everything going on. And she was on a kind of deadline. The sooner she finished this, the better. But she knew, in her position, in her station, she probably didn't have any choice. Not unlike the way Brandi had felt, shaking it for the Candy Kiss Crew before Randy walked up to her that night.

"It's not good to be lonely," she said.

She trailed him through a living room dominated by a black leather sectional couch and enormous matching recliner, into the great hall so big you could play three-on-three basketball with room to spare—she bet Randy had tried it, too, the asshole—and then up the stairs, her hand gliding along a gleaming mahogany rail. On the second floor, she peeked at the bedroom on the right, Madyson's, all pink and white, toys galore, the walls a vast mural of every Disney princess ever imagined skipping through a meadow. She turned and stepped into Randy and

Brandi's room. Randy was sitting on the bed, looking at her like a little boy on Christmas morning. He patted the bed. No sign of the gun.

"Can I see it?" she said, unbuttoning the top of her jeans.

"See what?"

"See your gun?"

"That's what I'm about to show you."

15

Sure enough, J. P. ended up at the Dutch House for lunch. He felt a little guilty, thinking about the enormous sandwich June left for him in the fridge, ham and cheese and salami and turkey and lettuce and tomato bulging between two slices of his favorite Italian bread, knowing how much effort she put into it. But he reasoned it would be perfect for lunch tomorrow, and perhaps a little less work than the meal she left him directions for, and then maybe they could have that meal when she came back, to save her some effort. Which would leave more time for baby-making. So there was that.

It was busy at the restaurant, with several people standing around by the cash register, waiting to pay or be seated. Some he knew, most he didn't. People came from Cleveland and Cincinnati and beyond just to eat here, it was so popular. Something about people and the Amish. When his turn finally came they gave him a booth by himself. He didn't bother opening the menu.

"June's off to see her folks?"

J. P. looked up as Tina appeared and set a glass of water in front of him.

"How'd you know that?"

"Word gets around."

"I guess it does."

"Anything besides water?"

"Just iced tea."

"How's your mom?"

"Pretty well. Keeping the boys in line."

"They need it," she said with a smile, and went to fetch his drink.

She was right: they did need it. Sometimes he wasn't sure how his mom managed. The lone woman, Executive Administrative Assistant II, in a highway department Quonset hut on the edge of Darbytown. Her coworkers a quarrelsome mix of drivers and road crew guys and managers. He'd been called out there more than once to settle the latest shouting match over scheduling and invoice responsibility. Even a fight about whose turn it was to ride shotgun on the paving jobs. The expectation after his father died had been that she'd quit, take the insurance money, and find something else, something not as volatile, maybe a little friendlier. But she surprised everyone and stayed on. "Place would go to heck if I left, and that's a fact," she said more than once. "I've got a certain responsibility to the boys."

Responsibility ran in the family, J. P. thought, trying to decide, as usual, if that was a good thing.

Tina returned with the tea. She set it down and retrieved an order pad from a pocket in her dress. "Ready, J. P.?" The only costumer she didn't call "Hon," in deference to them being relations.

"Meatloaf dinner. Corn instead of green beans. Mashed potatoes but can you put the gravy in a little bowl on the side?"

"Already wrote that last part down. Any bread?"

"Just a slice."

"Watching your weight?"

"June's watching it."

They both smiled.

Tina lingered instead of retreating to the kitchen. She was one of five waitresses on for lunch, all of them in the same gingham dresses and bonnets as they glided back and forth from table to table and into and out of the kitchen. They looked like real Amish ladies the way college kids wearing sheets and sandals looked Greek. But J. P. guessed the customers didn't mind.

"So, how's it going?"

"Going?" J. P. said.

"Downtown. With Marks and Vick."

"Same ol', same ol', I guess." But he was suddenly wary, and hid what he thought his face might be showing by taking a drink of tea. With sugar, the way he liked it, but that he knew Tina wouldn't have served all doctored up like that had he and June both been in the booth.

"I hear Marks is going to run for sheriff."

He nodded, frozen. It was news to him, but he tried not to react.

"What do you think of that?"

"Not much, I suppose. Out of my hands." That much was true.

"Why?"

He felt his stomach clench. Why were they having this conversation?

"He knows the right people, is why."

"And that's good enough reason to run?"

"Someone has to run, with the sheriff retiring."

"And that's another thing," Tina said. "Why's Waters leaving?"

"I don't know. He's sixty-two."

"Lots of people run again at that age."

"Maybe."

"I heard he was tired of dealing with the whole gang. That he's a little scared of Marks."

"His wife's been sick. And they've got grandkids."

"And you're just going to let Marks do this?"

"Me?"

"You heard me."

"What about it?"

Tina pushed a strand of hair back into her bonnet and rubbed her forehead. One of the things J. P. had always liked about Tina was the owl tattooed on her left shoulder, fierce looking, with a curved beak like a dinosaur claw and eyes as wide and round as buttons on a peacoat. Her favorite bird, she said, long before those owls in the *Harry Potter* books, a fact most people didn't believe but he knew to be true because growing up they hadn't been allowed to read those kinds of books because of church. The only reason she landed the job at Dutch House Inn was the collar of the dress was so high it missed showing the tufts of the owl's ears by a quarter inch or so. Tina still went to the same church, the same one he and June went to, and the elders still didn't think much of *Harry Potter*, though after the crap he dealt with every day, J. P. couldn't imagine what harm the books did compared to all that. They also still didn't think much of owl tattoos. But at eighteen, Tina hadn't cared what they thought. He would have. But she hadn't.

"It should be you," she said, slipping the order pad into her pocket in a single, smooth motion, as if she were holstering a gun. "You should be running."

"I'm not old enough."

She clicked her tongue. "And Marks is?"

"He's close to forty."

"Going on fourteen."

"He has more experience. And he saw, you know, combat."

"You're in the Guard."

"It's not the same thing."

"Says who? At least you help people here."

"That's not fair."

"Just think about it," she said. "I'm just saying, is all."

"Okay."

She left his booth and walked two tables over, where a couple in motorcycle chaps and jackets had just been seated. She smiled and listened as the man rattled off a drinks order, but as she wrote she glanced at J. P. and caught his eye, just briefly. And as she did, she rolled her left shoulder, like someone nursing an injury, and in that second J. P. caught a glimpse of the top of the owl's head as her collar shifted. He smiled, unable to help himself, and sipped some more tea. But he couldn't enjoy the sweet, cold drink, he realized after a moment. He set it down. Not after what Tina said.

Why wouldn't he run?

He knew the answer, of course. He just couldn't bring himself to tell her.

16

Penny took her time dressing. She knew she should feel guilty, taking her sister's clothes like this. But she hardly felt anything. The biggest problem, she realized, was deciding what to wear that was comfortable but didn't make her stand out too much. And that was an issue because, as she had to admit, Brandi had a lot of nice clothes. The dresses and blouses and skirts and pants had labels she'd heard of but couldn't imagine buying herself, in the same way you read about the names of kings and queens in places like Norway and Thailand but never imagined actually going there. She settled on two pairs of jeans, a red sleeveless blouse, and a light-green dress that had nothing to do with the job in front of her but which she thought she'd look good in.

As she wrapped her thrift store pants and shirt around her beat-up running shoes, the pair with the holes in the toes, she marveled again at the size of the walk-in closet. The space nearly as large as the bedroom she and Brandi shared as children. As she lingered, gaping at everything inside, she was interrupted by Randy calling her name. But not loudly. Because she'd warned him against shouting. She ignored him. He wasn't worth the trouble at this point.

She was a little surprised when he handed her the gun, just as she'd asked, right after she undid the second button on her jeans. "It's big," she said, smiling at him with her eyes open and her eyebrows lifted, mimicking the look she'd seen the girls give their boyfriends in the costume shop. "Sure is," Randy said, licking the underside of his top lip. He might have been about to say something else, probably something disgusting, but he never had the chance as she drove the side of the weapon hard against his left temple, hard and sure and without hesitation. She didn't know exactly where that impulse came from, but she thought about Myles in the hospital bed as she did it. Randy grunted as if he'd picked something heavy off the garage floor and fell straight over on the bed.

She thought about hitting him again, not to be sure, because he was definitely out like a light, but as punishment for dreaming she'd ever drop her shorts for him in a million, million years, gun and car be damned. That, and for all the dirty smiles he'd thrown her way in the long months Myles was gone, like he was some kind of prized suitor and she was nothing more than an object to be competed for. But she held off. He wasn't going anywhere.

The hardest part was undressing him as he lay unconscious, a few bubbles of spit dribbling out of his mouth over those red lips and onto the black, neatly trimmed beard. Naked like that on his back, his stuff just sitting there, tiny and floppy, you couldn't help but giggle. She thought about going to the garage or the basement for rope, but in the end settled on eight red First Ohio Bank shirts she found in his closet. She started with the dirty ones he'd wadded up and thrown on the floor, probably waiting for Brandi to wash them. She knotted the left sleeves around his wrists and ankles, two shirts per appendage, and then tied the other ends to the bedposts. She pulled tight, so that his arms and legs separated into a jumping jack kind of pose, except lying down and unconscious. Assured of the strength of the knots, she went downstairs, opened the refrigerator, and removed three bottles of beer. He drank St. Pauli Girl, which figured, the boobs on the

German girl on the label spilling out of her dress like balls of rising pizza dough. She opened them, went back upstairs, and poured them over his face, then his chest, then his junk, in slow but steady streams. After a minute he sputtered, opened and shut his eyes, strained at the constricting shirts, relaxed a moment, and then raised his head and looked straight at Penny.

"Smile," she said, and fired off a series of pictures with his iPhone. The one he placed on his nightstand after flopping down on the bed.

"What, the fuck," he managed.

"It would help if you held still," she said, taking a second series from an angle at the bottom of the bed that managed to capture both his junk and his reddening face, one in front of the other. She felt a little proud of that one.

"What are you doing? Cut me loose."

She took the last set with a photo of Brandi she took from the mantel downstairs, her sister smiling as she squinted into the sun on a boat on a body of water someplace. That was another thing about Randy. He boated. Penny set the picture down on Randy's stomach, which she noticed was a lot jigglier than when she first met him, and took three or four more photos. No need to overdo it at this point.

"You slut. You bitch. You whore." He struggled the best he could, but the knots were true and held, like knots on a sailing ship resisting the strain of an insistent, storm-brewing wind.

"Listen carefully. I'm borrowing the gun, like I asked. Just borrowing—not stealing or anything. And your car, since Brandi's not here. And I need some money. And a credit card. Which I already found in your wallet. Just so you know."

"Borrowing my ass—"

"I'll pay you back the money, and the gas." She hesitated, looking at the gun. "And any rounds. But I may be gone for a couple of days. So this is where you have to pay attention. Okay? If you call anybody, like the police or whoever, or try to find me, or anything, I'm going to send these pictures to everyone in your contacts. Everyone."

"You'll need my passcode," he said, smirking even in his condition.

"Tell it to me."

"Like hell—"

He gave it up in two seconds, staring at his gun in her hand pointed at his junk.

She scrolled up and down his contacts page. The phone so much nicer than her piece of crap flip phone. She stopped. "I'll start with this one. 'Bitch Boss.' Which is not a nice thing to say about your boss, just so you know. And then I'll probably go to 'Mom and Dad.'" She paused. "No, sorry. First 'Grandma.' Then 'Mom and Dad'"

"Listen," he said, panic filling his eyes. "I didn't—"

"Facebook, too. That's easier, because I can just post one picture and lots and lots of people will see it all at once."

Randy licked his lips. "I—"

"Same goes with Brandi. I know how she can be. She's going to want to do something. She's going to be mad at me. I don't blame her. We're a lot alike, believe it or not. But I'm serious." She held up the phone. "*Everyone*. Understand?"

He said nothing, just glared at her in rage and disbelief.

"And don't do anything stupid, like calling the phone company and cutting me off. I'm gonna text these pictures to my own phone as soon as I walk out of here. This phone goes dead, those pictures go out. You listening?"

He nodded, not speaking. And that's when she went into the closet, to pick out some clothes.

◆

"What?" she said, as she emerged a couple of minutes later.

"I have to go to the bathroom. If you could just"—he looked down at his right foot, wriggled his toes—"I promise I won't do anything."

"I don't have time. You'll have to hold it."

"I'm sorry, Penny. I didn't mean to, you know, before. What I suggested. It's just, the baby. Lonely. Like that. Please? I really have to go."

She paused at the door and held up the phone so he could see it. Get the message, one last time.

"Penny—"

She headed downstairs, gun and wallet balanced on top of her old clothes.

"Slut! Bitch! Whore!"

On the way out of the subdivision, she saw the same woman again, still walking her dog, rolled down the window on the shiny red Pilot, and waved. The woman waved back with a big, bright smile.

17

What would Myles do?

It's what Penny found herself thinking as she drove toward the highway. What's the first thing he would do?

She knew the basics, of course. She had to figure out where Pryor was staying, and how to approach him, and how to do that without her ending up in the same place Myles was at the moment. Or dead. Or in prison herself. She understood all that. But what she found herself concentrating on was: what would Myles do right away? How would he go about things? He'd have a plan, she knew. He always had a plan. Even yesterday, out jogging with somebody's gun, searching for Pryor no doubt, he'd had a plan. Maybe not a great one. But still.

Like the time the Bellamy kid stole Ma-Maw's car. Everyone knew who did it. No question about it. And Ma-Maw beside herself, because she needed that car to drive Clyde to the VA out on James Road for his appointments. Sure, they could take the bus if they wanted to ride two hours one way. A taxi or Uber out of the question because of the expense. Penny and Mama were all for going to the police, telling them what happened. But Myles had other ideas. Because Bellamy was stealing a lot of cars in those days. So he fixed it with his buddy Tom, and Tom found an old beater and drove it right onto Bellamy's property, right through the gate and past the ratty-looking mobile home that doubled as the junkyard's office, and asked if he was buying. And Bellamy looked at him like he was crazy, because everyone knew Tom ran with Myles, and Myles was connected to Ma-Maw through Penny, and what the hell was he thinking? But Tom was insistent, that he had nothing to do with that, that he needed the money, and was Bellamy buying or not? So Bellamy bought.

And late that night, after the yard was closed and everyone was gone, Myles popped open the trunk of the car from the inside and climbed out, a little stiffly after lying there all afternoon. But not so stiffly that he didn't remember to fling the steaks onto the ground right away, which was a good thing, because the dogs Bellamy kept were big and mean and liked meat. While they devoured the steaks Myles crept around the yard until he found Ma-Maw's car, none the worse for wear. There were nicer cars near it, and Myles thought about trading up, but he didn't want to seem greedy. Instead, he stuck to the plan. Drove Ma-Maw's car right up to the gate. Used the shears he brought with him in the trunk to snap the lock and slice a hole through the stiff, interlocking metal fencing. Then he walked back to the trailer serving as the office and doused the door with gasoline. From there he spread the fuel to the first pile of tires he found and from there to a row of old pickup trucks. Satisfied, he took out a pack of matches, scraped one against the sandpaper edge, dropped it and then hoofed it like hell to the car as the flames erupted. It was the easiest thing in the world to nudge Ma-Maw's car through the compromised gate and out onto the road. The last thing he saw as he drove away were the dogs, running toward the opening in the compound, away from the fire.

So Ma-Maw had her car back. And Bellamy didn't jack any more autos for a long, long time.

Now that was a plan. The kind of thing Myles excelled at.

But today Penny was by herself. And she had to find Pryor alone. What would Myles do, she thought again, pulling onto the highway. What would he do first?

18

After lunch J. P. drove the three-quarters of a mile into town, parked down from the coffee shop, and walked to the bank. He pulled open the heavy glass door on the right and went inside and stood in line for the teller. Thinking briefly of his conversation with June that morning. About the bank robber and the dead cop in Des Moines. He looked around. No sign of a security guard, as always. He'd talked to them about that, and more than once.

After a minute Jan waved him up.

"Afternoon J. P. How's your day going?"

"Not too bad."

"June's off at her parents, I hear."

"Mmm. That's right."

"How do they like it over there?"

"Like?"

"Living in Columbus. City living." Innocent as could be, blue eyes trained on his face, her blond hair a little shorter these days, thanks to the new gal cutting and treating it. A bit heavy on the makeup, especially the mascara, especially for a lady her age. At least according to June, who filled him in on stuff like that. Jan's sex life, for example.

"They live more east," he said. "In a suburb. Parts of it are like the country."

"I wouldn't care for it. All that traffic. And the crime. Aren't they nervous all the time?"

J. P. took the checks out of his wallet, smoothed them on the ledge in front of the security glass, and passed them through.

"Like I said, it's more a suburb. I don't think they mind."

"Don't get me wrong. We like going over for the football games. *Yo, Buckeyes!*" She laughed. "And German Village—you know I love Schmidt's. Course we're always going shopping there too. It's just *living* there I couldn't deal with."

"I know what you mean, I guess."

The truth was, he didn't, not really. Maybe it was because he'd been to Columbus more often since he met, then married, June. Or the fact that both her brother and her dad were huge Blue Jackets' fans and they'd braved the parking and the night drive several times to visit the hockey arena. Or the fact he traveled a bit with the Guard, even if it was only other places in Ohio. J. P. wasn't about to tell Jan this, but there were times he could see himself living there himself. Especially, come to think of it, if Marks were elected sheriff.

"June sell more doilies?" Jan said, running the checks through her machine.

"A few. Had some girls over to the house last week."

"More than a few, I'd say, this much money. She's so creative."

"Yes."

"Nice of you to deposit everything for her."

"Happy to, you know."

"Lucky man, J. P."

He nodded. He could guess where this was going, which was nowhere and everywhere at the same time. Jan was always saying kind things about June, her way of reminding him—as if he'd ever forget—of their brief time together in high school. Starting with the day his senior year Tina came up to him in church and told him he might be surprised by the response of Jan Gruning—now Rittmaier—if he asked her to homecoming. He *was* surprised, to be honest, just as he was surprised by how close she let him hold her during the dances and how long they sat in his truck afterward making out, and how happy she'd been to see him the following Monday in the school hallway. You could even say they'd gone out for a while, until one day they weren't anymore after Jan told him it wasn't him, it was her.

Fact was, he a little relieved. He could never quite abide her nonstop talking, which was ironic given who he married, a chatterbox if there ever was one. But unlike June, Jan was prone to gossip, and it made him uneasy listening to her, never knowing when it would emerge, like swimming in a creek you knew was filled with jagged old car parts lodged just below the surface. J. P.'s mother said it served Jan right, ending up with Hank the way she did. J. P. tried to be more charitable about it. But no question he won the lottery with June compared to Jan.

"Lucky man, I said," Jan repeated, smiling, handing him the deposit slip.

"I know. Thank you."

"Anytime, J. P."

He longed to turn and go. Instead, he forced himself to say, "How's things here?"

"Here?"

"At the bank."

"Oh, you know. About the same. Knock on wood."

"Sounds good. How's Hank?"

"Usual self, I guess. Think he's in the office, you want to say hi?" She gestured toward the far end of the bank. J. P. couldn't help but notice the way her eyes dulled at the mention of her husband. A nice enough guy, quiet, active in their church, always running errands related to the bank over in Columbus. A few years older than him and Jan, not that it mattered, he guessed. An ambitious man, it seemed. Except when it came to posting security guards.

"Some other time," J. P. said. "Need to get going."

"No problem."

"Thanks again."

"You're welcome. Don't be a stranger."

He breathed a sigh of relief as he escaped through the doors into the sunny afternoon. The only way the encounter could have been more awkward was if Jan's husband had poked his head out from his office on the other side of the lobby and seen him chatting with her like that. So maybe Jan was right, he thought, suppressing a grin. He was a lucky man, at least today.

Even though he was off-duty, once back inside his cruiser he rolled around the square once, just because, before heading back west out of town toward home. His test on opioids was Monday and he wanted to put in a little more book time before his shift started.

19

The first thing, Penny decided, was to fill up. The tank on Randy's Pilot was almost empty. Which figured. You'd think he'd be more conscientious than that, now that he had a kid and all. Right. She pulled into the same gas station where she asked directions on the way up. She considered charging it on Randy's bank card but thought better of it. She could tell by the look of slowly dawning terror on her brother-in-law's face, like a man who pulls himself back at the last second from an open elevator shaft, that he knew she was serious about texting the pictures. She wasn't worried he'd do something stupid. But there was also no point leaving any more of a trail than she had to. And she wasn't quite as sure about Brandi, because she knew her sister. She knew she wouldn't buy whatever story Randy concocted about how he ended up hogtied naked to their bed with his phone and car and wallet and gun missing and Penny's car on the curb. Brandi was a bitch but she wasn't blind. So Penny took two twenties out of Randy's wallet, put on the pair of Brandi's sunglasses she lifted from the kitchen counter on the way out and went inside the station and up to the counter where she gave the same boy as before the money. He didn't recognize her, what with the sunglasses and the new clothes and all. He didn't even recognize her chest.

Speeding down 270, traffic running light for a Friday, Penny delighted in how smoothly the Pilot handled. A long time since she drove a car she wasn't worried about breaking apart during a lane change. She thought about calling her mom, checking in, letting her know what was up, but only for a moment. She trusted her mother even less than Brandi not to do something stupid. To tell the wrong people what she was up to. Unlike her sister, it wouldn't be done maliciously. It would just happen, like a reed that bends at the slightest hint of a heavy breeze. But the result would be the same. Then she thought about calling the hospital, see if they'd tell her how Myles was doing. But she decided against that too. Maybe they had a way of tracing phone calls, or something. And she didn't expect to be away from him for that long. She couldn't afford to.

There was no way this was going to work if it took more than a day or two. Because by now Pryor knew Myles had survived. And he probably also figured out the cops weren't looking for him, just yet. Which would lead him to believe that Penny and company were scared enough that they weren't going to squeal a second time. All that was true enough. But Penny also knew Pryor wasn't stupid. That he'd be by Mama's house, just to check. See what he could see. And he'd figure out sooner rather than later that Penny was gone. And if she knew Pryor, he'd figure out Penny was hunting him. And at that point, the clock would start ticking and Penny's life would be worth less and less with every passing second.

She made up her mind. She thought of a place to start. It wasn't the best place, and not somewhere she wanted to go. But it was a beginning.

20

Michigan paced back and forth inside the barn, driving Pryor to distraction.

"Sit down."

"I'm starving," Michigan said.

"We just had breakfast."

"Coffeecake and bananas? That's girls' food. I need meat."

"We don't have meat."

"There's meat at that Amish place," Archie said. "It's 'filling.'" A pretty decent imitation of Robby.

"We're not going back to the Amish place," Pryor said. "Not now."

"Then what am I supposed to do?" Michigan said.

"Suck it up."

Of course, now that Michigan had brought it up, he was hungry too.

◆

One of the first things Pryor noticed was how clean the barn smelled. Clean . . . and something else. Old timey, but not in the way you'd think, not the smell of piss and medicine and fried eggs the way the place where they put his grandfather smelled. His mind recalling a small building and narrow halls and dark rooms and his mother shouting at him to shut the fuck up and stop crying as he whined all the way through the visit. No, this was old in a different way. He turned his attention away from Michigan and toward the stacks of straw piled up on a second level at the far end of the barn. Bales of straw, catching the sun coming in through a window near the top. Straw: how perfect. The bales sweet-smelling, not musty and moldy like you'd expect looking at the barn from the outside the building a dump just like the farmhouse, listing like a ship abandoned on the beach. Sweet-smelling and almost shiny and above all dry. He wondered what the straw was for. No animals here; he knew that. That had been one of the conditions. They weren't screwing around with a bunch of cows and pigs and shit. Horses once upon a time, years ago, Robby said, but none now. Without their own animals, it meant the old man and his sister must be keeping the straw for someone. Which could be a problem if someone stopped by. Which was why he felt good about delaying his plan that morning while Archie and Michigan slept. About keeping them around just a little bit longer.

"Maybe there's food in the house," Michigan said.

"What?" Pryor said.

"Maybe they have food over there. Did you see anything, when you were inside?"

The question careful. Pryor knew neither Archie nor Michigan wanted to ask him directly about what happened after he knocked on the door the night before and met the old woman cradling the shotgun. Not that he guessed either of them had any doubts, with night turning into morning without a peep from inside the farmhouse. They weren't that stupid.

"I wasn't really looking for food."

"So you didn't see any?" Archie, this time.

"I didn't say that."

"Could we try? Two people living there, had to be something."

"No."

"Why not?"

"Because I fucking said so."

But the damage was done, because now Pryor was hungry. Since he hadn't counted on the adjustment to their plan, spending the extra day here, he hadn't brought enough to eat. And they were stuck. It made zero sense to leave, to go to a store, to go anywhere they might be seen. Where the van might be identified. He needed it for one more day. After that, once the job was done and he was on his way south, he could ditch it and make other arrangements. But that was all beginning tomorrow. And he was hungry today.

"Stay here."

"Where you going?" Michigan said.

"Back over. See what they have."

"Can we go?" Archie said.

"No."

"Why not?"

He stopped to face Archie. The look on the man's face an infuriating combination of innocence and challenge.

"There wasn't a cop. Was there?" Pryor said.

"What?"

"Last night. With Baby. You didn't see a cop, did you? You just made that up. Because he's a pal of yours."

"I saw what I saw."

"If there was a cop, why didn't they come after us, when you gunned it out of there and Baby lying on the ground like that?"

"I don't know. Maybe we just got away."

"Bullshit. I think you do know."

Archie's brown face a mask, his eyes flat and empty of suspicion.

"I thought I saw a cop. So I got us out of there. It had nothing to do with Myles. So we're here now, instead of sitting in jail."

"And Baby's still alive."

"You don't know that."

"He's alive. Another second and he wouldn't have been."

"What are you saying? That I'm lying?"

"I'm saying I don't think you saw a cop."

Archie shifted his feet. Finally, a crack in his composure. A hint that he felt some fear, that he recognized what Pryor was thinking.

"I saw what I saw."

"I hope so."

"I wouldn't lie."

"You sure as hell better hope that's true," Pryor said, and turned and walked out of the barn and back to the farmhouse.

21

After Penny took the exit for Broad she made her way down side streets before turning into the neighborhood she wanted. Some of the small houses were tidy and pleasant and some had calf-high grass in the front yard and an array of vehicles and tools and furniture in the driveways, the kind of places a sheriff's deputy armed with an eviction notice tended to improve. She pulled up to a home the color of late summer pond algae that looked kind of in-between. Duct tape covered a crack on a broken bathroom window and weeds grew from the gutters. But the lawn was mowed and the driveway clear.

She tried the bell, realized it was broken, and knocked. She waited, listening. She could hear a TV. She knocked again. She rolled her left shoulder. Brandi's tan leather purse drooped from her elbow, a little heavy, the bag big enough for a water bottle and her knitting and the leftover pizza and Randy's gun. She was twisting the doorknob back and forth, left and right, wondering what it would take just to kick it in, when she heard a sound inside and stepped back.

"Penny?"

"Hi Lem. I need to know where Pryor is."

◆

She sat on a brown couch that sagged so low in the middle it felt like a hammock, watching men on TV playing golf someplace green and sunny and tropical, the ocean glittering blue in the background. She recalled the first time she saw Randy's clubs in his garage and realized what a truly strange world Brandi had slept her way up to. Lem Garretty sat on a thin wooden chair opposite her, rubbing his hands back and forth as if washing them in an invisible sink.

"He stopped coming by after Darren died. Couple months ago. That's all I know."

"Where'd he go?"

"I'm not sure. Someplace on the West Side. Or maybe Hilliard. He moved around a lot."

"How about Archie? Or Michigan?"

"What about them?"

"He stay with them?"

"Maybe. I don't know. After Darren, I just—"

"I'm sorry about Darren." Not really true, but whatever.

He nodded, not speaking.

"It wasn't your fault." That was definitely not true, depending on your perspective.

"I don't know. It's not what my sister . . ."

"Not what your sister what?"

"Not what she said."

"Which was what?" Penny tried not to sound bored. She actually was sorry Darren overdosed if she was being honest about it. He'd been a nice enough guy at one time. But the fact was, he was warned more than once not to hang around Pryor. Because hanging around Pryor was not an ongoing activity. It had a beginning and an end, a car trip followed by a car crash.

"She said I could have saved him."

"How?"

"The things."

"What things?"

"Medicine. Got it from the pharmacist. There's a law lets you do that now."

"What kind of medicine?" Penny nervously jiggled her right foot but made herself stop before she up and kicked Lem.

"Injector things. It brings them back. Like an antidote. If your relative or something, you know. If someone you know is using. You can get them, have them around, just in case. Here, I'll show you."

"That's okay—"

Too late. He was out of the room and down the hall. Penny sat and looked at the TV. Wherever they were golfing, it seemed like the kind of place Randy would want to go. Or maybe had been. She wasn't exactly sure he could afford all the trips he and Brandi went on, or the house, or the matching Honda Pilots, but it wasn't really her business.

"Here." Lem walked stiffly back into the living room. He handed her a box. His hands were shaking and she looked at him curiously, but he wouldn't meet her gaze. What was up with him? She opened the box and saw two widgets that appeared a little like needles. The labels said NARCAN. Now *that* she'd heard of.

"You can have them. I don't want them anymore."

"I don't want them," Penny said, setting the box beside her.

"I should have used them. It's just, I wasn't home at the time. And then it was too late."

"Where were you?" Penny asked because she knew it would hurt him, because she was growing impatient, and because everyone already knew where Lem had been the day Darren died.

"I—"

"Who would know?"

"Know?"

"Where Pryor is?"

"Why are you looking for him?"

A pause. "I need to ask him something."

"Is this about Myles?"

"I just need to ask him a question."

"You think he shot Myles? Is that what you want to ask?"

Lem's eyes glued to the floor as he spoke.

"I don't have time to explain. I just need to find Pryor. So either you know or you don't."

Lem looked like he was going to burst into tears. He looked that way a lot since his nephew died, but it was even worse today for some reason. His lined face sallow, his eyes sunken with exhaustion.

Lem said, "He's got a girl."

"What girl?"

"Girl with a funny name."

"Girlfriend?"

He shook his head. "She's, you know . . ."

"She's whoring for him."

"If that's what you call it. Didn't seem like she had a whole lot of choice in the matter."

"What's her name?"

"Something funny."

"You already said that."

"I know. It was like a—"

"Like a what?" she snapped. If this took much longer she was afraid she might say something to Lem she would regret. And given what people had said to him since Darren died, that was saying something.

"Like a month. Like April, or something. No, May. That's it, Mae. I can hear him yelling it. 'Get in here, *Mae*. Get in here, you slut.' You know how he is. I feel bad, tell you the truth. She seemed like a nice kid. They all do."

"All who?"

"Darren, Mae, all of them. It's the drugs that do it."

"Sure it is."

"I feel like I should have helped her. Done something. It wasn't right, how Pryor treated her."

"It's not right how Pryor treats anyone. Where can I find her?"

Lem pushed his hands up and down his face. Acne scars, four decades old, still pocked his cheeks. He had a smoker's yellow fingertips and thinning white hair and an old man's stoop and ears that jutted out like open doors on an abandoned car. He was wearing jeans and a faded Westland High T-shirt and scuffed work boots, though Penny couldn't imagine the last time he did the kind of labor they were made for. When Darren was still alive Lem worked the overnight shift at the Speedway up the street, but Penny wasn't sure where he worked now, or whether he did at all.

"Lem?"

Slowly, hesitantly, he explained where she might find Mae.

"Thanks." She stood up and headed to the door.

"Penny."

She turned.

"I'm sorry about Myles."

She didn't respond. She couldn't. She was at the door when he said her name again.

"Please, take these." He held out the box. The injectors. The things for overdoses.

"I don't want them."

"Then throw them away. I just want them out of the house."

"Throw them in the garbage, then."

"Please?"

"No," she said, and was outside before he could respond. As she drove the Pilot away from the curb she caught a glimpse of him standing in his doorway watching her. She thought he might have waved, but she was moving too quickly to be sure.

22

J. P. thought all afternoon about what Tina said. Standing for office. Him. For his father's old job. Going up against Marks, despite how tight he was with two of the county commissioners and the head judge. Tight with Vick.

He thought about it before and after a post-paint-scraping catnap. Thought about it while he read at the dining room table, more handouts about heroin and opioids and brain receptors, his mind wandering, his concentration minimal, his note-taking an embarrassment. He knew Tina was only saying what June always said, what she began saying almost as soon as they were married until he made it clear he didn't want to talk about it anymore.

He kept thinking about it on the range, where he shot so badly he cut the session short by twenty minutes and blushed when Feller told him he could come back another time, no charge, because everyone has that kind of day. You had to shoot ninety percent to requalify, which normally he could do in his sleep. A gun in his hand as natural as holding a baseball for other kids, though he preferred the feel of a shotgun, the weight and the heft. He wouldn't let himself dwell long on the reason for this preference, which came not from the weapon itself but from memories of crouching in blinds with his father on cold

December mornings. But nothing natural or comfortable today. He felt awkward and ungainly, fat, if you had to know the truth, already regretting the meatloaf dinner and the sweet tea and the slice of pie the day before.

J. P. was still thinking about it as he walked inside the county safety-service building and waited for Joyce to buzz him into the back and went down the hall, past the sheriff's large office, past the break room and the interview room, and into the back, with the lockers and the picture of his father and the bulletin board with the training updates and vacation schedules and car maintenance reminders. He was early enough he had time to go through the pile of warrants and organize them and toss out the ones that had been served and checked off but for some reason hadn't been filed up front. When he was done he scrubbed the coffee cups and plates in the sink, and washed down the counter. He couldn't ever remember dishes in the sink when his father—

"What are you doing?"

He turned. Vick limped into the room, ever present clipboard in hand, followed closely by Marks and the other three deputies on the shift.

"Just cleaning up."

"You bored, with the Mrs. gone?" Marks said. "That why you're here so early? Nothing to do at home?"

"That's right," J. P. said, putting the sponge into the sink and walking over to his locker. "Bored." Of course. Even Marks knew June was out of town.

He tried his best to ignore Marks while Vick read off the shift assignments. J. P. was surprised to find himself running radar out on 31.

"You don't need me to check up on Clayton and Priscilla?"

Vick shook his head. "They quit calling. Think they realized they was crying wolf one too many times. Unless you said something to them."

"I didn't say anything. Couldn't get a word in." That won a laugh from Livingston, sitting at the table studying his phone. "I looked around, couldn't see anything. Drove around to the back, where the tractor lane hits Red Hollow Road. Nothing there. If you ask me—"

"Sheriff wants at least six tickets," Vick interrupted. "Says he's seeing too many people over the limit, especially by the school."

"Why six?"

"What do you mean?"

"What if there aren't six people speeding?"

Vick stared at him. "It doesn't matter if there aren't six people speeding. It matters you get six tickets. Minimum."

"How many did you write yesterday?" J. P. said, directing the question at Marks.

Marks didn't answer right away. He was peering out the squad room door and into the hall where Joyce was walking past, slowly, wearing a tight T-shirt and a pair of jeans that fit her properly the way two pillows fit properly into a single pillowcase.

"Maybe it's none of your business," Marks said.

"Just a question."

"And I'm just telling you, it's none of your business."

So J. P. headed to 31 to run radar. Even though he thought it was his business to know, and if Marks stopped more than three cars he was a monkey's uncle.

23

Knowing about Mae helped, Penny thought. Because finding Archie or Michigan would be nearly impossible, like hunting a pair of rats in a sewer tunnel with lots of twists and turns and side exits. She thought about dropping by Archie's grandmother's house, see if she'd heard anything, knew anything, but that was an absolute last resort. She hadn't had anything to do with her grandson since he went from being William "Archie" Tolliver, a high school running back with a pile of recruiting letters so high they slipped off the dining room table and accumulated on the floor like leaves in October, to just Archie, fresh out of juvenile detention where he spent two years working off the boosting of a BMW downtown, over by the hockey arena, and the BMW's subsequent involvement in a drive-by shooting on the South End. All done in the service of a smooth-talking guy with short-cropped hair, hollow cheeks, unusually long ears, and one eye.

No, the grandmother could wait. How many times could an old woman's heart be broken without it killing her once and for all? So finding Mae it was.

◆

According to Lem, Pryor ran things with the girl for a while out of a room in an apartment building down Sullivant. That figured. Penny knew the place. Squat, square, two stories, with more than one window boarded up and the stucco exterior falling off in places like scabs that had been picked at too long. The cracked asphalt parking lot nearly empty when she pulled in fifteen minutes later, the new Pilot as conspicuous next to the beat-up wrecks beside it as if she'd set it on fire after placing it in park. Penny looked around carefully as she climbed out of the Pilot, making sure to lock the car and bring Brandi's handbag. She brushed her fingers across the Glock, reassuring herself it was there. Penny didn't think Pryor actually lived here, at least according to what Lem said. But she couldn't take the chance. She'd only have one shot at him. And she knew perfectly well she was a dead woman, or worse, if he saw her first. She didn't know that much about guns, and hoped she'd be able to use it when the time came. Because what choice did she have?

She stepped inside the open door on the left of the apartment building and found herself in a little foyer kind of space no bigger than a prison cell, two doors on either side. A and B, with a set of stairs in front of her. A smell of wet rot and smoke and used diapers. She hesitated, thought about it, and knocked on the door to the left. A. Nothing. She waited and knocked again. After a moment she tried the door on the other side. Same result. She examined the stairs, spying a broken needle halfway up and on the next step up, a used condom, coiled in a corner like the head of a pale snake someone crushed with his boot. She took the first step, left hand holding the purse strap on her shoulder, right hand inside the purse on the gun.

"Yeah?"

She started. A woman's voice above her. Penny looked up. A lady stared down at her, cigarette drooping from the left side of her mouth, eyes watery. She might have been Mama's age or she might have been Ma-Maw's.

"Looking for a girl named Mae."

"Mae?"

"That's right. She runs with Pryor."

"You know Pryor?"

Penny nodded, holding the woman's gaze. Her face a sickly and blotchy yellow, as if not all that long ago she was covered in bruises which had only partly healed.

"She ain't here."

"Do you know where she is?"

"No idea. Haven't seen her around."

"Have you seen Pryor?"

"Why are you looking for him?"

"I just am."

"So are you looking for Mae, or looking for Pryor?"

She hesitated, but only for a moment. "Pryor. I heard Mae worked here sometimes, that she might know where he is."

"You don't need to find Pryor, itty bitty thing like you. Why you don't you just go home."

Fuck you, she thought. *Itty bitty thing.* But she held her tongue.

"It's important."

"Well, he's not here either."

"You know where he is?"

"Not sure I'd tell you if I did, honey."

"Why not?"

"You have to ask, you must not know Pryor."

"I know him."

"Then you must be a lot dumber than you look."

Penny continued to hold her tongue, but she wasn't sure how much longer that would last. "How about Mae, then?"

"I told you, she's not here."

"Do you know where she went?"

The woman didn't say anything for a second. Ash shivered on the end of the cigarette and fell in a shower of talcum-like particles.

"Sorry about that," she said, watching the ashes fall.

"It's okay. So, um, Mae?"

"Saw her working down the street a ways, last night, maybe two nights ago. East of Central some place. Pryor sets her up there sometimes if it's slow."

"You know what street?"

"Not exactly. It's down that way," she said, pointing lazily through the apartment door across from her.

"Thanks," Penny said, and turned to go.

"Be careful, honey. Pryor ain't nobody—"

"I said thanks."

◆

Penny drove down Sullivant, stopped for the light at Central, and continued on. Middle of the day like this, she knew her chances weren't great. She'd seen plenty of them like Mae early in the morning and at night too. But this time of day they were either working in motels or sleeping it off or doing whatever it was people like Pryor told them to do. She didn't want to think about that part. She passed the hospital, trying not to think about Myles and all those tubes. She drove all the way down the street to Dodge recreation center, circled around, and drove back. Nothing. No one. Not the right time of day, even for something men bought every hour on the hour. She looked at the clock on the dashboard. A few hours still until evening came and Mae might come out again. If she was even around. But she was her one thread right now, and she was worth waiting around for. Penny rolled some things around in her head before making a decision. She turned and drove toward the hospital parking garage. What the hell? It might be the only chance she had to see Myles before it all went down.

24

"Hello, Penny."

She'd walked right past him, so focused on reaching Myles's room without being seen.

"Hi."

The Black detective. The one from last night.

"Back for a visit?"

"Yeah."

She was suddenly conscious of Brandi's purse hanging off her shoulder, realizing it was still unzipped from the encounter at the apartment house. The Glock, nestled barely out of sight next to a water bottle and a slice of pizza. Shit. She was pretty sure they didn't allow loaded handguns in a hospital, especially guns that weren't yours.

"In that case, you have a second?"

The detective gestured toward the little waiting room where they talked the night before. Reluctantly, Penny nodded and followed him, zipping up the purse as she walked.

"Have a seat."

Penny sat, trying to relax. There was a painting of a cottage in the countryside hanging on the wall across from her chair, where the detective sat down. Ma-Maw had a similar picture in her living room. What was the cop's name, on the card he'd handed her? Lesser? Lessner? And what the hell was he doing here like this, middle of the day?

He said, "How's he doing?"

"Okay, I guess. I was here this morning. He was still unconscious."

"That's what the nurse said. I mean, that you were here this morning."

She kept a poker face, playing it cool. The ploy obvious; they were keeping tabs on visitors, and he wanted her to know that.

"I like your outfit."

"What?"

"Your clothes. You like nice. Dressing up for Myles?"

She realized he meant Brandi's clothes. Did she really look that different in her sister's outfit? She supposed she did.

"Thanks."

"So, any more ideas about who might have done this?"

She shook her head.

"I went by your house this morning. You weren't there. Your mother said she didn't know where you were. I figured you might come here."

Thank you, Mama.

"I had to go out for a while."

"To work?"

"Just out. Run some errands."

"Where do you work?"

She told him about the costume shop. Except she probably didn't work there anymore, the way she ran out before her shift ended after Mama came bursting in. It didn't matter. She wouldn't be going back to help girls choose between slutty elf and slutty witch in either case. They would have to start making those decisions on their own.

"I see."

She tried to stay calm. It hadn't been the smartest idea, she realized, to come back like this. She should have left it at the goodbye this morning. She should have figured the cops might be keeping an eye on the hospital wing, curious to see who came to see Myles. She should have thought of that herself. She swallowed, trying to hide her anxiety, which was blooming in her like a bad smell she couldn't wash off. But it was impossible to relax, the detective sitting there, the sounds of the hospital all around her. This was where Pa-Paw died. Not at home, like he wanted to. Begged to. In a hospital bed stinking of urine and shit and with tubes coming out of him like some creature in a science fiction movie. The way Myles looked now. That was a bad enough memory.

But it was also where Mack was born, two months after they arrested Myles for the bank job. Sitting in jail, waiting for his trial, while she lay on a hospital bed with Mama and Ma-Maw holding her hands and her screaming her lungs out. She'd been furious at him; for doing the job, for being arrested, for sitting on his ass behind bars the day she needed him most. She pretty nearly called it off, then and there. Things not much better when she finally went to see him, two weeks later, able to move around for the first time. Her labor hard, the birth agony. Mack at home with Mama, too small to go out; not like she'd take him to a jail anyway.

"Ain't you going to say anything?" Penny had said, holding the phone as she stared at him through the thick glass window at the jail down on Jackson Pike.

"Like what?"

"Like, sorry or something?"

"Sorry?"

"About me, and Mack, and everything?"

"I said I was happy. A baby boy—what's better than that?"

"No apology?"

He gave her a look she hadn't seen before—or hadn't seen in a long, long time, his eyes brighter, and clearer, than she remembered them. "Would you accept it if I did?"

She hadn't known how to answer that.

And here she was back in the hospital, the place bracketed in her mind by death and birth. And now Myles was here, someplace in-between.

"Penny?"

The detective, looking at her funny.

"Yeah?"

"Are you all right?"

"I'm fine."

"Did you hear what I said?"

"Said?"

"I said there's a rumor going around."

"Okay."

"There's a rumor this was payback. For Myles's testimony. For what he said at the trial about Pryor. That was a big deal, wasn't it, him testifying?" He paused. "With Baby testifying."

"That's not his name," she snapped, unable to help herself.

"But that was his nickname, wasn't it? What Pryor called him? Why is that?"

"You know his nickname, I figure you know why."

"I don't. That's why I'm asking."

"It's a movie, all right?"

"A movie?"

"*Baby Driver.* It's about a bank robbery. This kid who drives is named Miles. But everyone calls him Baby. Pryor loves that movie. Satisfied?"

"Did Myles love it? Your Myles?"

"I don't know." Yes, dammit.

"About how you?"

I hated it from the first moment I watched it, which is the one and only time I ever saw it.

"Can't remember. Listen. I should probably be going."

"Where?"

"Stuff to do."

"Like what?"

"Just stuff." Stalling. Eying the corridor, like she might make a break for it and run. Real smart.

The detective wrote something in his little notebook. "The thing is, Penny. I'm worried about these rumors about Pryor being mad at Baby—at Myles," he corrected quickly, seeing the fire in Penny's eyes.

"I don't know nothing about any rumors. Everybody knew Pryor was mad at Myles. That's no secret."

"Myles just came home. Isn't that right?"

"Yeah."

"When?"

"Two days ago." She knew the detective already knew this.

"Did you see Pryor?"

"You already asked me that. Last night."

"That's right, I did. Well, I guess I'm asking again."

"See him when?" Carefully, not meeting his eyes.

"See him since Myles came home."

Just because you're out doesn't mean you're out.

"Like I said before, I haven't seen him."

"Okay. I got that. I don't mean to push the point. It's just that there's this rumor now. More than what I was asking before, which was just speculation. Now people are saying it *was* Pryor."

"Good for them."

"And there's still this other problem."

"Which problem?"

"The gun Myles had on him."

"I told you before, I don't know anything about that."

"Even if I say I believe you, I still have to wonder what Myles was doing with it. If he, you know, might have been trying to protect himself. Or something."

Or something. Actually, a good point.

"I told you I don't know."

"This morning. You said you were doing errands?"

"Yeah."

"What kind of errands?"

"Just stuff," Penny said.

"Well, I know what you mean, sort of. So much to do sometimes, it seems like. But it still seems funny you'd be out running errands, and Myles in there"—he jabbed a thumb in the direction of Myles's room—"not, you know, doing so great."

"I'm here now, ain't I?"

"Yes you are. Glad to see it."

"In fact, I should probably go in."

"Good idea. You mind if I come too? Just to see how he's doing?"

"I'd rather be alone with him."

"I understand. I just want to make sure you're okay, you know? And that you're not trying to help Myles in a different way. Doing something you might regret later. You know what I mean?"

"No."

"What I mean is, it would help Myles the most if there was something you knew that you could tell us. Because right now all we have are rumors."

"I already told you—"

But before she could finish the detective's cell phone went off. He looked at the number, sighed, pointed down the hall toward Myles's room, and turned away to take the call.

Penny stood up and walked toward the nurse's station. She wanted to keep going straight and then into Myles's room in the worst way possible. To see him, to place her hand on his cheek, to tell him it was going to be all right. To see him almost as desperately as she hadn't wanted to see him in the jail, that first time after Mack was born. Or the first time she saw him in prison. Before she started to see changes in him. Before she took Mack to see him the first time and they both cried. She wanted to see him in the same way you want that first glass of cold water after being out in the sun all day with nothing to drink.

Instead, she took a hard right and half-jogged to the elevator and jabbed the down button impatiently, one-two-three-four-five, looking over her shoulder, praying the detective didn't see her. The doors opened and she entered. An orderly in blue scrubs nodded at her. She nodded back. She pressed the button for the first floor and took shallow breaths while she waited for the door to close.

Just about the hardest thing she did all day was force herself to walk like a normal person back to the car and not turn around. Not once.

25

Afterward, Penny couldn't remember driving to the Kroger down the street in the neighborhood they called the Brewery District. Not that far from the downtown jail where they first put Myles, after the arrest, and where they kept him during the trial for easy transport. Ma-Maw had a picture of the old neighborhood from when her father worked in one of the breweries, and it didn't look anything like that now. All condos and restaurants and offices. Ma-Maw still had empties from those days stored in the basement, dusty glass Wagner's Gambrinus bottles lining the back wall. Ma-Maw just old enough to remember her father bringing them home full, in cases, to hand around to friends, but also old enough to remember when the last factory closed and her father came home and went in the backyard and drank a whole case himself.

Inside the store, Penny bought packages of lunch meat and cheese and two loaves of bread and some mayonnaise and grapes and two large bottles of a generic cherry pop the color of red wine that Myles liked for some reason, and a twelve-pack of bottled water. She wasn't sure why she was collecting all this, other than she didn't know how long this was going to take. And the encounter with the detective had made it clear she couldn't go back home, at least until she was finished, just like she couldn't go back to the hospital.

When she was done unloading the cart in the checkout aisle she looked in her wallet and counted up the cash she took from Randy, and decided to go ahead and use the credit card. She might as well test his willingness to cooperate, see if he understood she was serious about her threat. For just a moment, after she ran the card through and the little checkout screen said "processing transaction" she felt a thrill of panic like she was at the top of a big sledding hill and about to go down for the first time. She wondered whether Brandi overruled Randy after arriving home and they canceled the card, which was a possibility she hadn't thought of until just now. She cursed herself for not going straight to the ATM and withdrawing a few hundred dollars while she had the chance. Another password Randy had given up just like that. Getting the cash was something Myles would have thought of doing. She stamped her right foot in frustration, cursing her stupidity. But then the screen asked her if $67.32 was an okay amount, and she agreed that it was. She scribbled a name on the pad, took her cart, and left the store.

Randy's phone went off just as she finished unloading the groceries. The caller ID said, "Ball and Chain." It took her a second before she figured it out. Christ. What a dick Randy was.

"Yeah."

"The fuck you think you're doing?"

Brandi. "Ball and Chain." Sounding even madder than Penny expected. Taking a breath, she said, "I needed to borrow some things. I'm bringing them back. I told Randy that."

"That's not borrowing. That's stealing."

"I'm not stealing."

"Bullshit. You took my favorite jeans."

"Borrowed."

"Bitch."

"I told him not to do anything stupid. I warned him. And I'm warning you. I'll have everything back in a couple of days."

"Mama called."

"What?"

"You heard me. She was looking for you. She said a cop came by. I played dumb. Happy? She said she was worried, because she didn't know where you went. And Myles got shot? The fuck? You didn't think that was worth telling me?"

Penny didn't respond. She knew Brandi already knew the answer to that one. She wondered if her sister swore this much around Randy. That one, she knew the answer to.

"She told me everything," her sister said. "I didn't ask squat. So it was her, not Randy, who spilled the beans. I knew everything before I got home and found him."

"Good for you."

"So what I'm still wondering is, what are you up to?"

"Mama shouldn't have called."

"No shit. Look, I'm sorry about what happened to Myles. I really am. But you didn't have to do all that to Randy. You hurt his head, bad. And then you stole all that stuff. How the hell is he supposed to go to work?"

"Borrowed. And I'll have the car back by Monday. No problem."

"Stolen. And it's a big fucking problem."

Penny lost her patience. It was easy to do with her sister. Always had been, but it had been grown worse since Randy came into the picture. She said, "He wanted to fuck me for the gun. He tell you that?"

"You bitch."

"You weren't out of the house an hour and he's in your bedroom getting undressed wagging his tongue at me. All I did was teach him a lesson. Or would you rather I fucked him first?"

"I'm calling the cops."

"You do and I'm putting those pictures onto Facebook. All the ones I took of him on your bed. He tell you that part? And texting every friend he's got. And everybody at work."

"Like I care."

"Like you're gonna keep that house for two seconds if he loses his job." She paused. "Or you."

The phone went quiet. Penny could tell that her sister was rolling that possibility around in her mind. She couldn't believe it was the first time Brandi had thought about it, considered how precarious their situation was—her situation—in this economy, in that neighborhood, with the kind of guy Randy was. But it might be the first time she had hard evidence—like the sight of her scumbag cheating husband tied naked to their bed after trying to extort sex from her sister—that things might not be rosy forever.

Brandi said, "He'll survive, you put those photos out there." Her voice surprisingly confident. "He'll explain it away. You know how Randy is. But you won't survive the cops. Not with what Myles got into. Not for one second."

Penny made a fist with her left hand, squeezing it so tight she could feel her nails cutting into her palm. She fought off tears.

"Just give me the night."

"What?"

"Just give me tonight. I'll have everything back tomorrow. Good as new."

"Why?"

"Because I'm asking."

"Big fucking deal."

"Who's the bitch now?"

"He might have a concussion, you know. From you hitting him like that."

"He said the two of you don't have sex anymore. He blames Madyson. Is that the kind of father you want her growing up with?"

More silence. Penny sat and stared out the window of the SUV. Remembered long ago, playing with dolls with Brandi on the floor of one of the houses they lived in. She wasn't sure where. Not on Eureka. Maybe Harris or Terrace. They moved a lot.

"Tomorrow morning," Brandi said.

"That's right."

"Bright and early."

"Yes."

"Otherwise I call."

"Yes. But if you call before that, I send out the pictures. Promise."

"I don't care."

"You say that now."

"Bright and early, bitch," her sister said, and the line went dead.

Penny might have been mistaken, but it almost sounded at the end as if her sister was starting to cry.

26

Pryor walked into the farmhouse kitchen, sniffed, satisfied himself that the smell wasn't too bad yet, and walked over to the refrigerator. He opened it, looked inside, turned, and searched around in the kitchen until he found a plastic bag. He went back to the refrigerator and pulled stuff out randomly. Mustard, mayo. Three dried up tomatoes. A hunk of cheese. Everything went into the bag. No alcohol, not surprisingly. But that was okay. That was one thing he had plenty of. When he finished he opened the freezer door, pulled some things out, examined them, made some choices and filled the bag further.

Satisfied, he left the bag on the floor, grabbed another one, and headed to the basement. He took his time, being careful where he walked. He took a bunch more things out of the downstairs freezer. After that he selected three jars off the shelves along the back wall, placing them in his bag, shaking his head once more at the sight of it all. It was impressive, if you cared about shit like that. He had a dim memory of a similar sight in his own grandmother's house, the one in a holler in the woods in West Virginia. Deep in the woods. Abandoned now, but still livable. The kind of place you could hide out for a while. For a long while, actually, like riding in a fully stocked lifeboat in the middle of the green sea of all those hardwoods. The place nearly hidden even in the winter when the leaves were gone and the branches bare. Because there were so many fucking branches.

Yes, very impressive. And in the end, helpful to their adjusted plan, since as it happened there was plenty of food here, enough to last them through the next few hours. Just until tomorrow morning, he reminded himself.

Lifting up one shoe and examining it, then the other, scraping both carefully on the first wooden step, Pryor took the bag and went back upstairs. He retrieved the first bag and left the farmhouse and went back to the barn.

Tomorrow morning. First thing.

27

Penny lost track of how many times she drove up and down the side streets, looking for a girl who met Mae's description. All the while keeping an eye out for the cops. Wondering if the detective—Lessner, she'd found his card—had somehow tracked her from the hospital, used security cameras or something to identify her vehicle. She thought about what he said. About her trying to take care of Myles's problem herself. She guessed it didn't take a genius to figure out that her story wasn't adding up, running errands with Myles in the hospital. She could tell the detective didn't believe her when she denied knowing about rumors of payback. Or what Myles was doing with a gun, which ironically was the one thing she really didn't know anything about. Reminding her of Myles's stupid nickname was a smart move on the detective's part—if by smart she meant needling her until she might decide to crack.

She wasn't going to crack. She wouldn't change anything she'd done, other than not making the mistake of returning to the hospital again. Merely catching Pryor, putting him behind bars, wasn't going to keep her or Myles or any of them any safer. You might as well put a tiger in a cage and jab at it nice and hard and then forget to shut the door for all the good it would do you.

She went past the church three or four times. More accurately, down the alley that ran past the back of the church, the parking lot on one side, on the other an old concrete pad that used to hold the dumpster for a now abandoned convenience store. A common pickup and drop-off place. Empty now. She circled around again, taking a longer loop this time which brought her farther down Sullivant toward downtown, and this time she saw one or two girls, their stares blank as she went past them. A quick assessment, determining if the car was slowing, if a man was behind the wheel. When it was clear Penny was a girl and in any case wasn't going to stop they looked back down the street for the next car.

There was no one in the alley the first time she drove through, or the next time after that. She despaired a little. She thought about Archie's grandmother, how she was old enough to remember the real Archie, Archie Griffin, back in his glory days at Ohio State, how unstoppable he seemed. How much people said William reminded them of him. "Pure athleticism," Archie's grandmother said. "Only two-time Heisman trophy winner." All this spilled out to Penny on the bleachers at track practice, where the grandmother watched Archie practice his sprints in the spring. Before the boosting of the BMW. Penny was no sprinter, always a long-distance runner, eight hundred, mile, but only middling good. Nothing like Archie. Or Myles, for that matter.

The car was sitting on the concrete pad on what she told herself was her last swing through. Toyota sedan, new looking. She kept driving but slowed, keeping an eye on her rearview mirror. The sedan's front passenger door opened and a girl climbed out, slowly and stiffly. Penny braked, stopped, backed up. She caught the alarm in the driver's eyes before he backed up himself, gunned it into the church lot, swung a hard U-turn and went down the alley the opposite way. Penny backed all the way up to the pad, blocking the girl's escape, put the SUV in park, and hopped out.

"Mae?"

"What?"

"Are you Mae?"

"The fuck are you?"

"I'm looking for a girl called Mae."

"Why?"

"Doesn't matter. She around?"

The girl shook her head. "Got rid of her." Her voice husky and exhausted; the voice of a woman twice or three times her age.

"What?"

"You deaf? He got rid of her."

"Who got rid of her?"

"Pryor," the girl said.

28

J. P. gave the first guy a warning. He was in a suit with a bow tie with his nicely dressed wife beside him in the passenger seat and they were on their way to a concert in Columbus and didn't realize how fast they were going. Sun starting to set. Seventy-three in a sixty-five zone not all that bad. Seventy-four, maybe he would have written him up. Seventy-six, for sure. But now, as he watched the Accord pull back into traffic, J. P. realized he was no further along than when he began, since a warning didn't count for anything. Not when you needed six tickets, minimum.

The next car, a lady gave him the tampon line, a bit to his surprise. It seemed so old, like a joke you heard from recordings of comedy shows in the days of radio. "I'm really sorry, officer," she said, looking straight ahead, her cheeks burning. She was maybe early thirties, professionally dressed, with gold dangly earrings and a blue scarf around her neck. She lowered her voice. "I have my period. I don't have anything with me. This is so embarrassing. I was trying to make it to the drugstore in time." He fell for it just once, but was chastised by June when he relayed the story the next day. "That just doesn't happen, J. P.," she said, putting emphasis on each word, as if she were lecturing a tardy student. "You take it from a lady who knows." He apologized to the driver, not saying one way or another if he believed her, and waited patiently while she signed the ticket. When she was done she pushed it back out through her open window, miffed. He'd been rewarded with the same angry look before when he ignored the bee-inside-the-car line; the depositing-the-check-before-the-bank-closes line; and the so-mad-at-what-the-president-was-saying-on-the-radio-just-now-that-I-lost-track-of-how-fast-I-was-going line. He heard Marks boast that he kept packages of tampons in his cruiser and would hand them to the women after he wrote the ticket if they ever tried that with him. He also heard that Marks once asked a woman if she needed instructions for how to put it in, and maybe even a hand doing it, and that led to a complaint, but Sheriff Waters made it go away after a little while.

Occasionally, J. P. encountered the guy racing to the hospital to meet his wife in the delivery room, but he tried not to be a jerk about that one. He always offered to escort the anxious father-to-be straight there. That usually ended with a sheepish grin, a shrug, followed by the hostile thrusting of the ticket book back through the window. But you had to be careful with that scenario, to at least offer the escort. After all, his father had delivered two babies, once on the side of the road, once in a Kmart parking lot right off the 31 exit. So it wasn't a total myth, even if it hadn't happened to J. P. yet.

J. P. made five tickets by ten thirty, the last a legitimate ninety miles per by a dark-haired guy with that three-day growth of beard that everyone wore now, which apparently was cool but which always made J. P. think of unemployment lines and farmhands. He couldn't have pulled it off anyway, what with his little wisps of facial hair he only needed to shave every other day. The guy flew past in a red Audi that took J. P. almost two miles to catch up to and pull over. The driver, even-keeled, grinning a little when J. P. told him how fast he'd been going, giving the steering wheel a couple of self-congratulatory pats.

The blond in the passenger seat beside him in a short dress that matched the Audi not quite as happy. Though it was difficult to say if she was unhappy at being stopped or just bored. "Blond from a bottle," he heard June saying dismissively, a prejudice he never quite understood given how much makeup she wore. He told the guy to slow down and get there in one piece as he wrote out the ticket.

"Thanks, Deputy," the guy replied, drawing out the word *deputy* in a way that signaled disrespect, obviously, like he was some kind of hick police officer straight out of Mayberry. J. P. let it go because of the frown he saw the blond give the guy just before he walked back to his cruiser. That guy's evening was probably ending a lot earlier than he anticipated.

J. P. circled around to the little dip in the gravel berm past the bridge, repositioned himself and waited. And waited. Car after car, sixty and change. Sixty-five. High fifties even. Minute after minute. But nothing else to do, nowhere to go. *Six tickets. Minimum.* The county quiet, the radio almost silent except for Joyce sending Dalton to a domestic and three times asking Marks his 10-20. J. P. texted back and forth with June for a while. The visit with her folks going fine, but she missed him. He missed her too, he told her. Finally, twenty after eleven, a white Chevy Blazer streaked with rust, doing eighty if it was doing sixty, flying past. One brake light coming on briefly, which meant they'd seen him in the rearview mirror, then winking off again with no sign of a significant slowdown.

The Blazer was well past where he stopped the guy in the Audi when he finally pulled it over. He called the plate in and waited, starting to fill in the top of the ticket. Faster than he expected, the radio crackled and he heard Joyce's voice. She read off the name of the registration, paused, and said: "Unit 12, be advised there's a pending misdemeanor 10-50. Theft and receiving stolen property out of Columbus." Something funny in her voice, but she could be that way sometimes.

"Okay." Under his father, they were moving to plain English dispatching, trying to catch up with the rest of the country, which had slowly been ditching all the 10 codes after 9/11 and Katrina and all those problems firefighters had talking to police and other rescuers. But it was back to the old ways as soon as Waters took over as sheriff. 10-20: location. 10-50: warrant. Even a 10-11, as in report of a barking 10-11.

J. P. made sure his video cam was running as he climbed out of the cruiser. *Exited my vehicle*, he knew he'd have to write in his report to satisfy Vick. But it wasn't until he saw the dent in the Blazer's rear fender that he realized what he heard in Joyce's voice, and why. Tension. Wariness. Just like that his stomach tightened. He paused, letting a tractor trailer shift into the passing lane and rush past him in a cloud of diesel wind before he continued up the berm. Misdemeanor 10-50. The same return dispatch that his father received after calling in the plate that night. Also a Chevy Blazer. Open misdemeanor 10-50. Not on Route 31 but in downtown Darbytown, not two blocks from the station. His father barely halfway to the car when it suddenly took off, wheels squealing, filling the air with the smell of burning rubber. His father jogging back to the squad car as he keyed in his status.

"He took off," he had said, slightly out of breath. "I'm chasing him. Call for backup. Going west out of town."

J. P. brushed away the memories, like cobwebs from a doorway he passed through every day, took a deep breath, and approached the car.

29

After dinner Pryor left the barn again, just to check things out. No lights on in the farmhouse; he made sure of that. No lights on anywhere, with the exception of one large bright buzzing bulb on the side of the barn, just below the corner where the roof intersected with the sagging wall on that side. It cast long shadows across the driveway between the barn and the house. Pryor didn't think the light could be seen from the road because of the way the driveway sloped down onto the property, which was a big selling point of the place to begin with. But he still didn't like it. The darker the better, in his opinion. That was always how he operated in the city. The problem was he couldn't figure out where to turn it off. The switches they found inside the barn turned on a pair of single bulbs hanging from long cords from overhead beams, like nooses someone found another use for, but didn't affect the one outside. Nor was there anything obvious on the barn's exterior walls.

Back inside the farmhouse, Pryor tried the four switches just inside the front door. The wallpaper a bright blue striped business with a repeating pattern of white geese, trim and neat, no edges peeling, not what he expected when he first laid eyes on the property. Especially not when the door opened at his knock and the woman stood there, staring at him, her eyes like blue marbles pressed into dried-up pizza dough. The shotgun in her arms like she knew how to use it. Well, he'd landed on the truth there, anyway. The wallpaper in contrast to what he found inside the actual house.

He tried each switch in turn but activated only the porch light and a light in a closet to the left. The other two switches either not working or lighting something he couldn't see. He walked back onto the porch and shut the door behind him. He could do it with a gun, easily. Take the light out no problem. One shot. Despite his eye, since he'd learned to compensate for lost depth perception and peripheral vision over the years. But he didn't want to risk an outdoor shot. Not even this far out in the middle of nowhere Ohio. Instead, he cast around until he found some decent-sized rocks. The first throw went wide, missing by nearly a foot. He knew he shouldn't be mad, that it was dark and the ground uneven and he had things on his mind. But he'd brained squirrels off telephone lines that were just as high, if not higher, watching the animals drop like sock puppets, sometimes right to his feet. He liked to leave them where they lay and come back the next day, and sometimes the day after that, to see how long they remained. Sometimes they were there a long time.

He nailed the light on the third throw, the light blinking out in a sharp pop of breaking glass, the farmyard swallowed by darkness, the absence of the electrical buzzing a relief. Yet the sound of the glass breaking was also jarring, stirring up memories Pryor didn't expect just then. He stepped back quickly, nearly tripping, to avoid falling shards. It was important not to hurt himself at this stage. Who knew that better than him?

30

The stupid thing was, Penny saw attempts to mimic prostitutes in the costume shop every day. The dragnet stockings, the plunging necklines, makeup just short of clown face. *Which is sexier? Naughty nun or naughty nurse?* Which is dumber—your brain or your ass? So there were those imitations, so far from reality, and then there was the ragged-looking white girl standing in front of Penny on the concrete pad, wiping her mouth with the sleeve of her shirt. Jean shorts, the edges ragged, a too- small, faded Buckeyes jersey showing a little bit of tummy, and not flat tummy either, black eyes that might have been done up with mascara or might just have been two black eyes, teeth like something sailors had before they started keeping fresh fruit on ships.

"Got rid of her how?" Penny said.

"Not sure," the girl said after a moment too long.

"Please—I need to find her."

"Fuck off."

"It's important. I'm not looking for trouble."

"I said—"

"So you know Pryor?"

The girl stood there, swaying a bit, staring at Penny. "No," she said, finally.

"You with Pryor?"

"You need to get the fuck out of here."

Penny took a breath. She heard traffic passing on the south end of the alley, by the street. She probably didn't have much time, the way this part of town grew busy at night. But not with joggers and dog walkers. She opened her purse, pulled out her wallet, found Randy's last two twenties. She showed them to the girl, holding them tightly between her thumb and forefinger.

"What's your name?"

"Fuck you."

"Mine's Penny."

Another pause. "Ashley."

"I need to find Pryor. The only thing I know right now is he had a girl named Mae. That's all I need from you. Where Mae is."

"Why you looking for Pryor?"

The same expression on the girl's face as the woman at the apartment complex. The effect Pryor had on people like the fear of catching a fatal illness.

"I need to talk to him."

The girl laughed, except it sounded more like a cough. "People don't talk to Pryor."

"He shot my boyfriend."

That got her attention.

"When?"

"Last night."

"You want to talk to Pryor about him shooting your boyfriend?"

"Something like that."

"That's not such a good idea."

"You can have this," Penny said, moving the money in a little circle, like a magician about to do a trick. "I just need to know where Mae is. Where she really is, no bullshit."

"I don't know."

"Please."

A car turned into the alley a hundred yards up, headlights winking as it approached them, rocking on the uneven gravel surface. Could it be? Penny reached her hand into the purse, tightened her fingers around the Glock.

"Pryor sold her. That's all I know."

"*Sold* her?"

"What I said."

"I heard you. But what do you mean?"

"Couple nights ago. Mae was working down there." She pointed toward the street. "Pryor pulls up, and two minutes later some guy came by in a van. Green van with balls on the back."

"Balls?"

"Hanging from the trailer hitch. Like a guy's balls."

Penny nodded. Truck nuts. You saw them around the neighborhood. She was pretty sure Brandi made Randy ditch a pair she found in his garage, after they began dating.

She looked up the alley, staring anxiously at the approaching car. "So what about it?"

"So the two of them were talking, and then Mae started crying and shit, and then the guy handed Pryor a handful of cash, and they both pushed her into the van and the guy took off."

"You sure it wasn't just some john?"

"Not for that kind of money."

"You don't know where she went?"

Another pause. Penny showed Ashley the twenties again. The car nearly upon them. No way to see who the driver was. She would only have one chance. *Just because you're back doesn't mean you're out.*

"You better go," Ashley said.

"Where is she? Where'd that guy take her?"

"I told you—"

Too late. Dust rising as the car stopped suddenly, then inched forward, forcing them to move to the side. Nice car—newish Ford sedan. Penny saw a kid's car seat in the rear. The man behind the wheel stared at them. Well-dressed white guy—glasses, short hair, graying, wearing a button-down shirt. Old enough to be Ashley's father. She relaxed. Not Pryor. But trouble just the same.

"Haven't seen you around," he said to Penny. "How much? Whole nine yards."

Penny gave him the finger.

"Saucy. I like that. Hundred bucks?"

"Fuck you." She turned to Ashley. "If I give you my number, will you call me? If you change your mind?"

Ashley looked at the ground and then at the driver of the car, who was watching them both intently. Her face had gone dead at the man's arrival, her gray pupils dull as the backs of dirty spoons. She reached out and took the money from Penny. She put the bills in a rear pocket. Then she hugged herself so that her breasts bunched up under her shirt, and said, "Grand Knights Motel."

"What?"

"Hey—what's the delay?" the man said. "You getting in or what?"

Ashley held Penny's eyes for a second. Then she dropped her gaze, and walked around the front of the car, around to the passenger side.

"Where they took Mae," she said. "Grand Knights. Up north, by the highway. I heard them talking. Where 71 meets 161. Just down from Waffle House."

"They're working her out of there?"

"For now." Ashley opened the passenger door.

"What do you mean, for now?"

"For as long as she lasts. Lot of door knocks up there. Takes it out of you, what I hear."

"Pryor's involved in this?"

"Don't just stand there," the man said. "Get in the car." But he was looking at Penny, not Ashley, as he spoke.

Ashley shook her head. "I told you, Pryor sold her. He got rid of her."

"You know why?"

"Said he didn't need her anymore."

"Doesn't sound like Pryor."

"What I heard, he said he was tired of it holding him down."

"*Come on*," the man said, nervously.

"It?"

"It," Ashley said. "Mae."

With that, she climbed into the car and pulled the passenger door shut, staring through the windshield at something Penny couldn't see. The man drove off quickly, tires kicking up dust all the way down the alley.

31

Satisfied with the dark that finally enveloped the farmyard, Pryor went back inside the barn. He opened the cooler sitting next to the van, fished out two bottles of Yuengling and tossed them to Michigan and Archie. He returned to the van and found his bottle of Jack. Then he rooted around until he found his chipped Briggs High mug, filled it three quarters full with the whiskey as the others observed. He made sure they saw what he was doing. He took a long pull, and then another. The smell of cooked meat, the steaks they put on the grill he found on the back porch, filled the barn.

"What now?" Archie said.

"Now we wait."

"We've been waiting all day."

"We wait a little longer. Spend the night. Get up. Get it done."

"Why am I driving?" Archie said. Pryor tensed up. He thought they were done with all the questions.

"Like you're going to come in with us. A Black guy in an Amish bank. Might as well light you on fire, the attention that would bring."

"I thought you said it was a farmers' bank. Not all the farmers out here are Amish."

"You're an agricultural expert now?"

"I'm just saying—"

"You know what I meant."

"What about me?" Michigan said. "I'm inside?"

"That's right."

"I'm never inside."

"You are now."

"Doing what?"

"You're on the door," Pryor said. "You're the lookout."

"Lookout for what?"

Pryor took another sip from his cup before replying. Uncharacteristically, he needed a moment. Because he never, ever had trouble lying. It was as close to a birthright skill as he possessed. He had to teach himself to steal and kill. But lying just came naturally. Yet the incessant questions were threatening to crack the facade he'd successfully maintained over the past few days. Since he learned Baby was out.

You're not going to drive, he wanted to scream at the pair of them. *You're not going inside. I'm going to put bullets in both your brains as soon as I'm sure we're 100 percent alone out here and I don't need backup of any kind.*

But he didn't say that. Not quite yet.

"For trouble," Pryor said, straining to show patience. "For cops. For Amish guys with pitchforks. For whatever."

"He's inside, but I'm not?" Archie interrupted. "With his face?"

"He's the lookout. It's different."

"Bullshit," Archie muttered.

"I've never been inside before," Michigan. "It just seems—"

"Just seems what?"

"Not the way it usually is, is all." Pryor could tell Michigan was confused, but that he also didn't want to do anything to annoy him. Unlike Archie.

"That's because this is the big one. The last one. And it has to be different."

"I just don't have a grip on what I'm supposed to do."

"Just stick close to me," Pryor said.

"But—"

"Close," Pryor said.

Pryor handed around more beers. They talked a few minutes longer. With Pryor's permission, Archie and Michigan went outside to piss. When they came back they lay down since it was dark and there was nothing to do but take out their phones. Pryor kept an eye on Archie's face, illuminated from the glow of the screen. Watching porn—big surprise. He never used to worry about Archie. Michigan you could count on to be perpetually nervous, like a cat that never knows if you're going to open a can of food or kick it across the room. But more and more, Archie, all these questions. After a minute Archie looked at Pryor, as if he sensed his observation. They stared at each other for a couple of seconds before Archie turned back to his phone.

Now Pryor had to pee. He went outside and around to the back and unzipped his pants and let loose a long, satisfying stream, arcing his water toward the rustle of corn in the dark fields before him, waving it back and forth like a garden hose that's finally been unkinked, as if daring anything to emerge from those shadowy green depths to challenge him. Jack would never have made him go like that. But iced tea, strong and brown, which he made two days earlier to fill the bottle with, definitely had that effect. Compared to Jack it tasted like musty grass and leaves. But taste wasn't the point. Making it seem like he was drinking Jack was the point.

When he went back inside Archie and Michigan were asleep, snoring like downshifting dump trucks, the multiple beers and hot meat of the steaks and long day of boredom finally shutting their brains down. He went around to the side of the van and removed the three blankets he stole from Wal-Mart, one at a time over the past month. He was glad he had. There was the slightest chill in the barn, a hint of fall air creeping inside. He covered Archie and Michigan in turn, took a last look at the coals in the grill, the red glowing in the dark like some kind of underwater vent on one of those science shows, and lay down, using a shoe for a pillow and pulling his own blanket up to his shoulders. It was important to have a good night's sleep. They had a big day ahead of them.

He did, anyway.

32

The guy didn't run from J. P. He didn't race the engine and jam the gear shift into drive and spit gravel at the knees of the approaching sheriff's deputy like someone deciding at the last second, what the hell, to drive off a cliff. He just sat there, shaking, almost shivering, as J. P. came up to the driver's side and asked to see his license. He was a thin white guy with a spider tattoo climbing up his neck onto the left side of his face and a huge ring stapled through the septum of his nose. He was smoking nervously, the cigarette quivering in his right hand like a buoy bobbing up and down in choppy waters. An enormous woman sat in the passenger seat, her pink face fleshy and shiny and distended, holding a child wearing nothing but a diaper whose hands were gripping a bottle filled with something that looked like soda. The driver handed J. P. a license that expired two years ago. He didn't have insurance. Registration long out of date. The warrant was a misunderstanding, he said, not meeting the deputy's eyes. The baby began to cry.

A trooper arrived five minutes later as backup. J. P. knew that was thanks to Joyce, who was also on dispatch duty the night his father pulled the Chevy over. He conferred with the patrol lady briefly.

Brittany something. Relatively new to her post. He wasn't unhappy about the company, to tell the truth.

As Brittany watched, J. P. had everyone climb out of the Blazer. He cuffed the man for the warrant, searched him, found nothing but a lighter, and put him in the back of his cruiser. He cited the lady for child endangering for not having the baby in a car seat. He believed her when she said they couldn't afford one right now. But he didn't have any choice. The baby's safety came first. Brittany agreed to take the lady and the child to the post where she could call for someone to pick her up. After they left, J. P. sat in the front seat and listened to the man in back plead in a quiet, whimpering voice for one more chance while they waited for the tow truck to come and take the Blazer away.

"Please, man."

"I'm sorry," J. P. said.

"Kill you to help a guy out?"

"It'll be all right. You'll see."

A lie, and not even a white one, at that. *There's always a few that just can't get with the program.* Was that this guy? He didn't seem remotely evil. Just poor and downtrodden and stupid. But he could easily have gotten that baby killed under the right circumstances.

"Please?"

"You need to be quiet now," J. P. said.

It was nearing one o'clock by the time he finished the paperwork at the jail and went back inside the station and walked into the roster room. Deserted, as he expected. The whole building empty, except for the jail. Joyce long gone, since dispatch rolled over to the patrol from midnight to six A.M. Corey, the new guy, the lone deputy on overnight, out on the road someplace. At least not sitting in the parking lot working on "reports" the way Marks did on the same shift. J. P. looked inside the communal refrigerator, spied a lone Diet Coke, hesitated a moment, then took it anyway. It had been a long night. He sat down at the table, cracked it open, took a long pull, and checked his messages. During their texting while he sat on patrol, June filled him in on the party preparations and her parents and John and her nephews and nieces and her sister's financial troubles and all the usual stuff. He went silent once he made the stop and she sent a few unanswered texts, finishing with question marks, smiley faces, and hearts. He knew she was probably still thinking about Des Moines. He texted her a heart back, despite the hour. She could sleep through just about anything.

After he put his phone away he grabbed the list of reports piled high on a clipboard, each document looped through a round metal clip with two punch holes at the top. He idly flipped back through everything. There wasn't much to speak of. Traffic stops, warrants served, arguments tended to. Loose livestock observed, and then corralled with the help of a farmer. A mom who suspected her son of doing drugs, but without actual evidence. Going back another day, his check on Clayton and Priscilla Hartzell and their reports of a suspicious vehicle. The same call the day before that, and two days before that as well. Nothing today, he noticed. Well, yesterday, given the hour. He knew what he meant.

Their house wasn't exactly on his way home, but it was close enough. He probably wouldn't have bothered if June wasn't away, but now he was wide awake and just the tiniest bit curious why the cantankerous old guy stopped calling, cold, after several days of complaints. J. P. was also on edge, after the traffic stop. The misdemeanor warrant out of Columbus. The memories it revived so suddenly, like a waking dream.

"Car's off the road," his father called in about six minutes after the chase began, no jargon involved, just his regular voice, except for the note of urgency. "Smoke coming from the hood."

J. P. flipped back the top pages of the call log, straightened them so that everything was neat and aligned, stood up and took the clipboard and placed it on top of the file cabinet where it belonged. He went back outside, climbed into his cruiser, checked his messages one last time, pulled out of the parking lot, and headed west to London–Darbytown Road and the Hartzells' farmhouse.

33

It was past eleven when Penny took the exit off I-71 for Dublin–Granville Road. The motel sat a hundred yards away on the north side of the street, tucked back behind a service road that led to two other motels. Penny made a left onto the service drive and drove into the parking lot.

The building was laid out like an L. A small office occupied the front corner, a half-dead hedge running beneath the office's two windows. Penny couldn't see anyone inside as she drove past. The door to the first unit past the office was open, and she saw the blue flicker of a TV inside. The next two doors were shut, with window blinds drawn. The motel's outer walls were beige, the doors white and pocked with scratches and dents as if someone had beaten on them with chains instead of knocking. Penny passed another open door and saw, sitting just outside, a pair of small children playing with some kind of action figures despite the hour. She continued driving, trying not to stare, but also knowing she couldn't help but stick out in Randy's big, bright red SUV. Not as bad as at the apartment building where she searched for Mae. But close. For the first time that day she missed the Aurora; it would have fit right into a place like this.

She completed the long edge of the L, went left around the corner, and saw the green van right away. It was parked in front of the second to last unit. Sure enough, plastic truck nuts hanging from the hitch, big as swollen fruit. The door to the room shut and the blinds drawn, but a light was on inside. A man sat in the front seat of the van, smoking and talking on a phone. As Penny slowed, the man looked up and frowned. Without meeting his gaze, Penny stopped, reversed, and drove back up toward the office. From there she made for the service road, turned left, and then turned left again into a small shopping plaza on the other side of a through street from the motel. She parked in front of a business whose windows were filled with signs in Spanish. Farther down the row of stores, a Chinese place and a pay day lending business were still open, but most of the storefronts, including a shoe repair place, a nail salon, and a Somali tea shop, were dark. Penny killed the engine and threw the keys in her purse. She crossed the street and walked back toward the motel, stepping onto a dry patch of lawn littered with empty cigarette packs and plastic grocery bags. She paused in front of a Dumpster and a line of tall, conical bushes that hid the motel from the street. Penny took advantage of the protective cover it provided and stepped between two of the bushes. Now she was looking down the short leg of the L, the van at the end of her sightline. She waited for a couple minutes, trying to decide what to do. The irony, she thought, was that Myles would have known, would have understood their next move. But he wasn't here to make decisions. Of course he wasn't. That was the whole fucking problem.

◆

It hadn't always been that way. Time was, Myles's impatience took the upper hand. Almost always, like a nervous tick no amount of drugs would eliminate. Take track and field, in high school. Penny lasted longer than Myles, despite much less talent. She often wondered if Myles's decision to quit was less about his craziness in those days than because their coach insisted on him running the mile and the two-mile, which Myles couldn't stand. The coach a well-meaning guy, but his first love was coaching football. He took the job after a fair bit of arm twisting by the athletic director after the regular coach was caught under the bleachers with one of the girl long-jumpers the previous spring. You looked at Myles and you thought long distance, with his wiry build and his willingness to run lap after lap in practice without complaint. But the reality was, even white and skinny, he was as fast as any of the Black sprinters, including the hundred-meter guys, even in regular old running shoes without any spikes or starting blocks or anything. That's where he wanted to be. Going fast. *Baby.* But they had four good sprinters already, good not great, who all played for the coach in the fall under the stadium lights, and no milers and two-milers, and so there it was. And there it went for one season, until Myles just up and quit, right before districts. Sick of not being listened to and wanting to use his speed for more immediate gain. For boosting things from stores, for example, and being long gone before any lumbering security guard could round the aisle and see what happened. Speed that, a few years later, a guy named Pryor admired and mentioned when he started coming around regularly. And once Myles gave into that impatience and let Pryor into his life, it was a long time before Myles saw straight again. And by that time he was behind bars and Penny was home alone with their newborn son.

◆

The door to the motel room in front of the green van swung open and a man emerged. Penny held her breath, peering through the bushes. He was slight, vaguely Hispanic looking, wearing jeans and a blue work shirt. He shut the door hard behind him and glanced once at the van before walking up the sidewalk in Penny's direction. Before reaching her he turned to his right and walked to a small red car parked near where the two children played. Almost before he backed out and drove off, another car entered the parking lot, rolled down the long row of units, turned left, and pulled into a space beside the green van. A heavyset man climbed out of the car with difficulty, shut his door, and walked up to the motel room door. He had his hand on the knob when the man in the green van said something. The man pivoted, approached the van, stood at the window, and exchanged words. After a minute, the man stepped back toward the motel room, knocked, waited, and stepped inside as the door opened. As if that was his signal, the man in the green van started his engine and a few moments later drove out of the lot.

Penny steeled herself. This was it. She had to make her move, and fast. She might not have another chance. Who knew how long the man might be, when he might return? She remembered this one time when she and Myles were running the streets together, during her lost year, before she came to her senses and went back home. How he told her that the key to doing anything was overcoming the molasses of hesitation. What he actually called it. A phrase his grandmother used, from her younger days in Kentucky before the family up and moved to Columbus. How he said you had to decide to go all out or nothing good would come of your action. It was the feeling, he said, like when you lined up for a sprint and faced down the fear of the next few seconds. There was no room for deliberation, for plotting one's motives, good or bad. There was just the gun and the go.

Penny went. She pushed her way through the bushes, ignoring the brush of the prickly dry branches on her arms and neck, and emerged into the motel parking lot. She marched up to the door where the man entered a few minutes ago. Room 44. She put her hand on the doorknob. It turned. She took a breath and stepped inside.

34

It was a shame Baby wasn't along for this, Pryor reflected again, lying in the dark. Pryor certainly could have used him. But things had to be the way they were.

Strictly speaking, it wasn't true this was the last job. Not his last job, anyway. He had a bright future, the way he figured it. But a future that came in steps. First up, the chance to kick back for a while—a long while, sure—down in the holler, nothing to worry about, no one to bug him, no one to ask him a bunch of fucking questions all day long, until he decided what the next chapter would be. Solo, no matter what that future looked like. Archie and Michigan both liabilities now, after the other night. Archie especially, with that bullshit story about seeing a cop. Pryor knew for sure now what happened, what Archie was up to. Trying to save Baby's ass. Lying about a cop to rush them out of there to keep Pryor from taking the kill shot. Yeah, Pryor knew. And there would be a price to pay; make no mistake. The only question was when, and how. He glanced in their direction. Satisfied they were asleep, Pryor pulled his phone from his pocket and checked the time. Just a few more minutes. Long enough to ensure their breathing stayed steady, their snoring nice and loud, which would mean they wouldn't hear him coming. Same as Dawson hadn't seen it coming, come to think of it.

◆

Dawson. Good man. The way he placed his hand on the Bible and swore to tell the truth and nothing but the truth, and then looked the prosecutor right in the eye and told her that he and Pryor were smoking weed in his apartment at exactly the same moment the Eakin Road bank job went down. Dawson not exactly a pillar of the community, but not a guy with a criminal record either. Not like Baby.

What Dawson did have was a cute little grandbaby, two years old, darling little girl. A grandbaby that Dawson watched three times a week while his daughter went to work at the Target down by the university. A grandbaby that went missing for two hours one day after Pryor came by with Dawson's dope and kept him talking in the kitchen while Michigan came in through the side door and took the kid. Pryor explained the whole situation while Dawson sat on the couch and shook and swore and cried. Blubbering at the selfie Michigan took of himself holding the girl that he texted Pryor from the van down the street. The girl looking as terrified as if a bear had plucked her from her bed in the middle of the night. Though hard to say which was more dangerous, in Pryor's opinion: a bear or Michigan, with that crazy blue streak on his face and the perpetual sense he gave of having nothing left to lose.

When Pryor was sure Dawson understood what he was saying he texted Michigan back and not ten minutes later the little girl was in the house again, hardly the worse for wear, though her diaper could have used changing. And that's what it came down to. Dawson's word against Baby's—against Myles's. The alibi or his darling little grandbaby. His choice. Not that it wasn't a close call. Pryor had to hand it to the prosecutor. She made a good case. Pryor knew some of the jurors weren't buying it. But it didn't matter. Enough did that he walked away and Baby went inside, the plea deal he struck for testifying against Pryor suddenly not looking so rosy.

Pryor let some time pass and paid a visit to Dawson a year or so later. Told him he had one last job. Same kind of line he gave Archie and Michigan. Technically true. Afterward, nobody could believe Dawson would just up and leave town like that, with his daughter and granddaughter there and all the babysitting he did. But he wasn't from Columbus, after all, had migrated up from Kentucky, and maybe something happened to change his mind. It's not like there were any signs of struggle, or anything suspicious. His car was gone, and most of his clothes. The house tidied up, like a place you weren't planning to come back to for a while. And then there was the postcard his daughter retrieved from the mailbox a week later, postmarked Lexington, that offered a weak apology.

Yes, one last job. For Dawson. His job to fall down onto his knees in the middle of deep woods, clouds of mosquitos hovering in the air, as he cried and shivered, while Pryor told him to ready himself like a man. Told him he should be thankful for the service he'd done Pryor. Proud, even.

Nice thing about woods like that: no digging necessary. Who would ever come through there? And if they did, what would they see? Animals made sure of that.

Pryor checked his phone again. Listened to Michigan and Archie's rhythmic breathing, up and down, slow and smooth.

Five more minutes should do it, he thought.

35

"*Uhh-uhh-uhh. Uhh-uhh-uhh.*"

The inside of the motel room tiny, like pictures you saw of ship cabins. There couldn't have been more than four feet between the end of the bed on the right and the wall to Penny's left. The two of them on the bed, where the first thing Penny saw were the big, white, bobbing ass cheeks of the man as he thrust himself up and down. His white underpants were down around his left ankle and he was still wearing black socks. He'd pulled his shirt up and Penny could see a mat of thick dark hair on his lower back. "*Uhh-uhh-uhh,*" he groaned as he pumped the girl, his rear rising and falling so violently that the leg of the mattress frame closest to the door knocked up and down on the floor in rhythm with the thrusts. A sour smell of sweat and perfume and cigarette smoke filled the room. In contrast to the man's moaning, the sound the girl made beneath him was like the yelping of a puppy each time a boot made contact with its ribs.

Penny slammed the door behind her, shot the bolt and pushed the anti-intruder hinge over. At the sound of the door closing the man started so quickly he lost whatever equilibrium he had and slipped out of the girl and fell off the bed with a thud, like a duffel bag of dirty laundry hitting the sidewalk. "Jesus Christ!" he said.

But when he raised himself up he was staring not at Penny but at the Glock in her right hand. The girl lay on the bed, legs spread, not even bothering to cover her exposed, swollen sex. Not bothering, or not able. Pale and skinny and childlike, although Penny didn't think she was underage. Pryor wasn't stupid. Not that he cared, Penny figured, but he knew what lines not to cross to keep him from bigger trouble.

The girl peered at Penny in anticipation, as if her appearance was the most natural thing in the world. Penny looked from the girl to the man on the floor and back. Judging just by the size of his stomach, the man must have outweighed her by at least a hundred pounds. Penny glanced at the Glock in her hand and realized not for the first time in the past twelve hours that she didn't know much about guns. Except that most people looking down a gun barrel didn't think about whether you knew what you were doing.

Except for Pryor, of course.

"What the—" the man squeaked.

"Are you Mae?" Penny said to the girl.

"Listen. I don't know what this is," the man said.

"Shut up." Penny shifted the gun to her left hand, grabbed the crumpled top sheet from the right side of the bed and tossed it onto the girl. For a moment it just lay there, like a sheet thrown over a half-assembled mannequin in a department store after hours. Then the girl grabbed the edge and drew it up, covering her sex and knobby hip bones and small, hard breasts, but not in a gesture of modesty. Simply as if she were cold.

"I said, are you Mae?"

The girl looked past Penny, not to the man on the floor beside the bed, but toward the door. She nodded.

"You were with Pryor?"

Another nod.

"I need to know where he went."

"Who the hell is Pryor?" the man said.

Penny ignored him and took two steps toward the bed. The man gasped and in his panic farted, the sound like someone pulling up a giant strip of Velcro. Penny peered closer at the girl. There was something wrong with her face. Her eyes were dilated and her lips weren't the right color. Penny thought of Darren, Lem's nephew, who wouldn't listen to warnings about Pryor. Who had no one to blame but himself.

Thought about how uncharacteristically nervous Lem was when he saw Penny on his doorstep.

"Where he went," Penny said, shaking away the thought.

The girl said something Penny couldn't make out. She asked her to repeat it. She did, but what she said didn't make sense.

"Did you say a farm?"

The girl nodded again.

"What farm?"

"Went to a farm. In Darby County." The words barely above a whisper.

"Why?"

"Ain't sure."

"Now, listen." The man, still on the floor, glancing between Penny and Mae.

"Shut up," Penny repeated. To Mae: "Where? Where in Darby County?"

"I don't know."

"Who does?"

"Guy."

"What guy?"

"Some guy. Friend of Michigan. It's this guy's aunt and uncle or someone. It's their farm."

"What's his name?"

"Robby."

"Where's he stay at?"

"I don't know."

"Where can I find him?"

The girl didn't answer. Her eyes were shut now, her lips parted.

"Mae!" Penny said, sharply.

"Nuh," Mae said.

"Where can I find him?"

The girl licked her lips. "AFD."

"What?"

"American Farm Dairy. Way out on West Broad. We stopped there a couple times. Pryor made him give us free beer and ice cream and gas."

"Works when?"

"Not sure. Lot of nights."

"Overnight?"

After a moment she nodded.

"So he's there now?"

Mae pulled the sheet up higher, up to her neck, the contours of her body outlined beneath the thin covering.

"Maybe. Not really sure, though."

"What's he look like?"

Mae told her.

"All right," Penny said. The man was staring at her with an expression someplace between pissed off and dazed and confused. "All right," she repeated.

She took two steps back, toward the door. The man watched as she moved. Mae watched the man watching her. Without turning around, Penny reached behind her, swung the anti-intruder hinge back open, undid the deadbolt, and turned the knob. She opened the door. She stopped and frowned at the fat man. She hesitated. She thought about Lem Garretty, and Darren. She looked again at Mae. Something was wrong with her. Her eyes were shut.

No need to stay, Penny thought. She had what she came for. Robby at the AFD. Overnights. It was better than nothing. And she was running out of time. *Bright and early*, according to Brandi. Maybe a bluff, but the later the night went and the more tired Penny felt the less she could be sure. Brandi had worked hard for a house in the suburbs and she'd work just as hard to keep it.

"Don't do anything stupid," she said. She stepped outside and shut the door.

◆

The van with the truck nuts wasn't back. Penny counted herself lucky as she walked across the parking lot toward the dumpster and the cone-shaped bushes, back to Randy's car. Passing the garbage bin she caught a whiff of something bad all mixed together, rotting meat and diapers and spilled beer, and she stopped. She stood still for just a moment, her back to the motel, thinking. She thought about those white ass cheeks and that stomach and the look on the man's face. And of Darren. Such a loser. All she had in her life were losers.

"Shit," Penny said.

She turned around and went back across the parking lot and pushed open the door to Room 44. Inside, the man leaned over Mae, his right arm raised and Mae on her side, naked, the sheet gone, and she was raising her own hands, holding them over her face. Penny lifted the gun and pointed it not at the fat man's face but at his junk, and said, "Bathroom. Now."

"Fuck you, bitch," he squeaked.

She lowered the gun, because otherwise that's how accidents happen, walked up to him and kicked him, hard, the way Myles showed her, right between his legs, setting aside the molasses of hesitation that flickered in and out of her mind as she jerked her sneaker up where it counted. Setting the hesitation aside because kicking a guy like that was harder to bring yourself to do than you'd think, especially with the goods unprotected; it made you wince.

"Ooohhh!" the man said, doubling over. Penny moved closer, repeated her order, and waited while he half walked, half crawled into the bathroom. She yanked the door shut as soon as he was inside. She heard him moaning. She thought about trying something tricky like tying one of his pant legs to the knob and the other to the bed to keep him from opening the door right away—a version of what she did to Randy—but there was no time.

"Get your stuff," she said to Mae.

"What?"

"Get dressed."

"Why?"

"We're leaving. Move it."

"I don't want—"

"Now."

It took Mae a minute to find her clothes, bunched up on the floor by the bed, then another minute just to pull on her panties.

"Hurry up."

"I'm trying."

"Not hard enough."

After the girl finally pulled on her shirt and sweatpants, Penny gave up. She grabbed the socks from Mae's hands, stuffed them into the sneakers she lifted from the bedside and put her hand on Mae's left arm. "Let's go."

They emerged into the night air and the parking lot half-lit by a buzzing sodium lamp overhead, insects encircling the globe of light like flecks of February snow. Too late. Penny looked over and saw the green van turning and coming toward them. "Come *on*," she said, dragging Mae toward the dumpster. The flesh on the girl's arm felt strangely cold, as if she'd just emerged from a pool on a cool day. The van stopped with a screech of brakes and Penny heard the door open and the sound of feet hitting the asphalt.

"The fuck?" a man's voice said.

They reached the bushes and Penny dragged Mae through, ignoring the girl's cries of protests. She pulled her onto the through street and toward the shopping plaza. She dropped Mae's shoes and started running, forcing the girl to jog along beside her. Behind them, Penny heard something snap as the man made it to the bushes, followed by a loud exclamation and a curse. She didn't look back. She led the now stumbling Mae across a short tree lawn of grass and into the plaza parking lot and up to the Pilot. She fumbled in her purse for the key fob and keyed the door open. She opened the rear passenger door and was pushing Mae inside when she heard the footsteps behind her.

She turned, heart pounding with fear, and stared at the man in front of her. He was short, out of breath, maybe in his thirties—Pryor's age, more or less—white and chunky, what was left of his hair in a ponytail, wearing droopy cargo pants and a sleeveless gray wife beater.

"The fuck you think you're going?" he said, panting.

She hesitated.

"I said—"

"Pryor."

"What?"

"I'm going after Pryor."

"You know Pryor?"

"Unfortunately. You know where he is?"

"She's mine," the man said, ignoring the question, gesturing at the Pilot. At Mae.

"Not anymore, she isn't."

"I fucking bought her, bitch."

"You know where Pryor is?" Penny repeated.

"You can't just take her," he said, between labored breaths. "She belongs to me."

"You can't buy someone," Penny responded, though deep down she wasn't sure if that were true.

"Fuck this," the man said, and lumbered toward her. Penny reached for the gun again, dipping her hand into her purse, but realized only then that she was too slow and there wasn't time. He was too close and coming too fast. She backed up and tripped on a parking space curb and fell. And then he was on her.

36

Pryor awakened with a start. *Shit.* He hadn't meant to doze off. The iced tea masquerading as Jack was supposed to prevent that. He lifted his head off the boot he was using as a pillow, lifted his phone, and checked the hour. Middle of the night. He glanced at Archie and Michigan, satisfied after a moment by their snores and rising and falling chests that they were asleep. Well, now as good a time as any, he thought. Same line he used on Dawson, come to think of it. And Cousin Ed. Used on a lot of people over the years. And why not? Why tinker with success?

He threw off his blanket and made to stand when he froze, hearing a sound outside.

Bam-bam-bam.

Someone was knocking on the farmhouse door.

Bam-bam-bam.

Shit.

37

Penny looked up. Nothing happened. The pimp was just standing there, a few feet off, breathing hard, too hard, but not coming any closer. Making a strange wheezing sound. Gasping for air. In a way she'd seen before. It took her a couple of seconds to remember. He was gasping like she saw Pa-Paw before he went to the hospital the last time. In the days when he took off the cannula tube from his oxygen tank to use the bathroom and struggled even over that short time to return to his chair.

In front of her, the man dropped to his knees in slow motion, making elaborate heehaw sounds as his chest rose and fell. Now it came to her. Asthma attack. She'd seen it with the kids in her neighborhood. Mack somehow spared the problem, one of the lucky ones. She heard that it had something to do with bed bugs, or new carpet, or not changing the filters in the AC units roaring away in the bedroom windows day and night and which slowly clogged with mold.

The man's breathing grew heavier and more ragged, and the sound was almost exactly like one she'd already heard that night. *"Uhh-uhh-uhh. Uhh-uhh- uhh."* He looked at her, holding his hands out almost as if in supplication. As if he were pleading for something.

It had been a rainy summer, she thought, driving away from the parking lot a few moments later, going back west on Dublin–Granville Road. Headed for the highway and the American Farm Dairy on the far West Side of the city. Mae quiet in the back seat. Addressing the conditions that caused asthma was crucial, Penny thought, as she gripped the steering wheel. It was important to change those AC filters regularly. Or at least try to do something about bed bugs. And not just with that crap they sold at CVS and Walgreens, which was like using a squirt gun on a house fire. You needed to call an exterminator.

38

Bam-bam-bam.

Carefully, quietly, Pryor stood up. Stood still as a piece of rusted-out farm machinery and listened. Michigan and Archie's snoring softened to something closer to the breathing of people with heavy head colds. He waited a moment longer, then carefully walked to the back of the van. He opened the door, reached in, and felt around until he found what he was searching for. Not the knife, which he needed for something else. Something he should have been doing right about now. Not his biggest gun, either, the one he was saving for the bank. Sound was a factor here. Yes. Here it was. The .38 would work just fine. He took it and walked over to the small window in the side of the barn closest to the farmhouse. It was dirty and covered in spider webs and what looked like glops of bird crap, but still clear enough to see outside and across the gravel drive, even in the dark. He drew in his breath at what he saw, an involuntary intake of air. He berated himself, but it was too late.

"How?" he said to himself softly. He took another long look to make sure he was seeing right and turned around.

"Get up," he said in a loud whisper.

Nothing.

He tried again. Still nothing. His plan for the two of them was working exactly as he wanted, the multiple beers having the effect he counted on. To permit him to finish things quietly. But now, irony of ironies, after the trickiest part had passed, the dangerous stretch of daylight when someone might have come by, it was now that he needed them most. He looked back through the window. Goddamn it. "How?"

In the end he just left them sleeping. He could do this on his own. It would send a message when they woke up and saw what was happening. And that's when he'd need them more, anyway. It didn't fit with the plan. But what he saw through the window had just taken a giant shit on his plan, bigtime.

Pryor didn't bother putting his boots on. He needed to go softly. He watched through the window until he saw the door to the farmhouse open and then, after a moment, shut again. He strode to the far end of the barn, carefully opened the rear door, the one facing the cornfields, and stepped outside. The night air was cool and smelled of skunk. He felt the dew soak into his socks as he walked around the barn, over to the gravel drive, and quietly, quietly, tiptoed up the front steps.

◆

Pryor's hearing had improved after the accident. He didn't care what anybody said, what anybody thought about his theory. The body compensated. That was obvious enough. He noticed it the very day he came home from the hospital, still wearing the patch over his left eye. Over what used to be his left eye. Sitting in the living room, left by himself while the social worker talked to his mother in the kitchen, their voices low and hushed. A conversation that in the past would have been inaccessible, a jumble of sounds with maybe one or two words recognizable from time to time, like a TV on low two rooms over. But now, he was hearing entire phrases. *"Appointment with Children's Services,"* and "*misdemeanor child neglect charges*" and most often, "*fireworks.*" He must have heard the last word half a dozen times, sitting on the couch, gingerly placing a finger on the bandage, challenging himself to see if he could penetrate the medicated numbness surrounding the wound and feel actual pain. To his delight, he succeeded.

Oh yeah. His hearing was improved. He heard things, heard places people went, places people were, conversations people didn't want overheard, that no one else did.

◆

There were times—like approaching a dark house with a gun in your hand—when you had to make noise, Pryor thought, opening the farmhouse door, a lot of noise, because death wasn't a quiet affair and you needed to remind people of that, especially people who thought they were too good for dying. But there were also times when you had to be silent because while death wasn't always quick—and in that regard Pryor never liked to rush things—there were times when, regrettably, you didn't have any choice.

39

It was the light that caught J. P.'s attention. Or rather, the lack of light. So really, it was the darkness that led to the whole, sorry mess.

J. P. had traveled the road many times, in the day and in the night, and so must have seen the bright bulb on the corner of the Hartzells' barn out of the corner of his eye more frequently than not. It was visible through a quirk of the terrain from a quarter mile west, peeking through a gap in a stand of trees and the curve of the road, even though once you rounded the bend and approached the entrance to the farm the light was too far down the sloping drive to be seen. The light itself, that was. The smudgy glow it cast was almost always there as you rolled past the farmhouse, careful of the next bend approaching, sharper than the last.

That's what triggered the alarm for J. P. As he slowed, nearing the entrance to the Hartzells' driveway, planning just to creep past, it occurred to him how dark it was below. And that's when he realized he hadn't seen the wink of the farm light a quarter mile earlier. The grounds were completely dark—house and barn—and that didn't seem like Clayton and Priscilla, whose perennial fear of intruders trumped, if barely, their tight-fisted ways, which otherwise might have put a stop to a light jacking up their electrical bill by shining all night. J. P. braked, backed up, and drove down the sloping drive.

He put the cruiser in park in front of the farmhouse, leaving the engine running. He thought about radioing in. But to say what? He wasn't on duty. He wasn't responding to a call. He wasn't even sure anything was wrong. He just had a feeling. He could only imagine what Marks would say about that, or what the sheriff would say when alerted by Marks. The ribbing he would endure at the next roll call. "A feeling," he heard Vick say, the dry, inscrutable smile on the lieutenant's face like a weak bully telling tales at a bar.

No matter. It wouldn't take long. And he knew June would approve. Not because she cared for the Hartzells, who regarded most people in the county like scraps you dumped on the compost heap. The sentiment almost universally mutual. But because it was the right thing to do. Because it was odd that their calls for service had just stopped, like a radio announcer gone silent midsentence. J. P. could already hear June's favorable clucking as he related the story. He thought about their goodbye, the long kiss in the kitchen. It would be good to see her. To work on baby-making. But also just to be together again. She always snuggled a little closer and a little longer when she returned from her parents. Not that she didn't like spending time with them. But the visits made her feel like she'd been wearing church clothes for three days straight, with no chance to change into pajamas. "You're my pajamas," she said to him, more than once.

So now there was nothing to do but knock on the farmhouse door. He'd committed to it. The worst that could happen—and it could be pretty bad—was he'd undergo a tongue lashing from Priscilla for waking them in the middle of the night, and it wouldn't be pretty. He climbed the steps. He paused and looked around, took in the dark barn, the silhouette of Clayton's old Ford pickup truck beside it, and past that the tractor that J. P. knew was sitting in grass nearly to the top of the tires. Odd, the light on the corner of the barn's roof out like that. He went back to the door and knocked three times. He waited thirty seconds, knocked again. Repeated twice more. Going on five minutes now. Strange. Weren't old people supposed to be light sleepers? He tried the door. Unlocked. Stranger still.

"Clayton? Priscilla?"

He stepped inside, pausing at the squeak of a board beneath the aged white linoleum. Reflexively, he pulled his flashlight from his belt and turned it on, illuminating the space inside. In another moment the Sig was in his right hand. There was not overreacting and then there was being stupid. He moved the flashlight back and forth. He called the old folks' names again. Nothing. After a minute he stepped all the way into the kitchen, found the light switch. He thought about turning it on and then thought better of it. It wouldn't help matters, on the outside chance someone else was in the farmhouse. He moved the flashlight around the room but saw nothing unusual. Sink empty and scrubbed, though the counters were covered with stacks of clean dishes and plates and glasses. Completely covered, now that he looked closer. He called Priscilla and Clayton's names again. He raised the gun by a few degrees. He took a few more steps and walked into the living room.

He stopped, eyes widening. He'd never been this far inside their house. Now he wondered if anyone had, at least going back years. All around him, boxes and bulging black plastic garbage bags lined the outer edges of the walls, piled up on chairs and nearly enclosing an upright piano. How long since it had been last played, he wondered. J. P. tentatively pushed at one of the bags, pressing in with two fingers. He felt fabric. Filled with clothes, he was guessing. So the brother and sister were hoarders, on top of being paranoid and cruel and skinflinty. So much for the money rumors, all that cash under the mattresses. Turned out that they had been hiding things; just not what everyone assumed. J. P. wasn't surprised. He'd heard of such things, this kind of hoarding, though usually over in Columbus. Not illegal, necessarily, unless it resulted in living conditions so unsafe the county could make an argument that it constituted a public health risk.

Moving the beam of the flashlight around the room, J. P. doubted the Hartzells would meet that threshold. They were closer to pigsty. And God only knew, pigsties were everywhere in this county.

J. P. peered into the dining room, saw the same crowded conditions, more boxes here than bags, and headed upstairs. The going was narrow—but not unpassable—because of nearly waist-high stacks of carefully bundled newspapers on each step. He called the couple's names again at the top of the stairs. Still nothing. He poked his head into each of the four bedrooms, stroking the darkness with the beams of his flashlight. Two of the rooms packed with the same array of boxes and plastic bags and newspapers. The two others only slightly less crowded, enough space left to maneuver your way to narrow beds that, surprisingly, were neatly made up, each with a star quilt bedspread and a pair of pillows at the top. Both beds empty.

He went back downstairs, walked the length of the house again and reentered the kitchen. At the far end he saw steps leading down to a landing by the back door. To the left, the stairs to the basement. J. P. walked a little closer and saw that the basement door, which swung inward toward the stairs, was open. He wasn't sure what that meant. Was there a reason to keep the door closed, especially if you were running up and down those stairs all day long? He stepped onto the landing, sniffed and caught an odor of mustiness, and decided he'd answered his own question. You wouldn't want that drifting up into the kitchen.

This time he turned the light on. He had to be able to see. He grabbed the railing and started down the stairs. Each step creaked in protest. At the bottom, the musty smell was even stronger, the signature of a perpetually wet basement, even in the winter when the furnace should keep it dry. Mold and damp, and another smell too. Familiar, but one he couldn't place. He took in the space before him. To the right, a long top-opening chest freezer, its hum filling the room. Around the corner from that a furnace, a huge, ungainly thing with enormous ducts and pipework and dials like something from a movie poster for a cornball science fiction film from the 1950s. It was what he saw straight in front of him that gave him pause. Four wide, floor-to-ceiling wooden shelving units filled the entire back wall, each of them lined with jar after gleaming jar of canned goods. J. P. stepped a little closer, raised the flashlight and read the labels. Peas, beans, carrots. Tomatoes, corn, peppers. Zucchini, broccoli, cauliflower, spinach, potatoes, sweet potatoes. Then strawberry jam, blackberry jam, grape jelly, and grape pie filling. Apple preserves, apple butter, apple sauce. Dates on the labels all within the past year. No hoarding here. He realized that this is what they ate. What Priscilla and Clayton lived on, other than meat, which probably explained the freezer. He couldn't fathom how Priscilla managed it in that tiny, crowded kitchen. Another thing June would get a kick out of, as someone who took pride in canning her own spaghetti sauce and peach jelly but beyond that couldn't spare the time or energy.

J. P. lingered a moment, staring at the shelves, before taking one more look around, turning a full three hundred and sixty degrees. It was a neat basement, he concluded, for a pair of pack rats. Though perhaps Clayton was the real hoarding culprit and Priscilla put her foot down, down here, where the goods of her labors were stored and she needed easy access to them. He tried to imagine what that argument would have sounded like.

The last place he checked was a storage room to the left of the shelves. Maybe where the laundry machines were kept, although he realized that didn't jibe with the times he'd come out here and seen clothes flapping like pennants from a line stretched between the barn and the house. It was possible they didn't have a washer or dryer, that Priscilla did the laundry by hand in a washtub. His grandmother had been that way, even into the early 1970s. He heard about it from his mother enough times. He took a step toward the little room and his right foot slipped and he nearly fell and he looked down and saw what for just a moment his brain processed as a spreading pool of red paint, maybe a can falling off a shelf, the lid not tamped down tightly enough as sometimes they weren't. Then the coppery smell registered and he realized with a sickening drop in his stomach that most paint cans didn't hold that much liquid.

They were hunched side by side, slumped forward, facing the far wall of the little room, Priscilla to the left, Clayton on the right, filling the space between shelves on either side that held tools and plastic trays of bolts and screws and actual paint cans. The brother and sister jammed in tightly enough that their bodies supported one another even in death. The backs of their heads more or less gone, the floor wet and sticky with blood. As J. P. kneeled to see better, trembling but keeping his composure, remembering his training, he looked closer and saw that they were holding hands.

He gave a sigh and pushed himself back up, knowing he had blood on his shoes and on his uniform pants and there was nothing to be done about it right this second. He set the flashlight on a shelf outside the storage room and lifted his left hand to the radio intercom pinned just below his left collar. His right hand tightened on the Sig, the butt of the weapon comfortable in his hand. Reassuring. His thumb was on the radio transmit button when without warning he felt the hard barrel of a gun settle against the back of his neck like a drill bit finding its bore hole. The voice that spoke was close and calm and comforting and turned his insides to ice.

"Friends of yours?"

40

Penny was past the old Crew stadium, almost to Seventeenth Street, when Mae threw up the first time. It didn't sound good, like a combination of the dry heaves and a smoker's heavy, rattling cough in the middle of February.

"Jesus," Penny said, and took the exit and drove west for a hundred yards before pulling into one of the lanes that led to the fairgrounds parking lots.

"You all right?" she demanded, after she put the Pilot in park.

Mae didn't answer, just sat there, hunched over and shivering.

"I said, you all right?"

"Wha—?" she gasped, then lost her insides again.

"Do you want some water?"

Nothing. Penny swore, climbed out, went to the back and retrieved one of the water bottles she bought at Kroger a few hours earlier. She shut the rear door and walked to the passenger side, keeping a careful eye on her surroundings. The state patrol school was just around the corner, she knew, and this was not exactly a normal place to stop, especially this time of night. She opened the door, twisted the cap off the bottle and handed it to Mae. The girl took a few sips, swallowed, took a few more sips, and threw up again. She seemed to be shaking more and her skin looked paler than in the motel. Penny sat there a minute, stroking the girl's hair—it felt greasy, like it hadn't been washed in quite a while—and thought about what to do. For just a moment, she missed Myles as intensely as she ever had, even more than all those months he was in prison up in Mansfield. He would have listened to her as she debated aloud their next course of action. He would have helped her.

But now, of course, he wasn't there. Just when she needed him most.

◆

Sometimes it seemed to Penny as if she'd known Myles forever. As if there'd never been a moment when he wasn't in her life, starting in school when he would train his eyes on her so intensely that it became a physical beckoning, strong enough it could catch her attention like a sharp whistle, pulling her out of whatever conversation she was having with a girlfriend or her sister or just some random kid on the playground until she turned her head and there he was, homing in on her like she was the only person in a three-block radius. He held the gaze sometimes for three, maybe four seconds, straight-faced as a minister knocking on your door, until he couldn't play along anymore and broke into a grin and tilted his head as if to say, "Got you again."

In truth, it had been sometime in fourth grade that she looked up from her seat at the elementary school on West Broad and saw him two rows over and realized he was new. Not really *new* new, it turned out, because his family moved around a lot while his father tried to find work in various garages. He'd actually been at the same school for part of kindergarten and part of second grade, only she hadn't remembered.

From fourth grade on she didn't forget. They were friends when it was okay to have a boy who was a friend, walking up to Broad to buy chips and pop at the convenience store where they brushed past the wannabe dealers and crossed the street to avoid the real dealers.

Or walking down to Sullivant to buy soft serve at the Dari-Twist, sometimes daring each other at dusk to stroll as slowly as possible through Camp Chase cemetery, past the rows of little white square tombstones of Confederate soldiers who died in the prisoner of war camp, which always made Penny feel a little sad and made Myles wonder aloud if some of his ancestors were buried there. A little older, they met at the library, ran the gauntlet of high school kids standing outside cursing and smoking and chest bumping, and went inside and sat and read comic books and graphic novels and played on the computer, sometimes staying until the library ladies kicked them out at nine o'clock.

Ironically, it was at the library, sitting back-to-back on the carpet, sometime in middle school, reading a *Batman* (Myles) and a *Runaways* (Penny) that they first met Pryor.

"Nice tits," he said, standing over them.

Penny looked up, shocked. First at the word she just heard, then at the sight of the guy looking down at them. Something was horribly wrong with his face, with one of his eyes.

"Shut up," she managed after a second. She peeked at Myles, expecting him to share her concern. Instead, he was studying the guy, but as a problem or a solution, she couldn't tell.

"Not *you*," Pryor said, his voice mocking, as if at fourteen she was the last girl on Earth he'd accuse of having tits worth calling nice. "*Her.*"

She followed his gaze and saw he was pointing at the girl on the cover of the *Runaways* book in her hand. "Those are some serious jugs," the guy said. "Why aren't *you* reading that?" The comment directed at Myles, who didn't respond. Penny sneaked another glance at the guy. It wasn't that he didn't have a left eye, she saw. It's that what was there, what was in the space reserved for an eye, was like a thin, dried-up sliver of mud, or a jagged piece of charcoal, or half a walnut shell someone had slammed into the socket. Scar tissue rimmed the crevice. He had no left eyebrow either. The eye—the *thing*—winked with an obscene, involuntary twitch every time the kid laughed.

"You got any cigarettes?" the guy—Pryor—said.

Both mumbled no.

"You want to go get some?"

They shook their heads.

"You call this fun, reading books?" He looked to be high school age or a year or two older, short, brown hair, ears so elongated they made you think of tongues, wearing new sneakers and jeans and an Army shirt, all of which Penny instinctively knew he hadn't paid for. And hadn't borrowed either.

"It's okay," Myles said. Penny waited, hoping he'd say more. But he just ducked his head back into his book.

"Can you give me a dollar?"

"No," Penny said.

"How about you?" Pryor said to Myles.

"I don't have any money."

"Bullshit."

"I don't."

"I saw you buying ice cream just now."

"That's all the money I had."

But Penny was thinking: you saw us buying ice cream? Did you follow us in here?

"Liar."

Penny began to sweat, and it wasn't like the sweat from running around the track in practice, which was sweat she kind of liked. Sweat that made you feel healthy and strong and like you were accomplishing something. This was sweat you could smell under your shirt, sharp and sour, the sweat of shame and fear.

"I told you—" Myles said, but just then a security guy came by and told Pryor to either find a book or hop on a computer or go home.

Pryor said nothing but gave the guard the finger, and Penny gasped, because even in this neighborhood that was a shocking thing to see someone do to a security guard in the middle of the library.

"That's it," the man said sharply, grabbing Pryor by the arm.

"*Tits*," Pryor mouthed to Penny as he was led away, and this time it wasn't clear he was referring to the book. He gave them both double fingers as he rounded the corner and disappeared.

And what Penny remembered, even now, was that Pryor hadn't shown any signs of giving up about the dollar he wanted from Myles. Only the security guy's arrival interrupted him. And that turned out to be the way it always was. Pryor by himself, and with Myles, and with almost everyone else he dragged into his orbit. He pursued what he wanted and he didn't give up. And it seemed like there was nothing you could do to stop him. You could only hope, as sometimes happened, that he would disappear, like a recurring infection gone dormant, and you could take a breather while he was gone. Even all the way back then, it occurred to Penny that there might only be one way to make sure Pryor left you alone for good. And who would possibly be ballsy enough to do that?

◆

Penny looked up and saw a car's headlights coming from the direction of the patrol school. Screw it. She couldn't stay. She left Mae where she was on the seat, shut the door, went around to the driver's side and climbed back in. She made a sharp U-turn and headed to the highway.

She'd intended to go directly west, jump onto the outer belt, and jump off one exit south, back onto Broad and then over to the AFD and Robby. It was nearing one-thirty in the morning and she was running out of time. *Bright and early* was coming closer and closer. She didn't have a plan for persuading Robby to give up the location of the farm. She'd figure that out when she got there. If she got there. She put the thought out of her mind.

She took the exit for 670 West and was passing downtown when she realized how quiet it was behind her.

"Mae."

No answer.

"Mae." Still nothing. She looked in her rearview mirror. The girl's head lolled to the side, her eyes rolling back inside the sockets. Something white was trickling from the left side of her mouth.

"Shit," Penny said. She gunned it, pushing it to eighty, and drove without thinking until the West Side exit at Hague. She went a couple hundred yards and just before the railroad tracks pulled into an empty parking lot. She stopped the car, unbuckled, and turned around. "Mae," she said loudly. No answer. The only sound coming from the girl a harsh snoring that didn't sound like sleep.

She had to find the girl help. She had to take her to a hospital. She was either overdosing, having taken a hit sometime before the fat man entered the room and mounted her like an overweight beagle trying to climb stairs, or she had the DTs and was going into shock. Or five other things wrong with her. This was just what Penny needed right now. The problem, if she went to the hospital, was she couldn't just pull up and push Mae out. Not so much for Mae's sake, although that would be rough enough. But she'd have to go inside and find somebody and make a ruckus, with the Pilot sitting there in plain sight. The place would be crawling with security guards and security cameras and even if she were in and out in five minutes you knew someone would be knocking at Randy and Brandi's door in two, three hours, tops, and whatever motive they had for keeping their mouths shut would vanish. Same problem, doubled, tripled, if she called 911. She thought about the Black detective. *There's a rumor going around.* Penny lifted his card from the purse. His number right there in front of her. All it would take is one call. She picked up Randy's phone.

She thought of Pryor's Cousin Ed. And what's his name, the guy who testified at Pryor's trial. The one who swore the two of them smoked pot together the day of the bank job. Dawson. The one nobody had seen in a couple years. And of course she thought of Myles, breathing only because a ventilator was forcing him do it. Because he went out looking for Pryor—why play around anymore, clear as day what had happened? —with a gun no one seemed to know where it came from.

Or did they?

Time, moving faster and faster, an unforgiving train dragging her away from the job at hand, the task of ending their problems with Pryor once and for all. Time, she thought. The right time and the wrong time. She glanced in the back. Mae had gone silent, slumped over like a bag of clothing to be dropped at Goodwill.

She put the phone down and left the parking lot and drove away from the highway. She wasn't sure why, what it was she thought she owed the girl. But she drove on anyway.

She was at the house in less than ten minutes, but only because she hadn't seen any cops on the street which made it easier to burn down Broad at sixty.

"Penny?" Lem Garretty said, when he opened his door after nearly three minutes of her insistent knocking.

"Let me in. I need your help."

41

Pryor nodded at Michigan.

"You lying fucking piece of shit," Michigan said, as he pushed the red tips of the grilling fork into the fat deputy's arm and held them there until the smell of burning flesh filled the air. Again.

"*Ong*," the deputy said, reacting to the pain as he breathed deep and fast.

"Well?" Pryor said.

"*Ong*."

But nothing more.

Pryor swore and gave the signal again. He watched while Michigan handed the fork to Archie, who returned it to the grill, the one they grilled the steaks on earlier. Tines first, the flames shrinking by now but still steady from the new batch of charcoal they poured in on Pryor's orders.

"Who knows you're here?" Pryor said, for the third time.

The deputy shook his head, and to Pryor's disgust he saw tears in his eyes. He slapped him, open hand but hard. He wanted to try something else, something more persuasive, but for now he just needed to kill a little time, wait for the ends of the fork to glow red again.

"Do you not understand your situation?" Pryor said. "Did you not hear me before? You're gonna die with a bullet between your eyes like *that*"—he snapped his fingers right in front of the deputy's eyes, startling him. "Or maybe lying on the floor watching your intestines spill out, little by little, while I move my knife up and down like a paint brush. Know what way *I'd* pick, I'm in your shoes. You can choose, by telling the truth."

The deputy shook his head again, more wearily this time. Pryor nodded again at Michigan, who took the fork from Archie and found a promising spot on the deputy's other arm. He placed the tines just above the flesh until he saw the deputy's eyes settle on the sight, waited for his blond arm hair to shrivel from the heat, and then jammed the fork down, holding it even longer and harder this time. It smelled like a Fourth of July cookout. Which made Pryor even angrier, because Fourth of July was not a day he liked to be reminded of.

"*Ong*," the deputy grunted.

"Who . . . knows . . . you're . . . here?" Pryor repeated when he was done, leaning close to the captive's round face.

Nothing.

Pryor stood up straight. He didn't have time for this. He reached down, grabbed the deputy by the hair with his left hand, pulled hard, and forced him to stand up. It was a struggle with the deputy's hands bound behind him, but that was life. Once the man was up, knees shaking but at least steady on his feet, Pryor frog-walked him across the barn, past the shiny Darby County Sheriff's Office cruiser parked behind the van where they stowed it after Archie drove it inside. On the other side of the barn Pryor pushed his captive into an old horse stall that stank of dried manure and leather. The deputy fell to his knees with a groan. Pryor kicked him hard in the rear, aiming for his asshole, watching in satisfaction as the fatty tumbled forward with another groan. He bent down, gripped the deputy's hair again, and yanked him back up on his knees. He reached into his waistband, secured the .38, and jammed the barrel hard into the deputy's right ear.

"You got a sweet looking wife, you know that?" he whispered, leaning close. The man struggled, but Pryor applied more pressure to the barrel. After a minute, the deputy went limp.

"I saw her picture in your wallet. Big girl—how I like 'em. But real pretty too. Isn't she?"

When he didn't respond, Pryor repeated the question, then again, until finally the deputy moved his head up and down. Pryor thought he was sniffling. He could barely contain his revulsion.

"I'm going tell you something. When this is all over, I'm going to come back for her. I'm going to let myself into your house and wait for her to get home and when she comes inside I'm going to step out and surprise her. I'm gonna totally go all 'Here's Johnny!' on her. But before she has a chance to move a muscle, I'm gonna be on her. You know what I'm going to do then?"

The deputy shook his head.

"I'm going to do her on your kitchen floor. And then I'm going to do her all over again in the living room. And then I'm going to drag her upstairs and do her right on your bed. There's going to be blood. Do you hear what I'm saying? Because I'm going to be too big for her, I guarantee it. And if I'm not, this will be." He wiggled the barrel of the gun. "And the whole time I'm doing her, room to room to room, guess what?"

Nothing.

"Guess what?" Pryor said, louder.

Still nothing.

"*Guess what?*" Pryor screamed.

"*Ong,*" the deputy said.

Pryor leaned even closer, jamming the gun barrel farther into his ear.

"I'm going to be saying your name, over and over and over again."

The deputy tried in vain to struggle.

"Jerrod Paul," Pryor whispered. "Jerrod Paul. Jerrod Paul. Up and down, in and out, all day long. Your name from my lips is going to be the last thing she ever hears."

"*Ong,*" the deputy grunted.

42

Between the rolling waves of pain, J. P. tried to focus on something good. Something positive. Anything. On June, despite the horrible threats the one-eyed man was making. On his mom. How responsible she was, taking care of the boys down at the highway department. On memories of his dad, hunting trips, J. P.'s first buck, the day his dad shook his hand after he graduated from the academy. He tried to focus on those things. But try as he might, all that came to mind, despite his best efforts, of all people, was Marks. Looming over him, poking him in the chest, tugging on his baton. Saying those dumb things about him and June.

Marks. The last person he wanted to think about, especially if it was the last thing he ever considered.

"Ever wish you'd gone?"

Okay, okay. J. P. got it. He was too late for Iraq or Afghanistan. How many times did Marks have to remind him of it?

Not enough, apparently. When J. P.'s father was alive, the digs were infrequent and subtle, at least by Marks's standards. The occasional war story, at the end of a shift, in front of everyone, so it was hard to accuse him of singling J. P. out. *There we were,* he'd start in. Kicking doors down. Ripping burkas off women to find hidden guns. A guy they had to blow away because he wouldn't put his cell phone down fast enough. Choking dust clouds as they reentered Fallujah, sixty-pound packs on their backs, rifles at the fore, not knowing if they had five more seconds left on earth let alone the last five months of their rotation. It was gripping, even J. P. had to admit, and he found himself taken in, slack-jawed and wide-eyed, like the rest of them.

Marks's tales so different than the stories June's brother told. When you heard them, *if* you heard them, after enough pleading from one of the nephews, they were quiet accounts of other guys' heroism. Noble, like. Nonetheless, you could decipher John's own acts of bravery between the lines, like a figure hidden at the edge of a photograph you miss the first time around, and maybe the second and third as well. So unlike Marks's approach to his time in uniform. But that was just him, J. P. figured. Unlike June's brother, Marks had never done anything he wasn't dying to tell you about.

"Ever wish you'd gone?"

The question always casual, after Marks finished his own war stories, lobbed with the delicacy of a live grenade.

"I wasn't called up."

"You served, though, right? Didn't you clean up after some pretty bad tornadoes? Up by Toledo?"

"They were bad, yeah."

"No tornadoes in Iraq, tell you that. Too hot and too dry. Hundred and ten one time, two weeks straight. That's at night. Some guys were peeing brown, they were so dehydrated."

J. P. usually didn't respond after that. After the tornado question. He could have told plenty of his own war stories about those weeks up north. Because it had been very bad. Maybe not Iraq bad or Afghanistan bad, but bad enough. Trailers wrapped around trees like giant strips of aluminum foil. Knee-high piles of rubble where full garages once stood. The bodies of the wife and husband married forty years that he found, holding each other in the middle of a field, hardly a strip of clothing left. Or the wedding album he came across, buried under what used to be a dining room wall. The painting he uncovered by a shed, a priceless relic of a grandfather's wobbly attempt at watercolors in retirement. The family Bible, with births recorded in the front pages dating back before the Civil War.

And then there was the baby, pinned beneath a microwave, still alive thirty hours later, after everyone else stopped searching. J. P. hadn't given up. He'd been too late for Iraq. But not for the baby. For what that was worth.

Once J. P.'s father was gone, though, Marks's pretense at civility vanished like water boiling off the bottom of a pan.

"Must have been nice, just reading about it."

"I would have gone if they called me up."

"I hear that a lot. You can't imagine."

Vick grunted approvingly.

"I go ten months without so much as a hand job, and you're getting it from June what, every other night? How was that? I mean, did you ever think about us, over there?"

"I didn't know June then."

"Wow. Life before June. You must have had a hellavu pair of blue balls without her around."

"I would appreciate you not—"

"No ass in Iraq, tell you that. Nothing but men and sand and guns."

"I'm grateful for your service."

"People back here stuffing their faces at Dutch House and we're scraping goo out from MREs and trying to remember what a steak smelled like."

"It doesn't sound like it was easy."

"Damn right," Marks said, looking at Vick, who often witnessed the confrontations, but never intervened. Vick, who showed up after

J. P.'s father died, let go by some department near Cleveland under circumstances that were never too clear. But Sheriff Waters hired him right off. "Damn right," Marks repeated. "Must have been nice not to be called up."

"I was too late," J. P. said.

◆

Too late for Iraq. For Afghanistan. And now, too late for anything else. The only thing he had left was a single, solitary lie. No, not a lie exactly. A refusal. *Who knows you're here?* the one-eyed guy kept asking him. Had asked him since he forced him into the barn and the other two kicked him in the kidneys until he threw up and then bound his hands and feet so tightly he couldn't feel them anymore.

No one knows I'm here, J. P. said to himself. Because of June being gone, off to her folks. Even best-case scenario that June would panic after he didn't answer any texts or calls by noon and call somebody, he had entered a canyon of lost communication for at least twelve hours. He thought idly of Sasha, the pom, alone in the house, no one to let her out come morning, to feed her, and somehow that made everything so much worse. Just like his father: he'd run out of time. *No one knows I'm here.*

But he didn't say it out loud. Because keeping that truth hidden might be the only thing he had left in the world.

Another eruption of pain on his arm as the hot metal smoked flesh and sent flashes of agony leaping into his eyes. And then the walk to the stall and the new pain as he fell to his knees and something gouged his left kneecap, something small and sharp and metal leftover on the floor from who knew how long ago.

"Jerrod Paul. Jerrod Paul. Jerrod Paul," he heard, as if from miles away.

He shook his head and thought: *no one.* Not even—especially—June.

43

June stirred, opened her eyes, and rolled onto her back. She lay there a few moments, letting her sight adjust to the darkness of the bedroom, and then reached for her phone. Nearly four A.M. Nothing new from J. P.; nothing after his last text shortly before his shift ended. She pushed the comforter down and stared at the ceiling. Why was she awake? She always slept soundly, even at her parents' house in what now felt like a strange bedroom, her childhood room emptied, repainted, and transformed into a guest suite. But without question, she was now up and alert. And then, a moment later, it came to her. Someone had called her name; she was sure of it. Deep in a dream she couldn't remember, a voice had pierced the veil of sleep and dragged her into consciousness. But who? And why?

When she heard nothing more over the next minute she relaxed, assured it hadn't been one of her parents or John calling for her in the middle of the night. She padded to the bathroom, saw no other lights as she made her way to and fro, and returned to bed. Her next thought, which made her feel a little silly, but only a little, was the baby. Somehow, as new to the world as he was—she was certain it was a boy—the baby had spoken her name.

She hadn't told anybody she was pregnant, of course. She knew they would laugh. But she also knew that two days ago, right after they made love and J. P. propped the pillows under her rear and she moved his head to her stomach, and he said, "Sounds like gas," that it wasn't gas. She felt the conception as strongly and clearly as if someone scuffing his feet on a carpet reached out and shocked her with a forefinger. She thought about it the whole time she prepared for class after J. P. left that afternoon, and the whole time at Bible study and then church service that night, and at the Dutch House Inn later with her girlfriends where she limited herself to just half a slice of apple pie, because the diets she had them on had taken them this far and why look back now, and again when she heard J. P. creep in after his shift and slip between the covers.

And definitely the next morning when she slipped off her nightgown, the one with the fleecy pink sheep pattern, and pushed herself against J. P. to rouse him, and started the day just right. Because conception or not, they sure as heck weren't going to end up like Jan Rittmaier and that lump of a husband of hers. Only on his birthday, my foot. No wonder he drove over to Columbus on business so often. Probably needed the distraction. Yes, she thought about it the whole day. Smiling to herself when no one was looking lest she give the good news away.

On the way to her parents that afternoon after school let out she left the highway two exits early and bought the pregnancy test at a Walgreens where nobody would know her. It was too soon for those kind of results, she knew. As long as two weeks from conception before it would be accurate, according to what she read online. But that was according to the test. Not according to her heart.

She thought about what it would it be like when she showed J. P. the results. She knew he would be happy. But she also knew he would do his best to disguise the pain the news would inevitably inflict, because of his father. Because the baby would grow up absent one grandfather, and that absence wore heavily, so heavily, on his own heart.

She heard the whispers early on, almost from her first day in the classroom at Darbytown Elementary after she came to town. Certainly on the first day she laid eyes on him at church and asked her girlfriend, a fellow teacher who also attended, who he was. *Damaged goods*, they said. A good enough deputy, but he hasn't been able to move on. His father was the world to him. Be careful how you tread. You'll never have his full attention.

Well, turned out there were two sides to that equation, wasn't there? It was true enough that J. P. was a hard nut to crack. The combination of his innate shyness and the way he held himself in like a clenched fist over what happened to his father—to the sheriff—acted like an invisible forcefield for quite some time. June practically dragged him kicking and screaming to their first date, a picnic on the town square one Sunday after church, just the two of them. And it's not like he warmed up after that. For a long time she felt as if she were the only one invested in the two of them.

"Are we dating or not?" she asked herself, lying in bed at night, more than once. Of course, when he did come around, that was all she wrote. J. P. didn't do things in half measures. One minute he was supposed to pick her up at her apartment to go watch the Buckeyes at the assistant pastor's house, again, and then next minute asked her to pack an overnight bag instead and forty minutes later to her utter amazement they were standing on the threshold of the cutest little farmhouse Airbnb she thought she'd ever seen, with the sound of the opening act of an outdoor country music festival trailing across the field and two tickets materializing in J. P.'s outstretched hand.

"You arranged all this?" she said, wandering wide-eyed around the house.

"Yup."

"Why?"

"Because I may be slow," he said, coming up from behind and putting his arms around her waist. "But I'm not stupid."

They had a good start on practicing baby-making that weekend.

So that was one side of the equation. The battle to crack open the inner J. P. Ironic that though she might have begun the process, he sure as heck finished it—at least when it came to acknowledging how much she meant to him. The other side, of course, was a little more typical. *Damaged goods*, it turned out, was both a semi-accurate description of the weight J. P. carried around, and a red herring. Because it didn't take June long to see once they fully came out as a couple that one of the reason the other girls at church warned her off was because they wanted their own shot at him and no outsider was going to take that away from them.

Well, too bad. Move your feet, lose your seat.

When it came right down to it, she wondered how those other girls would have fared. It was one thing to dream of life with a big, strong cop and another to live it day to day. The weird shifts. The unexpected extra hours. The moods that came over him after responding to a particularly bad scene. Just because it was Darby County didn't make the gore any tidier. And of course, the tiniest hint of fear each time she said goodbye to him. And not just because of his father. Because of the life he chose. Don't tell me the girls whose boyfriends and husbands schlepped off to jobs that didn't involve carrying a gun and walking up to cars with no idea what was about to happen next shared the same concerns each and every morning.

True, June had some experience with worry because of John and his deployments. But somehow, because he was abroad so much, it was less of a constant reminder. With J. P., with police work, you just never knew, day to day, hour to hour.

"Not a life for everyone," J. P.'s mother said to her one weekend, shortly before the wedding. "But I can see you already know that."

"If it's life with J. P., that's all that matters." She realized as soon as she said it how corny it sounded. But it also happened to be true.

"If that's your attitude, I believe you're going to be my favorite daughter-in-law, June."

"And also your only one."

"Don't split hairs with me. It's the truth. I like a girl with some steel in her spine. And that's you all the way home."

"Thank you, I guess."

"I mean it. Not like some of these other gals. They talk a big game, but they wouldn't last a week with the life you and J. P. have made."

"I'm not sure that's true," June lied.

"No offense, June, but that's where you're wrong. Way I see it, most of the ladies getting married these days are looking for one thing and one thing only. They want a sperm donor with an ATM attached, pure and simple, and the sooner they move into their four-bedroom, two and a half bath the better. Ridiculous. They think it's love but they're one missed mortgage payment away from hating each other's guts. J. P.'s father and me, we lived in a trailer the first two years we were married. Try that on for size, these girls, and see how they like it."

"Two years," June said politely, as if hearing the story for the first time. But secretly she was pleased as could be with the compliment she'd been paid. Especially because it wasn't the life she envisioned. Even until not that long ago. Her brother's military service or not, marrying a cop was the furthest thing from her mind when she decided to take the job in Darbytown. All she anticipated was a change in perspective, both because she liked the town and the community and because it was time to put some space between her and her parents. Beyond time. Reality was, she wasn't even sure she would marry, before all this happened. She was kind of satisfied with life the way it was.

She loved teaching. She loved work. She loved her mother, but she also saw her struggle to find herself after she and John hit high school and the nearly fifteen years she spent out of the workforce suddenly hit home. No, that was never happening to June, marriage and kids or not. Regardless of the eye-opening experience of seeing J. P. at church that first Sunday in town and saying to herself, "Well, hello there."

She blinked, wondering at how her mind had wandered. She yawned and brought herself back to the issue at hand. She was awake because someone called her name. Not her parents or John. And not the baby. That left only one person, and the truth of the matter hit home in seconds and threatened to overwhelm her. J. P. It was J. P.'s voice she heard, calling out in her dreams. Of course. But what did it mean?

June reached for her phone again and for a few seconds debated calling him, no matter the hour. She wasn't superstitious, but she also believed in signs, including ones God sent you. Was that what this was? But she relented in the end. She couldn't see herself waking him up on a whim, especially when he'd probably only been asleep a few hours and was looking forward to a long, uninterrupted Saturday morning lie-in. She knew she would have. She held off texting, too, since he never put his phone on silent mode in case he was called out in the middle of the night. Even the single tone of an arriving message might stir him.

Instead, she replaced her phone on the nightstand, and said a little prayer for his safety, and curled onto her side and pulled the comforter back over her and shut her eyes again. Morning would come soon enough, and then she could reach him and tell her about the dream, about hearing him call her name, and everything would be all right. Everything would be fine.

44

Lem Garretty's eyes widened as he stood in his doorway and listened to the wild tale Penny was telling and the request she was making.

"I can't. I'm sorry."

"Yes you can. But it has to be right now, or it's going to be too late."

"It's already too late—"

"It's never too late, goddamn it. Can't you get that into your thick skull?"

Penny thought about pulling the Glock on him, recalling the effect it had on the fat man in the black socks at the Grand Knights Motel. She decided against it, not the least because she was worried about handling it, as upset and as tired as she was. That, and one other thing she had noticed. That guns were useful on people with lots to lose. But they had little if no effect on people with nothing to lose, and Garretty had looked that way for a long, long time.

"I can't," he repeated.

"Wrong answer," she said, and pushed past him and entered the house.

"Now wait a second," Garretty said, but she was already through the living room and down the hall.

It was a calculated risk. Odds on, the injectors he showed her earlier in the day, the ones she refused to take, were in the bathroom. That's where people kept that kind of stuff, even more so in this case since it was often the cabinets over the sinks where all the medicine resided. She knew from experience that people around here who wouldn't dream of allowing a drop of alcohol in their houses kept prescription bottles of Oxy 80s in their bathrooms that were capable of three times the damage of a fifth of Wild Turkey. So many bottles that a couple pills from each were rarely missed.

She threw open the door of the cabinet over the sink, its mirror flecked with dried water spots and specks of toothpaste, and ran her eyes down the shelves. Aspirin. Ibuprofen. Cortisone cream. Box of bandages. Vicks VapoRub, bottle of hydrogen peroxide, a floss dispenser. Fingernail clippers rusted at the joint. An old black comb on its side. A lady's purple razor, which gave Penny pause when she thought about the childless, widowed Garretty. No injectors. She'd seen signs for them at the health clinic where she took Mack for check-ups. Heard people talk about them. The granddaughter of someone Ma-Maw knew was saved in the nick of time with one. Made for junkies. She turned, frustrated, feeling her stomach tighten. She opened the door of a utility closet and found herself staring at neatly folded towels and wash clothes, two identical hot water bottle boxes and a plastic bin containing five rolls of ace bandages.

"They're not here," she said aloud.

"I know."

She whirled. She hadn't heard him come in.

"Then where the hell are they?"

He held the box up in his right hand before she could finish.

"Refrigerator. Where they said to keep it."

"Come on, then."

"You take it," he said, extending the cardboard tray.

"You have to do it. I don't know how."

"I've never done it. I already told you—"

"I know you've never done it," she shouted, patience draining from her at last. "Everyone knows. Because you won't stop fucking talking about it. But you know how to do it, don't you? You had to learn? Because of Darren? Just in case?"

"Yes, but—"

She grabbed him by the shoulders, turned him around, and forced him down the hall. He stumbled, they were moving so fast. Not fast enough by half, Penny said, cursing. *Bright and early.*

She forced him all the way outside, down the porch steps, onto the lawn by the Pilot. She opened the back door and dragged Mae out. She felt cold and clammy. Only when Penny sagged under the girl's weight did Garretty step forward, hook his left arm around Mae's waist and half-push, half-pull her onto the grass in the dark where she lay motionless as a rolled-up rug.

"Hurry," Penny said.

Garretty started to cry.

"Now."

"Darren. I meant to. I know I shouldn't—"

"You shouldn't have gone to the casino. You're right about that. Who goes to the casino at seven in the morning after work? You go home. That's what you do. You go home and you go to sleep and then you get up and go to work again. But people aren't supposed to shoot up at seven in the morning either. That's not your fault. That was Darren's fault. And that happened."

Happened because of Pryor's unblemished record of supplying people their drugs whenever they called. As Darren had called, time and again.

"I'm sorry—"

"Do it!" Penny yelled.

Groaning, Garretty lowered himself to his knees. He pulled the small, white plunger from the box, positioned the nozzle inside Mae's right nostril, and pushed down. He repeated the gesture with a second plunger in her left nostril. Nothing happened over the next ten seconds. Fifteen. Twenty. Tears dropped from Garretty's red eyes, though he didn't make a sound. Then he sighed and Penny recoiled at his bad breath. She tried to remember Darren, who could only have been a year or two older than her. But all that came to mind was the shadow of a boy, thin and pale, eyes as dark as mud, hugging the lockers as he floated down the halls. Afterward, after he died, Garretty couldn't even afford an obituary.

At thirty seconds Mae's eyelids fluttered and her breathing returned, raspy and jagged.

Penny stood. "Call 911."

"What?"

"She needs to be in the hospital. I can't take her there. I need to go."

"I can't do that. I'll be arrested."

"For what? Saving her life?"

"You know what I mean."

"They can see what she is. They're not stupid. Tell them you just found her lying there. They're not going to care. They see this every day. Every hour. Just make the call."

"Why can't you?"

"I'm not done yet."

"Done with what?"

"It was you, wasn't it?" Penny said, ignoring his question.

"Me what?"

Beside them, Mae coughed and blinked her eyes and struggled to raise herself. Penny unconsciously reached out and brushed the hair out of her eyes. The girl relaxed at the gesture and lay back down, staring at the few stars visible through the glow of city lights.

"You gave Myles the gun, didn't you?"

The stricken look on Lem's face, as if she'd just delivered the news of a relative's passing, all the confirmation she needed.

He nodded, eyes bright with tears again.

"When? At the party?"

It came to her now. Lem and Myles standing in the far corner of Mama's yard, talking in whispers, just before the welcome-home dinner was served. Mack clinging to Myles's leg, begging for attention. Penny watching them, annoyed that Lem had the gall to stop by at all. Seeing now how that annoyance blinded her from understanding what was really going on.

He shook his head.

"Then when?"

"Next day. After you'd—"

"After I'd gone to work."

Of course. Meeting up while she was out of the picture. Ma-Maw useless in that situation. Even if she suspected Myles was up to something, nothing she could have done about it.

A deep sigh from Mae.

"Where am I?" she said.

Penny wasn't sure what was worse. That Myles had been stupid enough to think a plan like that would work—going after Pryor alone, on foot, with no backup—or that he undertook it without telling her. Without saying a word. Without trusting her.

Actually, not true. She knew damn well which was worse.

"He killed Darren," Lem said hoarsely.

"Pryor's killed a lot of people."

"I wanted him to pay for what he did."

"But not do it yourself?"

"I thought if anyone could, it would be Myles."

"Guess you thought wrong."

She regretted the remark as soon as the words left her mouth. Because Lem hadn't thought wrong. Not exactly. Because if anyone could have killed Pryor, using a borrowed gun from a dead addict's uncle bent on revenge, it would have been Myles.

Except he hadn't. And now she was the only one left who could try.

"Penny?" Lem said as she stood up.

"Call 911," she said, looking down at Mae looking up at her. "For the girl or for yourself. I don't really care anymore."

45

"Wait," Archie said.

"What," Pryor said, not bothering to disguise his impatience.

"Listen."

"What?"

"There's nothing."

"What?"

"There's nothing to hear," Archie said. "There's nobody coming."

Pryor stood there, the barrel of the gun in his hand under an inch from the fat deputy's squishy brain, trying to figure out what Archie meant. And where he came up with the nerve to interrupt him. Him, of all people. *There's a cop.* After a moment of indecision, he relaxed his finger and removed it from the .38's trigger. But he kept the barrel in the sheriff's ear.

"What the fuck are you talking about?"

"I timed it."

"Timed what?"

"You woke us up forty minutes ago," Archie said. "Quarter to two. I checked my phone."

"So?"

"So, how long before that did you hear him knocking?"

"I don't know. Ten minutes?"

"So nearly fifty minutes total. But do you hear anything now? Sirens? Helicopter? There hasn't been a single car drive along the road other than this guy since midnight."

"What's your point?"

"My point is, no one knows this guy's here. He's all alone. He's like a kid in a well that nobody gives a shit about because they all think he's at somebody else's house. Isn't that right?"

The deputy didn't reply. But something about his eyes and the way his shoulders suddenly sagged told Pryor that Archie might be right.

"You don't know that for sure," Pryor said, testing.

"Pretty sure."

"And why's that?"

"Because this guy's a complete pussy, is why," Archie said. "He was pissing his pants the second the fork went on the coals. He had anything to tell you, we would have heard it by now. There's nothing to hear. He's all by himself."

"All the better reason to shoot him. We get a head start on anyone looking."

"That's your call. Do whatever you want. You're the boss. I'm just saying, they're not coming for him."

Damn right I'm the boss, Pryor thought, but didn't say anything. Because he hadn't expected this development. Up until now, his only real concern was that someone else would demand to do the killing. Michigan, for example. Because Michigan hated cops more than he did, which was saying something. Michigan hated cops the way you hated not breathing when somebody pushes your head underwater and you'll do anything to fill your lungs with air. It was one of the few things—maybe the only thing—the guy was good for. Pryor had thought about turning the gun over to Michigan at the last second. Because Michigan would have enjoyed killing the deputy. Michigan, who still wasn't over the cop who gave him his nickname in the first place. The guy bawling to anyone who would listen in the booking room that the kid with the blue streak and the blond hair had the same colors as Ohio State's football rival. And there was Michigan, aka Jimmy O'Brien, thinking he looked like a Scottish warrior. Instead, he had a roomful of Ohio State fans laughing their asses off at him. And there was no going back. Not with a tattoo like that. Not with how much it cost.

But now Archie had stopped everything in its tracks. And it was in that moment while Pryor was deciding what to do—give Michigan the gun, strangle the deputy with his bare hands, kill everybody all at once and be fucking done with it—that he had another idea. An addendum to the plan. Normally he shied away from last-minute changes to an operation the way he avoided girls with sores on their lips. But this might work. It would complicate things later on, because he should have taken care of business by now. He had the deputy to thank for that, which he'd make him pay for at the very end. But for now—

Yeah. This might actually work.

"That true?" he said to the deputy. "No one knows you're here?"

The slow nod of the head. The sag of the shoulders.

"All righty, then," Pryor said, removing the gun from the deputy's ear. "Don't get the wrong idea here, Jerrod Paul. I'm still going to kill you. And I'm still going to do your wife. We're just going to take a little break for a while so I can think about some stuff."

"*Ong*," the deputy said, which was the last thing out of his mouth for a while. The blow Pryor aimed at his head saw to that.

46

When J. P. opened his eyes again it was so dark he thought at first he must be blindfolded. Then he thought he must be dreaming and wasn't awake at all. Then he realized he was staring at the sidewall of a car tire, and after he blinked he saw the car's brown paint and realized it was the tire of his own cruiser. He must have been dragged beside the car after everything went black in the horse stall. He lay without moving. He let his eyes adjust to the light and soon saw that while it was dark in the barn, still the middle of the night by the feel of it, it wasn't the absolute blackness he first imagined. The sound of slow, heavy breathing all around him, as if he'd awakened in a manger. He heard rustles and creaks, the music of a barn as old as this one, and guessed at mice and night breezes and bats. His hands and feet were still zip-tied, tingling as feeling passed in and out of them like an intermittent electrical current. His head throbbed from the blow he received before passing out, his left knee ached from whatever gouged it earlier in the empty horse stall, and his arms were burning from the wounds from the heated barbecue fork.

He tried to figure out what was going on. He'd obviously stumbled onto a gang of some sort. The irony, he thought, that Clayton had been right all along about someone watching his place. His mom's favorite saying, down at the garage: *Just because someone's paranoid doesn't mean they're not out to get you.* But what were they up to? Robbing the old couple? If so, joke was on them. The only thing the dried-up pair hoarded, apparently, was clothes and trash and canned vegetables. So in that case, why kill them? There were two possibilities, neither of them much comfort. One, whoever these people were, they needed this property for something—the barn in particular—and wanted the brother and sister out of the way. A hiding place? But if that were true, why not just tie them up and leave them in a bedroom? That raised a second possibility, that Clayton and Priscilla were killed just because. And that wasn't hard to believe when he thought about the leader, the man who made the threats about June. The one-eyed guy. He acted like someone who would kill for the sake of killing. What was the word for it? He'd seen it in one of his textbooks. It came to J. P. after a moment: psychopath.

Again: what were they up to? And who were they? He'd caught a glimpse of a Black man, the one who intervened in the horse stall, maybe saving his life, for a few minutes anyway. And an odd-looking guy with blond hair and a blue mark on his face. And then there was the guy with the gun, unremarkable in every way except for his huge ears and that deformed eye, if that small slit of scar tissue like a badly healed exit wound could even be called an eye. If he meant for the sight of his face to unnerve people, it was working. J. P. was certain he'd remember seeing a person like that before. But he didn't recognize anyone. He doubted they were from Darby County. Dayton, possibly, or maybe Columbus.

Slowly, very slowly, he tried moving his hands, then his ankles. No luck. Both were bound tightly the way only zip-ties can manage. Adjustable vises, but adjustable in only one direction: pain. He felt numbness creeping up his arms and legs. It was nothing like the movies, where he might be able to wriggle free somehow and limp his way to safety, find a gun, and shoot his way out. He was trussed like a hog awaiting the bolt pistol. Still, he wasn't ready to give up quite yet, even if he saw no way out in the long run. His last-second commutation in the horse stall ought to be worth something, and not just relief at another chance at life. It had exposed the slightest chink in the leader's armor. Even in his dazed condition, J. P. could tell the one-eyed guy had been fazed by the Black man's logic. The only question was what to do about it. He was guessing that begging wouldn't work, nor would bargaining. His trump card, the idea that people would search for him, had been lost by the Black man's accurate conclusion that no one knew he was there.

Perhaps if he could deny the one-eyed man the death he wanted for him. Struggle and fight up until the moment of extinction. Embrace it. Somehow foil their plan by taking too long to die. Delay things by a few minutes. Even a few seconds. Rob them of the time they needed for whatever it was they were up to. A death almost the exact opposite of that suffered by his father, who to judge by the reconstruction of what happened that night spent his last few seconds on Earth doing his job not only with no concern for his own safety but no understanding that the end was so near. There was a moment captured by the cruiser's dash cam video where his father turned and looked in the direction of the camera. Not in any conscious way, but a movement borne from the difficulty of the task at hand, the awkwardness of trying to free the driver's twisted body from what was left of the front half of the SUV. A movement that illustrated the nonchalant nature of his father's final moments. He had shown not the slightest fear or expectation that he was close to death. His face was that of a man who's been working outside all day, perhaps digging a trench with a shovel or rototilling the garden, and has paused, just for a moment, to both rest and gather energy for the next phase of the job.

J. P. decided to experiment. He tried to see if he could raise his knees. He took comfort in knowing it would please June that he attempted it, if somehow she should ever learn that fact. It took him a minute, as he flinched and gasped from the kicks he took to his back when he was first brought inside the barn. But finally he did it. Slowly, slowly, he drew his knees toward his chest as though doing a sideways crunch. He relaxed them, did it again, then a third time. He breathed in and out at the pain. After a moment, relaxing until the bright colored pinpricks cleared from before his eyes, he tried just as slowly to bring his chin down, toward his chest. Pain flared like a spike through his brain and he stopped. But after a moment he tried repeating the gesture and this time was successful. He could move his head up and down. His arms were the hardest, with the wrists bound behind him, but he found that with a lot of effort he could extend them away from the small of his back nearly five inches. He repeated the motions. Knees, head, arms. Knees, head, arms. Finally, he called it quits and went still. It was possible. He could put up a fight. It wouldn't be much. But it would be more than nothing. It would steal a little time from them. It would be a death that meant something.

47

Penny sat in the Pilot in the parking lot of the AFD, stalling. She was parked three spaces down from the entrance but could still see inside. She saw who she guessed was Robby, a tall pudgy guy wearing a red apron, lounging by the checkout counter. She should go in. But she wasn't ready yet. Her fatigue had chased any plan out of her head. That and the scene at Lem Garretty's house. The enormity of what he did hitting home. *I thought if anyone could, it would be Myles.* No, not ready yet. She needed to think.

She pulled out Randy's phone and tapped on Facebook. No privacy setting. Typical. She scrolled through the feed, searching for signs that anyone knew something was amiss. She recognized very few of the people whose pictures and updates she was looking at. The people posting on his page seemed to consist of either relatively buff young guys like Randy or pretty moms like Brandi with kids about the same age as Madyson. A lot of the moms' pictures were selfies at zoos and ballparks and the downtown science museum and some beaches at sunset that sure as hell didn't look like anyplace in Ohio. A lot of the guys shared links to articles that mocked Democrats and gay people and welfare recipients and immigrants and anyone still wearing a mask in public. Penny wondered if Randy knew how long she and Brandi had been on public assistance when they were kids, or if he realized that Mama—his mother-in-law—was on food stamps.

She kept scrolling, and after a minute started as she came across a photo of her and Brandi. She recognized the black-and-white picture immediately. It was taken right before her sister met Randy, at one of those photo booths at the state fair. Both laughing as though they didn't have a care in the world. Her sister posted the photo right at midnight, just over two hours ago, tagged her, and added a three-word message: "Bright and early."

Even at that time of night it received seven likes.

Penny dumped the phone in her purse in disgust and looked inside the store again. Now Robby was standing behind the ice cream counter, his back to her, mixing up a shake. He was waiting on a heavy-set guy with a biker vibe—chaps, jacket, beard—standing at the checkout counter. Penny searched and a moment later located the man's Harley two spaces down. On the other side of the store a second clerk, a Black woman, was stocking items on a shelf. One other customer was inside, another guy, removing something from the cooler.

She was wide awake again thanks to the photo and her sister's warning. Fatigue gone like a jacket thrown off on a spring day turned uncomfortably warm. She knew she had to think of something, and fast. The business of driving Mae to Lem's house and the ordeal of forcing him off his ass to help the girl and his confession about giving Myles the gun had cost so much time. She balled up her fists. There were so many people in her way, making her life hard. Falling short. She knew she should feel good about saving Mae—from the fat john, from the guy in the green van, from a fatal overdose—but nothing was registering. All she could think was that Mae cost her a good thirty minutes, time she couldn't spare. Time neither she nor Myles had. *Bright and early.*

She looked out at the street and saw a white Columbus police cruiser go by. She tensed, and then relaxed as it continued on, stopped at a red light, and turned right into Lincoln Village. She thought of the Black detective, Lessner, the things he said to encourage her to help them. Help them catch the person who hurt Myles. *I just want to make sure you're okay, you know? And that you're not trying to help Myles in a different way.*

She took a breath and climbed out of the Pilot. She double-tapped the key fob so the SUV beeped and its lights flashed as it locked up. Inside the store, the air conditioning was cranked up so high the place smelled like a cold morning in February. Penny blinked in the glare of the overhead lights. She walked over to the beer cooler and studied the shelves while she glanced toward the cash register. The biker guy was paying for his shake. He said something to Robby she couldn't make out, and Robby laughed and told him to have a good night. The other customer stepped up and put three cans of Red Bull on the counter and handed Robby a bill. Robby rang up the drinks, made change, took a plastic bag from beneath the counter and put the cans in it. The guy grabbed the bag and turned and walked out without saying anything.

Penny counted thirty seconds in her head, reached into the cooler, pulled out a six of Bud and walked to the counter.

"Hey," Robby said as she slid the beer toward him.

"Hello."

"Will that be all for you?"

"No."

He waited, bored.

"I need to know where Pryor is," she said.

48

Pryor tried to figure out what the hell the deputy was doing. Pulling his knees toward him and pushing them away. Bobbing his head. Extending his hands behind. Some kind of exercise? What was the point? Like doing jumping jacks on the gallows. He didn't bother investigating further. He was too comfortable, drifting in and out of sleep as he waited for dawn to come. For the final enactment of his newly revised plan. He wasn't worried about ol' Jerrod Paul pulling anything. He zipped his hands and ankles himself, the usual way, and they weren't bonds you were going to break. What puzzled him was what the deputy's squirming reminded him of. He knew he'd seen something like it before. But where? It was like déjà vu, a feeling Pryor had never liked. Because he didn't appreciate the thought that he might have repeated himself in some way. He liked the idea that everything he did was new.

The movement stopped after a bit and in another moment Pryor dozed off.

He woke up. He remembered.

49

Robby stared at Penny.

"What did you say?"

Penny repeated the question.

After a moment, he said, "I don't know anybody by that name."

Now it was Penny's turn to stare, finding it hard to believe he'd spoken so formally, so like the way they said things on TV. *I don't know anybody by that name.* Gimme a break.

"Don't lie. I just need to know where he is. That's all. Nothing more than that."

"I told you, I don't know who that is." His voice a little more forceful, his stare stronger. She felt her heart sink. The exhaustion was starting to come back.

"Listen—"

"The beer's $7.99. Cash or credit?"

"I just need a little help. That's all."

"Either pay for the beer or I'll have to ask you to leave."

Penny hesitated, fighting the fatigue gripping her like a swimmer who's ventured out too far, too late, and realizes she can't see the shore any longer. She turned toward the door and as she did watched the Columbus cruiser reappear from a side street and roll past the store, headed east. Something clicked inside her. *I don't know anybody by that name.* She thought of Myles, the things they planned to do now that he was out. Jesus. This was such bullshit.

"There's this girl, Mae," she said, turning back to face Robby. "I think you know her. Knew her, I mean. She hooked for Pryor."

"I don't know anybody named Mae or Pryor," Robby said, though his eyes flickered hearing the prostitute's name. Interesting. "Are you going to pay or what?"

"Here's the thing," Penny continued. "Mae's dead. Somebody gave her something bad and she turned blue and that was that. They look like they've frozen to death when they go that way. It was pretty awful."

"Like I said—"

"And the problem is, I was sort of there at the time. Nearby. And that could get me in a little bit of trouble. A lot of trouble, actually. Because I have this possession thing hanging over my head. First-degree misdemeanor, but it's like my third one. Cops are talking about making it a fourth-degree felony instead."

"I'm sorry, miss, but—"

"Unless, I mean, unless I help them figure out what's going on. Because they don't give a shit about someone like me getting caught with a couple of balloons in my bra. They're not stupid. They want something bigger."

"I told you—"

Behind them the door opened. Penny turned and saw two Latino guys walk in. They nodded at Robby and made for the beer coolers.

"But the thing is, I don't have anything to give them," Penny said, warming to the task. Almost enjoying herself. "You know what I mean? I tried telling them about my girlfriend, because she knows somebody who's got fentanyl, but they weren't interested. They said they could find that stuff blind folded on East Livingston at noon and not break a sweat. So where does that leave me?"

"I—"

"Looking at a fourth-degree felony with two priors unless I hold up my end of the bargain, is where. And I don't have jack."

"Es-cuse me."

The two men were behind her. One was wearing a bright yellow soccer jersey and the other a green golf shirt with a landscaping company's logo over the upper left side. They placed two six packs of Modelo on the counter and a bag of pretzels. Penny made eye contact with Robby before stepping aside while he waited on them. She kept her left hand on the counter and tapped her ring finger and middle finger nervously, *thip-thip-thip*, while she waited. The first guy, who'd asked her politely to move, stared at her as he turned to go.

"So anyway," Penny said, once they were through the door and in the parking lot. She was on a roll now. At first she wasn't sure where it came from. But then she realized it was like running. Sometimes, starting out, you feel like shit. It's hard to take two steps. But eventually, settling in, you hit a groove. Begin to flow. Overcome the molasses of hesitation. Like what was happening now.

"That's where I was until Mae died," Penny continued. "Needle stuck right in her arm. Yesterday sometime. And the cops want to know what happened. I kind of played dumb to give me more time. And I got to thinking. What if I gave up the guy who gave her the smack? *Her* dealer. That's like negligent homicide, maybe even manslaughter. That ought to be worth something. They like going after those guys. That's a lot better than fentanyl. And that takes me down on my stuff to what, maybe third-degree misdemeanor? Maybe not even. Maybe I keep myself clean and they leave me alone."

"I'm done listening to you. Okay? Now get out."

"So here's what I decided. I'm going to give them you."

He stared, as if hearing her for the first time since she started talking.

"Me?"

"I'm going to tell them that this guy Robby, who knows Pryor, gave Mae the stuff that killed her. And you know what the name Pryor means to the cops, right? That's like a bank alarm going off. You know Pryor, you're for reals. They're going to take that seriously."

"I never—"

Penny held up Randy's phone. "Don't bother. I've made up my mind. I'm gonna call this drug squad lady who's been riding me." She thought about the lady detective in the hospital the night Myles was shot. Her blond, spiky hair, roots starting to show. The fake tan. A lady who nonetheless looked like she meant business. "I'm gonna tell her about Mae. And then I'm gonna tell her that you got the stuff from Pryor and sold it to Mae, and you're working right now at an American Farm Dairy on the West Side. I'm going to tell her that you're"—she paused just for a moment, realizing again how exhausted she was, wishing she could just go back home and lie down and forget everything—"that you're dealing stuff you drop into ice cream cones if the customers know the code words."

"Please leave. Please."

"But that's not all I'm gonna tell her. Because I can't afford to screw this up. I'm also going to explain you're a little nervous after what happened to Mae and you might try to get rid of everything and it would be good to get over here fast. Like, *really* fast."

"Jesus Christ. You're crazy."

"I mean, they're not going to have a warrant. I understand that. But it's still going to look funny, all those cops here. You have to report that, right? Or does it matter? *She* will if you don't, right?" She nodded at the other clerk, who was hunched over, rearranging bottles of pop on a shelf.

"Get out." Pleading now, voice dropped suddenly to a whisper.

"Unless," Penny said.

"I said, get out."

"And I said, unless."

"Unless what?"

The other clerk walked up, sensing trouble. She stood to Penny's left, eyeing her.

"Everything okay?"

"Fine," Robby said.

"Doesn't sound fine."

"It's nothing. It's okay."

"That all you getting," the clerk said, pointing at Penny's beer.

"I also need a shake."

"A shake?"

"Mint chocolate chip. Do you have that?"

"You know this girl?" the other clerk said to Robby.

"Yes," he said, after a pause. "Um, could you fix that for her? Do you mind?"

"Me?"

"Yeah. If you could."

Penny thought she was going to make a scene, but she just laughed and shook her head and walked toward the ice cream bins.

"Unless what?" Robby said.

"Unless you tell me where Pryor is."

"I already told you—"

"I know he's on a farm. In Darby County. Your uncle's. All I'm looking for is an address."

Robby swallowed. "How do you know about the farm?"

"Mae told me. Right before she died. With the needle in her arm with the stuff you sold her."

"I didn't sell her anything."

"Just the address."

"Hey," the other clerk yelled. "We ain't got mint chocolate chip. Is regular chocolate chip okay?"

"I guess," Penny said.

"Good to hear," the woman said.

"I just need the address," Penny repeated. "Then I walk out of here and leave you alone. But without it, I call my drug squad lady and she and her boys pile in here and even if the only thing you're dropping in ice cream cones is Reese's Pieces they're going to be here for a while and it could be unpleasant. And anyway, you do know Pryor, don't you?"

Robby took a deep breath. "I don't know the address."

"Bullshit."

"I'm telling the truth. It's on some country road, off Darbytown–London. I've always just driven there."

"What's the road called?"

"Did Mae tell you I know Pryor?"

"What's the road?"

"Prairie something. Prairie Acres."

"Prairie Acres?"

"No. Alkire. Prairie–Alkire. It's Prairie–Alkire Road."

"What's your uncle's name?"

He told her. It was an aunt and uncle, but not married. Brother and sister. A great-aunt and -uncle, actually. They weren't very nice people, and he didn't know them all that well. He made both points a few times. He only went out there because his father made him go check on them, because no one else wanted to. Because they were so mean. Penny looked up the names on Randy's phone and found the address. She showed him the screen. He studied it for a minute.

"Yeah. That's it."

Regardless, she made him describe the road in detail, the turns and the signs and the distance from Darbytown–London Road and where the farmhouse and the barn sat, going over it once, then twice, then a third time.

"All right," she said. "You better hope I find Pryor there. Or I'm making the call."

"I thought you just wanted to know where the farm was."

"I want Pryor. I could care less if he's on a farm or on the moon. And by the way."

"What?"

"You tell him you saw me before I get there? I'm not calling the cops at that point. I'm sticking your head down a garbage disposal. Promise."

"I didn't sell anything to that girl."

"I know." She reached out and took the milk shake from the other clerk.

"You do? Then the cops will know you're lying."

"It doesn't matter," Penny said. She took a long pull of the shake through the straw. She couldn't help it. She was famished, and the combination of cold and sweet going down her throat was electrifying. Famished and exhausted and out of patience.

"Sure it does," Robby said. "You're the one who's going to be in trouble—"

"It doesn't matter," she repeated. "Not after what you did."

"I told you I didn't do anything."

"Not to Mae. I was bullshitting you anyway. She's alive." He protested but she cut him off. "I'm talking about what you did to your aunt and uncle."

"I didn't do anything to them."

"Sure you did. You told Pryor where they lived. That's the worst thing you could have done. That's like pushing wood into a buzz saw. You're going to wish Mae did die, the trouble you're going to be in after this."

She left the beer on the counter and took the shake without paying and walked out of the store. She drove quickly out of the parking lot. A quarter mile west she pulled into a gas station and parked over to the side, by the cooler holding the bags of ice. She fumbled with Randy's phone until she found the GPS and typed in the address of Robby's uncle's farm and pressed start. Then she removed the lid from the shake cup and sucked the last of the ice cream out of the straw and tilted the contents of the cup down her throat and finished it in four long swallows. She dropped the cup on the floor behind her where the mess Mae made when she threw up was still drying, stinking up the car. She lowered the windows despite the chill in the air and made sure she was only one or two miles per hour above the speed limit and drove west in the direction the phone told her to go.

50

Cousin Ed, Pryor thought, studying the deputy squirm on the barn floor, twisting his body like a pedestrian in his final convulsions in the middle of the road after a hit-and-run. The movement reminded him of Cousin Ed.

Pryor had been thirteen, a little small for his age, except for his ears, which if you thought they were big now were like elephant ears back then. *Hey Dumbo, you gonna fly?* His fists sore from the number of noses he bloodied from all the teasing. And still it continued. Cousin Ed one of the worst. Not really his cousin, he guessed, but some kind of relation to his father. A drunk no one seemed to like except his mother, who liked him a lot and so he was around a lot. Out in the back yard on July Fourth that year. Darkness fallen and the neighborhood filled with pops and bangs and whooshes like a scene from some B-grade war movie. Ed, half a case of Miller Lite in, taunting him, teasing him. *Dumbo. Mickey. Ross Perot,* whoever the fuck that was. Daring him to set off one of the big rockets, one of the ones Ed bought over in Indiana that you weren't supposed to have without a license. His mother egging him on too, arm around Ed's shoulders.

To this day he couldn't remember lighting the fuse, though so many people told him afterward what happened that it was like he actually saw it, as if he were watching a movie with himself in it. Something he peered at and studied, like some kind of scientist looking at evidence. In truth, all he really remembered was waking up in the hospital afterward.

Children's Services. Misdemeanor child neglect charges. Fireworks.

He bided his time. Not the summer of the accident, obviously, or even the next summer, when he was still trying to figure out the whole one-eye thing and growing tired of pounding the kids who kept coming up to him and pointing at his patch and yelling, "Argh!" Worse than *Dumbo* in its own way. Rather, it was the summer after that, the summer he turned fifteen, three inches taller and thirty pounds heavier, that he decided he was ready. It wasn't a long walk to Ed's house, maybe six blocks. He left his place after dark, just to be sure, the house where he and his mother were staying. Baseball bat hanging easy from his hand, no big deal. Not that his mother kept track of him. It was hard to keep an eye on stuff when you were passed out so often.

It was easier to pull off than Pryor expected, although the fact that Ed was totally blotto when he arrived didn't hurt. Ed started a bit when he opened the door, swaying back and forth, and saw Pryor standing there. Staring at him with his eye, the patch off. The last time he wore the patch, come to think of it, so pleased was he with the look on Cousin Ed's face.

"Pryor?" he managed.

In his condition Ed went down like an old lady on ice when Pryor responded by tapping him in the middle of the forehead with the bat. *Thud*, right onto the living room floor. Pryor inside and shutting the door in a flash. Ed weighed a shit ton, which made pulling him by the feet through the kitchen and then easing him down the basement stairs, head going *thunk-thunk-thunk* on the steps, more of a chore than Pryor had counted on. But the reward, once he gagged and trussed him with twine, was worth it. The more efficient plastic zip ties out of the question, since they would melt but not totally disappear. The basement shelves were loaded with leftover fireworks, including some of those big sons of a bitches that cost Pryor his eye. He took two of those and jammed them both down the front of Ed's pants, the man's eyes wide now, Ed awake and sobering up quickly. Stuck a bunch of other ones up Ed's shirt and between his feet and then all around him. Finished, Pryor went back upstairs to find more combustible material, which Ed had plenty of in the form of newspapers and magazines and a bunch of paperback books, the pages specked with mildew. Satisfied, Pryor returned to the basement and piled the stuff around Cousin Ed like one of those pyre things you saw on the Internet in India or some other crazy ass place like that.

"Please," Ed said as Pryor worked. "You don't have to do this."

"That's where you're wrong," Pryor said.

Matches in hand, he stood and looked down at Ed. Ed looked back at him, squirming to try to free himself.

And that's what the deputy reminded him of, Pryor realized. Cousin Ed, shifting back and forth like a trussed-up dog. Stopping just for a second after Pryor caught his attention and pointed at the place where his left eye had been.

"I'm sorry," Ed said, seeming as if he wanted to say more, but Pryor shut him up right quick, kicking him hard in the face. Standing back, he admired his handiwork. Then he lit two Roman Candles and threw them on the pile and added a burning ball of newspaper and retreated up the steps, fast. Ed moaning with pain and squirming like it was going to make any difference. Like he had any chance left in the world.

The firefighters did what they could, though the house went up quickly. It wasn't until hours later that they found what was left of Ed. Which wasn't much. A drunken accident, the coroner concluded, piecing together the few remaining bits and pieces of the body and considering the obvious—the shelves and shelves of illegal fireworks.

Indeed, Pryor thought, leveling his eye at the sheriff lying beside his cruiser. He looked just like Cousin Ed squirming before the explosion.

Maybe déjà vu wasn't such a bad thing after all.

51

At some point J. P. fell asleep, despite the pain, worn out by his exertions. Hopelessness had fallen over him like clouds overtaking a harvest moon, the feeling of defeat and surrender overpowering and with it a welcome descent into unconsciousness. But he woke again soon enough, prodded out of sleep by the burning on his arms and the ache on the side of his head. He stared at the cruiser tire and then at the shadows of objects seen through the undercarriage of the car. The barn still filled with the sound of deep breathing and snores. Other sounds too, the creaks he heard before, and something scurrying along the side of the cavernous space. He wondered how long until the moment came to struggle for his last bit of life. He was feeling worse and worse from being beaten and burned and hog-tied, and knew instinctively that where his injuries were concerned, time was not on his side. He gave a deep sigh.

◆

J. P. had never been the kind of guy you'd imagine coming out on top in a final life-or-death battle; never thin, never prone to athletic accomplishments. Not much good at anything, really, other than tagging along with his dad. He was chunky as a toddler and downright porky in elementary school. He graduated to beefy in seventh and eighth grades and then to nearly semi-fit in high school, thanks to football practices that kept the weight off so he looked halfway decent in his uniform while he rode the bench. Maybe that's what attracted Jan Gruning Rittmaier all those years ago. Or maybe not. Because he hadn't been what you'd call super muscular either. The most weight he ever lost was in his first year with the Guard when he was more or less ordered to slim down. After his father died he ballooned again and he struggled right up until he married June. June had other ideas. For the first three months after the wedding they ate tilapia three times a week. So much tilapia. He never even heard of it until the moment she set it down in front of him as he tried to explain that he didn't eat fish.

"You do now, Deputy. We both do."

He had to give her credit. He was on his third size uniform pants on the downward trend, and she'd cut two dress sizes. He was still overweight and June was too, he supposed, or at least pleasantly plump. But he felt better. He moved better. Even his marksmanship improved, though he couldn't have told you what connection slimming down had with hitting a bull's eye a hundred yards away. June kept commenting on it whenever they went to bed. "The new you." Going to bed happened more and more, the more weight he lost, even before the baby-making began in earnest. Under the covers, June said things to him that in his wildest dreams, waiting to be picked last for dodgeball or kickball or soccer year after year, he couldn't imagine someone would ever whisper in his ear. He blushed more in the first six months of married life than the whole rest of his life combined. It was almost, he thought, as though June were rewarding him for losing weight. Almost. Because he could tell that most of the time, that sing song noise she made as her breathing deepened was not something she could just pretend about.

◆

He felt an urge to roll over. He'd been lying on his left side for what felt like hours. He wondered if he could do it, and whether he should. Whether the sound of his heavy body changing directions would awaken everyone and hasten the end. He decided he didn't care. He was too uncomfortable. But he was cautious nonetheless and made the transition in stages. First, ever so slowly, he shifted until he was lying very nearly on his back, his hands trapped painfully beneath him. He held that position until his arm muscles screamed and he felt something pop in his hands and he thought he would scream himself, and then slowly rocked to his right. He rolled over with a slight thud, completing the turn. He heard someone cough. He held his breath and waited. A minute passed. Then two. At three minutes the breathing in the room returned to its uneven rhythms. Satisfied, J. P. took in his new vista.

He was facing a wall without door or window. From the wall hung a series of strange shapes he couldn't identify. They came into focus after a moment, like objects revealed as a fog begins to lift. A horse-drawn plow that must have belonged to Clayton's father, or more likely *his* father. What J. P. thought was a scythe. A curved, wooden yoke, which he knew only from schoolbooks, meant to drape over the neck of an ox. Old-fashioned stuff that had little bearing on a modern farm. He thought about what he saw inside the farmhouse, the bags and boxes crowding the living and dining rooms and bedrooms upstairs, and it made a little more sense. Clayton couldn't give stuff away. He had to have it around. He may have starved his horses near to death, but he didn't want to forget them. Long ago, the Darbytown vet told J. P. that Clayton was one of the best farriers in the county in his day. Could pop a horseshoe like flicking a dandelion off the stem. J. P. took in an old leather halter and a shelf that held bottles and cans and several license plates nailed to the wooden planks. Below those, shovels and pitchforks and hoes hung straight up and down like bars on a Wild West jail cell. Then he saw someone looking at him.

He blinked. He lost the spot on the wall and squeezed his eyes shut tightly and reopened them and tried again. Sure enough, a pair of eyes was peering into the barn. To the right of the scythe and the left of the halter. Peering through a gap in the boards in the side of the barn the size of two horseshoes end-to-end. Maybe the gap began as a knothole and then grew over the years as birds flew in and out and Clayton left it unrepaired, until it merged with a separating of boards warping with age and now opened up like a small, a very small window. A window someone was looking through at this very moment, staring at him. His heart raced for a minute, thinking wildly that it was June. Overwhelmed with relief at the thought of seeing her, then panicked at the idea of her being here, of encountering the one-eyed guy after the threats he made. Those horrible threats. J. P. calmed down after a moment, realizing that didn't make sense. No one knew he was here, least of all June. It was early on Saturday morning. She was asleep at her parents' house, probably deep asleep, taking advantage of a weekend morning off without the dog to care for or J. P. to put to work or the house to clean. The dog—another thing to worry about. He thought briefly of the mess June would come home to, with Sasha alone like that. He opened and shut his eyes, forcing himself to focus. Forget Sasha. Concentrate on the gap in the side of the barn.

Whoever it was, he couldn't tell if it was a man or a woman. Or what they were doing there. For a dreadful second he thought of the bodies in the basement storage room and wondered whether he was seeing the eyes of Clayton or Priscilla. He blinked again. No. That was impossible. He'd seen the coagulating pool of blood seeping across the floor for himself, the pints and pints of it. The disaster that was the back of their heads. People in that condition didn't stand up and walk outside and look through gaps in barn walls.

No. It wasn't Clayton or Priscilla. And it wasn't June. June didn't know where he was. No one knew where he was, he reminded himself. No one in the whole world.

No one—except the three men asleep on the barn floor, and whoever was looking at him this very second through a hole in the barn.

52

Penny lost her way twice. Once, when the GPS froze and she exited early onto the London–Marysville road and went almost two miles before the satellite kicked back in and the voice on the phone said things about turns that didn't make any sense. And then a second time, when a car came up behind her just before she signaled to turn onto Prairie–Alkire and she panicked and went straight instead, and drove another mile and turned onto US 40 in hopes of losing the vehicle, which as it happened quickly blew past her once she was on the four-lane road. Five minutes after that she was back on Prairie–Alkire and two minutes later she came up on the entrance to the farm. She slowed, confirmed via the mailbox that she had the right place, but didn't stop. It was pointless going in the front way. With Pryor around, that was the equivalent of a fly winging it straight into the middle of a spider web. It didn't matter if it was a falling down drug house with knee-high grass in the heart of the city or a farmhouse in the middle of the country. You'd be dead before you put the car in park.

Instead, she drove a full mile farther down until she came to a crossroad. She stopped, looked in both directions, and turned around. Cool air filled the car, smelling of green and dirt and worms as in the city after a cleansing summer rain. Night clear and the sky splattered with more stars than Penny thought she'd ever seen. She shut off her headlights for the second pass. She had to be careful, because driving without lights was a surefire way to draw attention out here if someone passed her. She decided to risk it. What choice did she have? She passed the driveway again and slowed but didn't stop. She almost missed the lane two hundred yards past the entrance to the aunt and uncle's house on the left. Not much more than a wide rut between two fields of tall corn. She slowed, braked, turned. She inched her way forward, the Pilot rocking on the uneven ground, trying to make out the way ahead. Resisting the temptation to turn the lights back on. The leaves of corn brushed either side of the SUV when she maneuvered too close to the left or the right. She drove like that for almost a minute, calculating the distance from the road to the farmhouse, knowing she was driving parallel to the driveway that Robby had described as nearly a hundred yards. At last she stopped, rolled down the windows with the engine still running, and listened. Night breezes rustled the corn. Far off, she heard a chorus of yipping that momentarily chilled her. Without knowing why, she understood that they were coyotes. She'd been in country as deep as this maybe three times in her life, and it felt as alien as if she found herself transplanted to the seashore. Yet oddly enough, as she listened to the sound of the wild dogs, she didn't feel all that scared. Nervous with anticipation of what lay ahead, but not at the strangeness of her surroundings. She looked to her left, through the open car window. The farmhouse was that way. It couldn't be far.

It took her another five minutes to turn the Pilot to the east, backing into the field, pulling forward, cranking hard to the right, backing up again, until she had the SUV at a ninety degree angle to the lane, its rear bumper facing the direction of the farmhouse. Slowly, she backed into the field, feeling the tall, thick stalks of corn give way behind her with a gentle *thud-thud-thud* as she drove farther and farther back. It felt as if she were backing the car into a wide, green lake. When she could no longer see the field opposite the lane she stopped. She killed the engine. She left the Pilot and walked forward and gathered up as many of the felled stalks as she could manage, some easy because she'd snapped them like twigs, others stubborn as saplings, unwilling to let go their hold on the earth. She made three trips, stacking them along the front of the SUV until it was almost hidden. Then she walked back to the lane. She nodded in satisfaction at her handiwork. In daylight, it probably wouldn't fool anyone, a glint of the Pilot's red metal exterior a sure giveaway. But for now, and for the next few hours it would work. The car was hidden, and it was pointed in the right direction for leaving there fast.

She went back to the car and retrieved the gun and the phone. She looked idly at Myles's unfinished sweater—the bunched-up wool and the needles—and found herself wishing she could bring that as well. Something familiar to comfort herself with. A ridiculous thought, but no more ridiculous in its own way than dragging the knitting along in the first place on this trip. She shook her head, shut the car door, pushed the keys into her jeans pocket, and made her way through the corn.

It took her less time to reach the barn than she would have guessed. One minute she was blundering her way through the thick stalks, swearing silently each time she felt an ear knock against her face, and the next she was staring at a gray building looming up in the darkness directly in front of her. The first thing that struck her was how dark the property was. No lights on anywhere. That meant one of two things. Either Robby was wrong, that Pryor hadn't made it out here. Or, as she suspected, that Pryor was up to his usual tricks. He was not a person who advertised his presence even if he was standing right behind you. Especially if—

Penny glanced around quickly. But all she saw were tall stalks of leafy corn.

It was possible he'd positioned lookouts, in which case the whole trip was a waste of time. But who? Archie and Michigan had their place in Pryor's hive of worker bees, but she couldn't see them staking out a field of corn in the pitch dark in the middle of the country. Not that Pryor would take their nervousness about such a job seriously for a second. But he might recognize that their fear could jeopardize whatever mission they were on. And Pryor himself sure as hell wasn't one for guard duty. No, Penny decided, she'd have to risk it, just as she had driving without lights down the dark, country road.

Staying inside the perimeter of the corn she walked down a row to the right until she was at the far end of the barn. The wall on that side an unbroken expanse, windowless, like the hull of a beached ship finally pushed over by a month of tides. She tightened her grip on the Glock and crept out of the field. Two seconds later she cried out as something ran in front of her. She took two steps back and nearly slipped on the wet, dewy grass.

"Shit," she whispered, almost in tears. She kneeled, waiting for her heart to stop hammering. She looked to her left and followed the small bundle scurrying away from her. Just a raccoon, and a little one at that, nothing like its enormous cousins that roamed the alleys up and down her neighborhood, plump as bear cubs, darting from storm sewer grate to trash bins and back. She stood up. She took a breath. She was going to have to do better than that. Jumping at the sound of coyotes and the sight of a raccoon was small change when you were going up against Pryor.

She moved forward, eyes up, ears taking in every sound. The air was cool and sweet-smelling. She hadn't experienced smells like this in years. The last time, a cross-country meet far out in similar territory miles from Columbus—she couldn't have said where—her junior year, her third and last season. She finished thirteenth out of thirty but didn't care about the place. It was so nice to be away from the city for a change. It wasn't the trees or the fields or all the space she noticed. It was the sound. Or rather, the absence of it. No sirens, no rush of traffic up on Broad, no angry shouts between neighbors. No nothing.

She moved closer and closer to the barn, pausing every few steps, waiting, advancing, waiting again. She saw the hole in the barn wall from twenty yards out. She didn't approach it directly but shifted to her right and came at it on an angle. She stood and listened. Still nothing. Finally, satisfied, she inched all the way up to the hole.

At first she couldn't make out anything. Like looking into a black cave on a deserted island. Slowly, as her eyes adjusted to the light inside, she made out objects. And the very first thing she recognized was a sheriff's cruiser. The hell? Had she missed something here? Was Robby's great uncle a police officer? No, she decided. That didn't make sense. So: what? Did the police beat her to it? Received some kind of tip and rushed in and arrested everyone? She thought furiously of Brandi, of her threat over the phone. Of Detective Lessner. *There's a rumor this was payback.* No, she thought, relaxing just a bit. That didn't make sense either. If the police had come there'd be a shit show by now: cars, cops, and above all lights everywhere instead of this all-consuming darkness. She was puzzling over everything when she caught a glimpse of movement on the floor near the cruiser's left passenger tire. She pulled her head away, flattened herself against the wall and moved her eyes left and right. After almost a minute she turned and looked again. And nearly had her second heart attack of the night. Someone was lying on the floor. She pulled away again, trying to control her breathing, taking in the darkened fields before her like a sea before a storm. Again, she peered back inside. She stared at the figure on the barn floor and a moment later realized he was staring back at her. She froze, just for a second. But didn't turn away. She saw that his feet were bound and his arms drawn behind his back, out of sight. He was a prisoner, and he was wearing a deputy's uniform.

Slowly, she tried to parse things out in her mind. Who was he? How had he come to be there? Why, if he somehow stumbled onto Pryor and his gang, was he still alive? She couldn't begin to imagine. But instinctively she knew it was important to keep looking at him. To maintain eye contact. Because of something she sensed that filled her with both hope and a deep dread. That they each might, just might, have something to offer the other.

53

Pryor looked down in disgust at the long, blue tattoo on the sleeping man's face.

"Wake up."

"Mmph," Michigan said.

"Now."

No reaction.

"Now."

Nothing. Then: "Why?"

"Because I said so."

"What time is it?"

"It's time to wake up."

"Give me a couple more minutes."

"We don't have a couple more minutes."

"It's too early still—"

Michigan yelped as Pryor kicked him in the side with his right foot, or more accurately, with his right foot encased in a steel-toed boot. The boots some of his most prized possessions. Authentic leather construction boots that once belonged to Cousin Ed. Grabbed on a whim as he ran out of the house, the sound of explosions coming from the basement. Explosions and something else that might have been a scream. Pryor grinned at the obscenity Michigan flung at him as he sat up and rubbed his ribs.

"That's more like it." He turned toward Archie, but he was already stirring, eyeing Pryor warily. He sat up, yawned, stretched, and reached for his own shoes. Archie had been uncharacteristically quiet since Pryor lied to him and told him he wasn't going inside the bank; that Michigan was going instead. And Archie was a quiet guy to begin with, except when he started up with the questions. So quiet that sometimes you didn't know what he was thinking. Pryor didn't like that in a man. Never had. A man working for him, anyway.

"Where are you going?" Pryor said, catching sight of Michigan by the barn's rear door.

"I need to take a piss."

"Do it in here."

"In here?"

"You heard me."

"I might have to take a crap, too."

"Do them both here. We don't want to attract attention."

"There's nobody around."

"We don't know that."

"You really want me to—"

"Use the stall," Pryor said, jerking his head toward the room where he dragged the deputy earlier in the night, ready to blow his brains out with the .38 if he didn't start explaining himself. Michigan bitched a little more but went ahead and did as he was told. Archie did the same afterward, dragging a bale of straw into the stable to cover the mess.

What the hell, Pryor thought, something dawning on him as he took his own turn. Archie was right after all. It was quiet as a mausoleum, inside and out. At least two hours had passed without any sign of backup. It was true: no one knew the fat deputy was there. Which made what he had in mind all the better.

"All right," Pryor said, coming out of the stable. Patting the .38 tucked into his waistband, assured by the comfortable way it sat in the small of his back. "Let's go."

"Where?" Michigan said.

"Him." Pryor gestured at the deputy.

"What about him?"

"Get him in the van. It's time."

"For what?"

"For story hour, asshole. What do you think? Just do it."

"Oh," Michigan said, eyeing Pryor's gun. He licked his lips. "I get it."

54

Penny was back in the SUV. Sitting in the back seat so she could turn without too much trouble and look at the barn. In her hands her knitting, Myles's sweater, taking shape at last. Almost done. It was absurd, she knew, to sit there like that, manipulating the needles in a quiet, quick rhythm with the object of her hunt so close, just a few dozen yards away in that barn. But she needed to think, and she needed to stay awake, and she doubted she could accomplish either laying low in the corn and just waiting. The deputy changed everything. She had to reconsider how to do this. She wasn't particularly concerned about his welfare. But there were advantages he might be able to offer, if only she could figure it out. Determine the best moment to make her move.

◆

She learned to knit from Ma-Maw, picked it up as a girl on overnight visits when Pa-Paw was still around and healthy enough for visitors. Long before Clyde entered the picture. Her first creation a scarf that looked like somebody knit it in the dark without a clue for shape or color. Her second and third attempts better, but only marginally. Someplace along the line she knitted Myles a winter hat. Just handed it to him one day, one cold winter morning, not his birthday and not around Christmas. Tenth or eleventh grade, she couldn't remember. Just gave it to him.

"Here. I made this."

"Thanks," he said, giving her that look of his.

He had it until at least the end of high school, wearing it on the coldest days in January and February.

She began the sweater the day he went to prison. Three years. A bargain, his public defender said, given that he was facing twenty for accessory to armed robbery, and maybe the same again for negligent homicide because of the woman who died. The agreement to testify against Pryor changing all that. The deal looking pretty good until Myles walked off the stand and Dawson walked on and the whole thing went to hell.

Penny wanted the sweater to mean something. She didn't want to finish it too quickly, and she wanted it to be nice. To be done the day Myles walked free. So sometimes she set it aside for a few weeks, if she came too close to finishing. Randy, the creep, teased her about it when he visited with Brandi.

"You finish that in time, maybe I'll try it on," he said once, when Brandi was out of earshot, arguing with Mama about something in the kitchen.

"Not a chance," Penny said, pausing so the needles stood up straight in her hands, their sharp ends glinting under the light of the lamp beside her chair.

She unraveled a third of it that same night, not willing to give Randy the slightest hint of satisfaction that she might ever take him up on the offer. Or on any of the offers his lecherous smile always implied.

She planned to give it to Myles the day he came home, in front of everybody at the party. But things became too hectic, and she was too tense. Which may also have explained why she missed the significance of Myles and Lem talking in the far corner of Ma-Maw's yard. And then she planned to give it to him after she returned from work at the costume shop that second day. And then—

She still planned to give it to him, she told herself, needles clicking furiously, like the champing of tiny teeth. He'd receive the gift, no matter what. Because he was going to be fine and soon they weren't going to have anything to worry about ever again.

55

J. P. tried his best. He felt certain of that. He took what little comfort he could knowing that in the hour of his death he didn't give up. But it didn't take him long to realize his best was one thing and his best in the condition he was in compared with the reality of three grown men with boots and fists and one with a gun was another thing altogether. He took satisfaction in watching the one-eyed guy stagger in surprise as soon as they had him on his feet and J. P. jerked his head backward, catching him on the chin with a satisfying cue ball-like *thwock* and then throwing his full weight against Blue Streak. But he paid a high price a moment later with a blow to the side of his head so hard he momentarily lost consciousness. When he awoke he thought he'd gone partially blind until he realized he was seeing the world through blood streaming down his face.

"By the cruiser," the one-eyed guy said.

"What?" the Black man said.

"Put him by the cruiser."

"We're shooting him there?"

"Prop him up somehow. Make sure he doesn't fall over. I need him standing up."

"It's going to be messy."

"Roll the barn door open, just a little bit." This last order to Blue Streak. "It's too dark in here. We need more light."

"Can I do it?" Blue Streak asked.

"Do what?"

"Shoot him. Take the gun and make him suck on the barrel and wait until he's gagging and then do it. Like that."

"Just open the door."

J. P. struggled again as the Black man and Blue Streak wrestled him toward the cruiser. Why not? The pair cursed and shouted at him as they tried to maneuver what he knew was just over two hundred pounds of dead weight. But then the one-eyed guy marched over and without speaking kicked him in the groin with his boot and a thousand explosions of tiny lights blew up in his brain and J. P. felt himself fall and after that vomit all over himself.

"You don't stop fucking around, the next time you're going to be chewing on your balls," the one-eyed guy said.

When J. P. came to again he was propped against the side of his cruiser and the three of them were standing in a semicircle, observing him like people in a museum studying a statue they don't quite understand. J. P. gazed back at them blearily. But he tried not to focus on their faces. He tried to imagine June, and his father, and his mom, instead.

"All right," the one-eyed guy said, raising his right hand. "Let's make this count."

56

Sounds, coming from the barn. Penny craned her neck and listened, lowering her head. Something was happening. She heard shouting. That didn't sound good. She thought of the deputy. She thought of Pryor and his permanent squint, like a man born looking into the sun. She tried to decide what to do. She picked up Randy's phone. Text messages from Brandi filled the screen.

Where are you?
You're out of time.
I'm going to call.
What the fuck where are you?

Penny jammed the phone into her jeans without replying. She set the knitting down, picked up the Glock, and left the car. She crouched down the way you saw in movies and moved out of the field and across the short lawn to the barn. Now or never, she guessed.

She made it to the spy hole she found earlier and flattened herself on the wall beside it. But what difference did it make, trying to shield herself in broad daylight? She was completely exposed, like a butterfly pinned to a sheet of cardboard. Anyone coming around either side of the building would see her and have an easy shot, the kind you barely had to aim for. She kept the gun loose in her hand, turned and looked through the hole. Inside, it was much lighter than she expected. She puzzled at this until she saw that the main door at the front had been rolled open. Across the barn Pryor and Archie and Michigan stood with their backs to her, facing a van. The van Pryor drove two nights before, when he woke them up at midnight, the day of Myles's homecoming. Beyond them, partially obscured, she saw the deputy, propped in the open side door of the van, leaning motionless against the front passenger seat like some kind of giant carnival toy. Blood streaking his face, which even at this distance she saw was swollen and bruised. Penny pushed her face into the hole as deep as she dared and tried to make eye contact, tried to renew the connection they had earlier. But he was staring at something else now, something she wasn't sure was even in the barn.

Pryor held something in his right hand, but it wasn't a gun. It didn't look good, whatever was going on. Penny knew what she had to do. She was going to have to take action.

Her first thought was to bolt to her left, dash around the corner of the barn, burst through the open door and hope her aim was good enough to do a little damage before they realized what was happening. She dismissed it just as quickly. At best she'd manage a few shots, sprayed in the right direction if she were lucky, before one or more returned fire. And the three of them didn't spray.

There was only one other choice: shoot first, through the hole, praying she could nail each of them in turn. That was a stretch, she knew. The first shot, even if it took one of them down, would probably send the surviving two out the door and around. But it was worth trying and the slightest bit safer than attempting to get the jump on them inside. Even if, as was likely, she managed to hit only one of them, she still had the protection of the barn wall and the safety of the field to fall back on, assuming she could sprint out of there faster than they could tear from the barn and chase around to the direction the shots were fired from.

She raised her gun, and set the barrel on the bottom edge of the hole. She sighted Michigan, then Archie, then Pryor. It would have to be Pryor first. You didn't shoot the bitch when the alpha male was right in front of you. She saw that on Discovery or Animal Planet or National Geographic, one of those.

"All right," Penny heard Pryor say, watching as he raised both hands. "Let's make this count."

She adjusted the gun one last time and brought the sight to the back of his bony, shaved head. And fired.

57

If not for the sound of the shot, Pryor might have thought a wasp stung him. The pain was that bad. But there was no mistaking the noise that accompanied it. And there was also no mistaking the fact that the entire operation, not to mention his life, depended on what happened in the next two seconds. Left hand clamped on his ear, already slippery with blood, he knelt, pivoted, yanked the .38 from his waistband and returned fire in one, smooth motion, peppering the far wall of the barn.

"Go, go, go," he yelled at Michigan and Archie. They went.

Crouched, eye trained on the wall and the large hole right in the middle that he was seeing now for the first time, Pryor crab-walked from barrier to barrier—the deputy's cruiser, an old tractor, a pair of straw bales—until he was just below the mess he made of the boards shooting at whoever shot at him. He held his breath and listened, ignoring the agony that was the left side of his head. If there was one thing he could do, it was hear things. But the only sounds that came to him were Archie and Michigan crashing into the broad field of corn and swearing as they ran to and fro. Idiots. Why not ring bells while they were at it?

Slowly, slowly, Pryor rose until he was even with the peep hole. He stepped toward it, inch by inch, listening intently. Blood streamed down his cheek and his neck but he held his position. He once detected a gunner on the other side of a closet door just from the nearly imperceptible inhalations of the man's breathing, so quiet that no one else in the room detected. But Pryor did. Unfortunately for the gunner. But once again, he heard nothing but the thrashing of Michigan and Archie out in the cornfield. He shifted closer, and closer again, and risked a quick glance through the hole. Nothing. No one—just a wide, thick sea of green stretched out for acres and acres.

Pryor found a bottle of water in the van and, using the van's driver side mirror to guide him, cleaned what remained of his left ear. The shot, whoever took it, severed the flesh cleanly; at least the bleeding had stopped. He used his knife to tear a strip off the blanket Archie slept beneath and wrapped it around his head, binding the wound tightly. Despite the pain, he was pleased with the result when he examined it in the mirror. Very Apache-warrior like, if he did say so himself. But what the fuck: first his eye, now his ear? Someone was going to pay, big time, and when he was finished with them, it was going to make what he did to Cousin Ed look like a walk in the park.

Finished doctoring himself, Pryor approached the deputy laying on the floor beside the van. He retrieved the phone and examined the picture he took just before the shot. It was good. Actually, more than good. Exactly what he hoped for. He replaced the phone and stared down at the deputy.

"Jerrod Paul," he said. "You sure as shit better hope you didn't have anything to do with that."

The deputy looked up at him wordlessly. Pryor considered retrieving his knife from the van and removing chunks of the fat fuck's flesh until he explained why Pryor now lacked a left ear. But no. The deputy would get what was coming to him, soon enough. First things first. Without another word, Pryor left the barn and jogged around to the field to see what the hell was going on out there.

58

Penny ran.

She ran and she cursed and she ran.

She should have anticipated this. She should have guessed that even a wounded Pryor would retaliate hard and fast. But still, the speed with which he responded stunned her. If the image of Myles and his reminder about the molasses of hesitation hadn't popped into her mind at the instant she saw Pryor's head twitch after she fired, she'd be dead. If she hadn't had the good sense to duck and roll, somehow surviving the barrage of gunfire that splintered the boards she was standing in front of just seconds before.

She ran wildly at first, flailing through the corn, but corrected herself soon enough. That was the quickest path to suicide. It didn't take long to hear the sound of pursuit behind her—Michigan and Archie, she was guessing, though maybe Pryor too—and know that the more noise she made, the better chance they had of finding her. So she slowed to a steady trot, easing her way fifty feet down one row, hanging a left into the next, following that another fifty feet, and so on.

She didn't dare head for the Pilot. Talk about suicide. It was one thing to hide the vehicle so well that no one would see it. Another altogether to attempt to drive out of there with a wounded Pryor and his two henchmen on the warpath, in quarters so close. She'd be lucky to make it halfway to Prairie–Alkire. Instead, she zigzagged away from the farm lane and out into the field, farther and farther from the barn. She ran until she had to stop and catch her breath. Which was not like her. She had good lungs and good legs. But she also didn't anticipate the toll the one-two punch of terror and defeat would take on her. She crouched and held her breath and listened.

It wasn't hard to hear them. At least she was quiet. The men chasing her were like bumpers whacking at pinballs for all the care they took to disguise their progress. At least she'd see them before they saw her. She gripped the gun, waiting. And sure enough, a few moments later, there they were. Michigan, then Archie. Crashing through the rows of corn indiscriminately. A few dozen feet away at best. Both of them panting, their faces shiny with sweat. And something else. Fear, she saw after a moment. Fear, not of what they might encounter. Fear of what would happen at Pryor's hands if they didn't find her.

She pressed herself as flat as possible onto the cool earth, trying to detect a third set of feet. It was hard to tell anything inside what amounted to a cornfield maze from hell. But she was pretty sure it was just the two of them, and her. That was good and bad. Good, because two were easier to take out than three, especially if one of them wasn't Pryor. She felt sad, just for a second, thinking about Archie, and his grandmother, but she let it go. She wasn't running a charity here. She had only herself and Myles and Mack to think about. Archie had made his choice. But the bad part was, if she had to shoot the two of them, that would signal Pryor as to her location as clearly as if she stood up and rang a gong. And she knew for damn sure that Pryor wouldn't let her successfully draw a bead on him a second time.

Closer and closer still. The two of them glancing from side to side. Both of them carrying, but she decided she wasn't going to worry about that. This wasn't going to be a shootout, a duel at high noon. If she had to, she wasn't providing any notice. She was just going to shoot.

Closer, closer still. And then: in the distance, a long, sharp whistle.

The pair froze. They looked at each other, and then away. Penny extended her arm, sighting on Archie. Best if she did him first. She didn't want to run the risk of listening to him beg for his life. It wouldn't change what she had to do, but it would make it all the harder. They didn't move, and she raised the gun just a little higher. She thought of Myles. *The gun and the go.*

The whistle again, a second or two longer.

"Shit," Michigan said. He lingered another second, and then turned and walked in the opposite direction. Back toward the barn.

Archie stayed, casting an extended, searching glance around him. Then, for just a second, he stopped and it was Penny's turn to freeze. He was peering right at her. Was he? She was almost certain of it. No. Yes. She braced herself, and heard a third whistle. Archie blinked, his eyes still on her, spun around, and caught up with Michigan.

When the master called, the dogs came.

Penny collapsed, breath leaving her as if someone fell hard atop her, almost sobbing in relief.

And then she heard the two shots. Followed by a third.

59

Pryor looked to the left and the right as he hurried out of the field, still listening. And still nothing. Yet another advantage to being out in the country. Who gave a crap about a couple random gunshots in these parts?

He felt a little bad about Michigan. He wasn't half the driver Baby was, and that damn tattoo made him useless in five other ways. But he had a vicious streak Pryor could appreciate and who couldn't admire a guy who hated cops that much? Before whatever the hell just happened and someone took that shot through the barn's peephole, Pryor had half a mind to let Michigan do the deputy himself, however he pleased, as long as it was quiet. He would have killed Michigan anyway, of course, because that's just how this plan ended up working out. But it would have been nice to admire his handiwork, like watching a condemned artist work up a sketch just before the gallows' dead drop.

Instead, Pryor put him down first as he crept through the maze, one shot in the back of the head. Exactly what whoever the shooter out there was had planned for him.

Archie was a different matter, Pryor thought, turning and shooting him in the thigh because he had just a couple things to say first. Well really, just one.

"There was no cop, was there?" he said, leaning over the fallen man and retrieving his gun.

"What the fuck are you talking about?" Archie gasped.

"After I shot Baby. There was no cop. You just made that up, didn't you?"

"Listen, Pryor—" he said, and grasped his leg, grimacing in pain.

"No, you listen. That wasn't a field trip we were on that night. It was a safari. And safaris only end one way. And you fucked that up. You let your feelings for Baby get in the way of the job we had to do."

"Please—"

"Baby was mine to deal with. My problem. My shot."

Archie went still, his eyes suddenly bright with rage. "Myles saved your ass going to prison for you, motherfucker. And that's how you paid him back? Shooting him down like a dog? You're goddamn right there wasn't a cop—"

"Thank you for telling the truth," Pryor said, and shot him between the eyes.

Any other day, he would have continued this particular safari. Find whoever shot him and send them to hell. But he had a schedule to follow and he'd already lost too much time with the whole severed left ear complication. He'd figure out later who was responsible, and how to pay them back. For now, Pryor had the deputy to deal with and a quick trip into town to make.

He hadn't done a half-bad job, he thought, glancing at the photo on the phone one more time as he reentered the barn. Which in fact was the deputy's own phone, which Pryor played with for quite some time earlier in the evening, and not just to ogle pictures of the deputy's not half-bad-looking wife as long as you were into big girls. Phones could be valuable things, he found over the years. They contained useful information about people's lives, even when—or especially when—the people themselves weren't around anymore. Opening it as easy as bending the deputy's thumb back so far he hoped it might snap, then relenting long enough to press it down on the pad to unlock the phone.

He had some experience in this area, so it worked just fine.

What he was starting to explain to Michigan before all hell broke loose was the photo was their—well, *his* key to safe passage. Both Michigan and Archie looked at him as if he were out of his mind when they realized they dragged the deputy all the way to the van just for Pryor to take a picture instead of putting a bullet in his fat head.

"I nearly ruptured my scrotum dragging that sack of shit for a selfie?" Michigan said, and despite himself, Pryor had to laugh. It was a funny line.

"Not a selfie. More like a passport."

Which was right when someone took off his left ear.

But the concept still stood. When the correct moment presented itself, likely five to ten minutes after he left the bank, Pryor planned to send that picture to the proper authorities. All of them, all the way down the line. The Darby County sheriff, whose cell he found in the deputy's phone. Some lady trooper he probably had a hard-on for. The Darbytown police chief. And so on and so forth. They were all receiving the picture, with a warning. If anyone came close to him, if he saw a single flashing light, whether fire truck or ambulance or highway truck, he was pushing the deputy out the door at eighty miles an hour right after passing a tractor trailer and good luck identifying the remains.

But of course, the deputy wasn't going to be in the van. Pryor was making that part up. He had other plans for him, he thought, scrabbling up the ladder to the loft and pulling down the first bale of straw.

60

A thud, from the other side of the barn. Something heavy hitting the floor. J. P. flinched and craned his neck to see—an inch, then two, then . . . back down again. It took so much effort to move now, so dazed was he from the blows to his head and to his groin, from the blisters on his arms where the red-hot fork tines cooked his flesh, and perhaps first and foremost from the terror of knowing he was likely to die, and soon. There was only one thing he thought he understood at this point, which was the reason he didn't shut his eyes and give up for good. Something had changed. Something had happened, probably bad, and now he was alone with the one-eyed guy.

He was almost positive the person he saw looking at him through the hole was related to all the commotion in the past few minutes—the sound of a gun going off and the yelp the one-eyed guy gave—which came down shortly after he took the picture of J. P. propped against the van. The rush outside and a few minutes later what sounded like more shots.

J. P. could guess what happened to the Black man and Blue Streak out there, which would explain why they weren't back inside the barn. Good riddance, he was tempted to say, though he knew his father wouldn't have approved of such a sentiment, even under these conditions.

J. P. could also guess what happened to the person on the other side of the barn wall. Him, her, whoever they were, he mourned.

Now the one-eyed guy was inside the barn again, moving fast. And up to something. Dragging bales of straw down from the half attic and placing them in a tight circle around J. P. Finished, he went to the blue-gray van and opened the back. J. P.'s brain, thick with fog, struggled for a few seconds to identify the acrid smell of the liquid his captor poured over each of the bales, drenching them, a manic grin on his face. What was happening?

It came to him with the force of a dream you can't wake up from, the dream you kill someone in, the death you deeply regret but can't do anything about. Of course. Gasoline.

Bracing for what came next, he followed the passage of the one-eyed guy as he left the barn gasoline can in hand, sunlight flooding inside from the opened door. Nearly five minutes passed. Then the one-eyed guy returned, doused J. P.'s cruiser, and set the gas can down. A few moments later J. P. smelled smoke and heard what sounded like a window breaking, and even in his reduced state realized what just happened. The one-eyed guy had set the farmhouse on fire. He thought of Clayton and Priscilla, their bodies in the basement. How long it would take the flames to reach them.

A second after that, a shadow fell over J. P.

"Jerrold Paul."

He looked up.

"Was that you?"

He squinted, not sure he heard correctly.

"I said, was that you?"

"Was that me what?" J. P. croaked.

"Whoever shot me." He tapped the left side of his head where red bloomed from the makeshift bandage wrapped around his skull. "Did you have something to do with that?"

J. P. thought of the mysterious stranger.

"I wish," he said, slowly.

"You wish what?"

"I wish I did. And believe me, I would have taken off more than your ear. But no."

"Liar."

"I'm telling the truth." Words coming as grudgingly as splinters yanked from his flesh. "I truly wish I did. I wish I'd done it myself. But I didn't."

"You know what's going on here, right?" The one-eyed guy narrowed his single orb into a squint like a twitching gash.

J. P. shook his head.

"I'm having myself a pig roast, is what. It's not a pleasant way to go, Jerrold Paul. I know because I have some experience in these matters. But I have a proposal. Tell me who shot me, and how you pulled it off, and I'll let you live."

J. P. smiled at that, despite all the pain he was in, the lie so brazen.

"I wouldn't," he said.

"You wouldn't what?"

"I wouldn't have missed."

"Too bad we'll never find out," the one-eyed guy said, lighting a match, dropping it on the straw and then stepping back quickly as the gasoline vapors ignited. Flames grew fast and faster, and leaped around the bales circling J. P. like flames at a South Seas ceremony trotted out for tourists. Soon they spread to the floor, devouring loose clumps of straw that the one-eyed guy scattered here and there, and then jumped to the walls, and to the roof.

Flames everywhere now. Smoke filling the space. The sounds of the barn door rolling shut behind the one-eyed guy, the bolt being shot, and the van's engine roaring into life.

So, J. P. thought, looking around in terror. Fire and fuel. Just like my father.

61

Penny felt the phone buzzing in her pocket as she hid in the cornfield, frozen, watching a blue-gray van roar up the drive as smoke rose from the farmhouse, trying to fight off the molasses of hesitation and figure out what to do next. Brandi—what a bitch, she thought, connecting.

"I said I'd be there," she hissed. "I fucking said—"

"Penny?"

A man's voice.

"Penny? It's Detective Lessner."

She didn't say anything. She held out the phone, looked at the caller ID. Number blocked.

"Penny?"

This was a waste of time. She couldn't afford to go over everything with him again. The rumors he heard. The payback. Yes, she knew he was just trying to do his job, but—

She stopped. The realization hitting her like a smack on the back of the head. Lessner. Calling her on Randy's phone. Which meant—

"I know what's going on, Penny. At least I have a pretty good idea. And what I need for you to do right now is talk to me. Tell me where you are. Let me help you."

She didn't speak. She followed the smoke rising above the barn, and after a moment heard something unexpected. A loud thump. She listened intently, but it didn't repeat.

"Penny? You there?"

It had been so hard with Myles at first, him gone away like that, locked up, Pryor free as a bird if the bird was a hawk and you were a wounded rabbit, waiting for the inevitable. The feeling she couldn't shake that Myles betrayed her, leaving her alone and vulnerable. And then not alone because she had Mack, though at times that made it even worse. But then things went better, eventually, sitting in the visitors' room at the Mansfield prison, talking out their positions, and they reached a kind of accord. Their ability to breathe just a little and dream, just a little, helped significantly by the fact that Pryor seemed to be biding his time.

Shared responsibility for Mack bound Penny and Myles at first, but later on something else grew between them, something that went beyond their boy. The recognition that they were on a journey together, one helping the other along, and it seemed like a waste of a thousand shared footsteps just to chuck it all after they came this far.

So why did Myles have to go after Pryor like that? By himself, with Lem's gun? Couldn't they have gone together?

"Penny?"

Lessner.

"Listen to me. This is not some *Thelma and Louise* thing. Life's not like that. This is real. I can help you, but you have to talk to me. Your mom's worried about you. Your sister too."

"Bullshit." She couldn't help herself.

"It's true. She says she forgives you, for what you did to her husband. She just wants you to be okay."

Was that another thump?

"You're lying," she said, distracted by what she thought she heard.

"Myles does too. He's awake. I spoke to him myself."

In a funny way, the sweater was the turning point in their new life. Something of her own, something she alone could create and use as a way to mark time. The act connecting her both to Ma-Maw, who taught her how to knit, and to Myles as the recipient. And to all the people who commented on it over the years as she labored away, even the ones teasing her about how long it was taking. Even, she reflected, creeps like Randy, despite his deranged belief she'd ever let him wear it. A gift for Myles and Myles alone.

Watching the barn burn Penny thought fondly about the sweater: the tight rows, the deep blue color of the yarn, the sleeve she was almost finished with . . .

Thump.

Thump.

"Penny?"

Thump.

Oh, shit.

"Goodbye," she said, flinging the phone as hard as she could into the sea of green and sprinting toward the barn.

62

Fire and fuel. Just like his father.

J. P. held the thought like a flower he was ready to drop onto a grave, but only for a moment.

He flipped himself over from his left side onto his back and then over onto his right, grunting with pain, then did it again. He paused, trying not to inhale the smoke, and flipped once more. The circle he was trapped inside was so small, more movement than that was nearly impossible. He felt how intense the flames were, like sitting too close to a midsummer bonfire, and flinched as burning straw fell atop him. It was possible his shirt was now on fire. He flipped himself again, smelling scorched hair as he bumped up against the fiery bale. He rested and prepared to do it again. Why not? Man was heavier than straw. It was only a question of pushing the bale out of the way and rolling on the floor toward the door faster than the fire could follow him. That the one-eyed guy had bolted the door behind him was barely a concern. He knew he was doomed. But he wasn't going down without a fight.

No, he thought, gathering his strength. Not like his father.

63

Penny stood and gaped. Before her, flames engulfed the farmhouse porch and licked angrily in and out of broken windows and gushed from a corner of the roof like some kind of monstrous genie. Black smoke poured from the open door and she heard loud cracks and pops. She couldn't believe it was going up this fast. She prayed that no one was inside or if they were, that they weren't alive to face a death by fire.

Thump.

She turned and looked at the barn. Out of an upper window smoke rolled up into the sky like blood clouding blue water. But lower down, that sound again. Like something being thrown against one of the inner walls, over and over.

Not something. Someone. Someone was inside trying to escape.

The deputy? The man she stared at through the hole in the wall? Was it even possible?

Penny ran forward, grabbed the door's bolt and tried to shoot it, but cried out instead, recoiling from the touch of hot metal. She backed away, shaking her hand, rubbing it on her jeans. She spun, searching for something, anything, to aid her. But nothing lay in sight to pull the door open with. All the available tools and rope and pieces of cloth were going up in flames inside the barn or the house.

Thump.

She thought for a moment and sprinted back into the field. She threw open the SUV's door and grabbed the sweater and ran back to the front of the barn, gasping from the exertion. Bunching the sweater around her hands she reached forward, seized the bolt, and pulled. It wouldn't budge. She tried again in vain. Flames darted out of a crack in the door and the sweater started to smoke. The bottom of the door shook as the person inside struck it again. She yelled and tried once more and after several seconds the bolt slid over. She rolled the door open, coughing as smoke enveloped her and took three giant steps back.

Penny didn't see him at first, fixated as she was at the sight of the conflagration inside. Flames devoured straw bales and dry wooden boards and the heat and smoke was so intense she couldn't tell whether she stepped away from the hot wave of air or was pushed back. And then she nearly tripped as something hit her shins. She looked down in shock. There was a man on fire at her feet.

The deputy was big, much bigger than he appeared as she stared through the hole in the wall. She tried dragging him but it was like trying to pull a fold-out couch across a living room floor. There was no way to lift him, and anyway his pants and part of his shirt were on fire. As was the sweater, lying on the ground beside him. The sweater—three years' work gone. The deputy was moaning something she couldn't quite make out. She jumped over him and crouched behind and clapped and slapped at the flames, and at the same time pushed, and yelled, "Roll, damn it. Roll!"

He rolled. Once, twice, a third time. He rolled and she pushed until at last he flipped over onto a patch of still dewy grass between the drive and the cornfield. She helped him rock back and forth until the flames on his uniform were out. But he was still moaning, and he was still bound by his feet and hands. She had to cut him loose. And she was losing time she could have spent following Pryor. So much time she nearly shrieked in frustration.

Penny stood and jogged back and forth, like someone warming up for a race, trying to figure out what to do. She ran as close as possible to the burning house, then back to the deputy, then to the edge of the barn, scouring the ground with her eyes. She felt something crunch under her feet. She looked down and saw shards of glass. She bent over and picked one up and examined it. Raising her eyes, she saw a shattered light fixture at the top of the barn. That explained the darkness, in part.

It took what felt like an eternity, sawing away at the plastic ties binding the deputy's hands so tightly they seemed to have lost color. She cut her fingers three times on the jagged, misshapen piece of glass before the first zip-tie finally gave. She drew in breath at the line of red constriction encircling his wrists. The work of Pryor, no doubt. Who else?

The deputy's feet, entrapped by three of the plastic bindings, were a little easier. She helped him sit up and he kept himself propped in a sitting position with his hands behind him on the ground, palms flat, while she worked, repressing a sudden memory of Ma-Maw cutting the strings on a piece of meat she roasted one holiday.

"You're bleeding," he said, voice cracked and dry.

She looked at her hands, slippery with blood from the glass shard cuts.

"And you're on fire," she said, slapping at a puff of smoke on the bottom of his pant leg.

"Thank you."

"Your father," Penny said. She finished cutting and the zip ties around the deputy's feet fell loose.

"What?"

"He's not in there, is he?" The barn now a roaring hill of flame whose heat baked the side of her face, even sitting so many yards away. Smoke billowing into the sky, higher than the highest tree around.

"No. Why are you asking that?"

"'Dad,'" Penny said. "You kept saying, 'Dad,' just now."

"Dad," the deputy said, moving his head up and down.

"So he's okay?"

"No. He's dead. He died a few years ago."

Penny stood. "Well, I'm sorry about that."

She looked at the barn, thinking about the deputy's narrow survival. If he hadn't made that noise trying to escape.

"That was you, wasn't it? Looking at me through the hole in the barn?"

Penny told him it was.

"I thought so. It gave me a little hope, just so you know. So thanks for that as well."

"You're welcome," Penny said, not feeling as if she'd done a damn thing.

"The other two," the deputy continued. "The Black man and the guy with the blue streak on his face."

"Archie and Michigan? They're dead."

"Did you—?"

"Almost. But Pryor got them first. I'm not sure why. Except he does that sometimes. Just ups and shoots people."

And I'm probably next, she thought.

"That's his name. Pryor?"

She nodded, suddenly exhausted.

"He was on about something with them. Especially the Black man. He kept saying something about a cop, and someone named Myles. Pryor seemed to think the Black man, Archie, did something to keep him from killing Myles. From finishing the job."

"He said that? Pryor did?"

"That's what I heard. That Archie pulled away too soon."

"Oh, God," Penny said, choking back a sob.

"What's wrong?"

She felt a torrent of tears inside her, ready to burst forth like water inside a long-blocked pipe. Archie, of all people. Saving Myles, and now lying dead in a cornfield miles from home and his grandmother—

No. It wasn't the time. She had to pull herself together.

"Did he say anything else? Pryor, I mean. Like what he was up to?"

"Not exactly."

"What's that supposed to mean?" Penny snapped, immediately regretting it. But if the deputy noticed he didn't seem to care.

"It means I figured it out, by stuff they were talking about."

"Stuff like what?"

"Like the fact I think he's planning to rob a bank."

64

Pryor pressed his hand to the left side of his head and pulled away a barely bloody palm. Still painful as a sonofabitch but the bleeding seemed to be easing. So that was one good thing amid seventeen other disasters in the shit show this day turned into.

He knew the deputy was lying about the ambush, about whoever shot him. He had to be. Because how the fuck else? As he drove toward Darbytown, keeping just under the speed limit, he regretted not staying just a few minutes longer to stand outside the barn and listen to Jerrod Paul's screams as he was roasted alive. He also regretted the fact that he would not, in fact, be able to do the deputy's wife like he threatened, given how far away he'd be in just a few hours. Well, not do her anytime soon. But life was long. For some.

One thing was certain: he felt liberated with Archie and Michigan out of the way. Talk about dead weight. They served their purpose along the way, sure, and he even congratulated himself on keeping them alive long enough to help with the deputy after Pryor discovered him knocking on the old couple's door and sneaked in after him, and then marched him out of the basement and into the barn with a gun against his neck a few minutes later. It had been useful to have three people for what followed, that's for damn sure.

Not that any outcome other than what happened in the field was ever in doubt, despite the pair's temporary usefulness. In the end, Archie and Michigan had the same problem as Dawson. And Cousin Ed, and even Mae, come to think of it. All were witnesses. And witnesses talked, as Pryor learned the hard way when Baby took the stand. Talk about some unfinished business.

But first things first. Despite the cock-up back there, the ambush, the loss of his ear, the unfortunate executions outdoors where someone could have heard, he was still on track. He knew this because of the thick plumes of smoke he saw in his rearview mirror roiling into the sky. The fact no one was following him. And because, ahead of him, he heard the sound of a siren coming his way.

He thought back to the deputy. To Jerrold Paul. Pryor had always liked puzzles. Not asinine puzzles like crosswords in the paper, all those words. But games of strategy, like chess or checkers, which also contained the wild card of never knowing exactly what crazy thing your opponent might do. Weirdly, he thought of the deputy that way, even though he had the drop on him from the moment the knocking on the door awoke him. Somehow, the deputy still managed to pull something off that ended with Pryor wrapping part of a shoplifted blanket around the bloody stump of what used to be his ear. It was a puzzle still waiting for a solution. And one day, he promised, he would solve it. And someone would pay.

But first, the bank. He was almost there.

65

"A bank?" Penny said.

"Pretty sure." He explained his theory based on what he heard the trio discussing inside the barn.

"How far's the nearest one?"

"Few miles. Right in Darbytown. I'm guessing that's it. Why else would he be out here to begin with? So we just need to call for help, tell someone what's going on."

Penny thought of Randy's phone, lying someplace in the cornfield. She wondered how long Detective Lessner stayed on the line until he realized Penny wasn't there anymore.

"No phone."

"The radio. In my cruiser."

Penny looked at the inferno before them. What used to be the barn. She shook her head.

The deputy said, "Then we can stop at a house along the way."

"Wouldn't it be faster to drive straight to the bank?"

"Faster, maybe. But we need reinforcements. I mean, what would we do just by ourselves? Especially in my condition?"

"We could get him," Penny said.

"Get who?"

"Pryor."

"Get him or stop him?"

"Let's go," Penny said, reaching down and collecting what remained of the sweater. "We're wasting time. We can call on the way."

66

Looking at the line of people waiting for Darby Farmers National Bank to open, Pryor smiled for the third time that morning.

The first time was at the sight of the farmhouse going up in flames so quickly. Even with all the gasoline he poured inside and out, and even with all the bags and papers and boxes the crazy old couple had accumulated, he was pleasantly surprised at the speed of the blaze. But what really made him smile was the fact that he predicted this to them, to the shriveled-up man and woman, as he forced them to kneel in that room next to all those jars of food. "The flames will rise so high," he said, lifting his voice over the old woman's keening.

The second time he smiled was when he was nearly run off the road and into the fields not once, not twice, but three times by fire trucks and sheriff's cruisers barreling past him on their way to the farmhouse and barn. After the last near accident, he checked out his rearview mirror again where he saw thick, gray plumes rising in the sky, the scene like those pictures you saw on the news showing the smoky aftermath of multiple Middle East car bombs. Pryor grinned at the sight of the chaos he'd created. Grinned and then very nearly giggled when, a minute later, two more sheriff's cruisers blew past, lights and sirens wailing, one and then another. Pryor was used to his plans working. No shit.

But this was unfolding perfectly, like a vividly imagined dream coming true after you wake up. Draw the cops out of town with flames, leaving the bank as exposed as a deer in the middle of a wide-open field.

And now this. A line of people waiting for the bank to open. A woman at the head of the line, rocking a baby stroller as she balanced a boy of about two on her hip. Behind her, an old lady, white-haired and frail, leaning on a cane. Behind her, a dad trailed by three kids, two girls and a boy, each dressed in red soccer uniforms and cleats. Behind them, a farmer in overalls, and then two Amish men with their dark clothes and suspenders and hats and those weird wizard-y beards with the upper lip bare. So many people. So much money. And no one around to stop him. Because everyone with a gun and uniform in town was at the fire.

Pryor put the van in park, reached onto the seat opposite him, grabbed the plastic sack he retrieved from his backpack, and pulled out the mask. The one he bought months ago in the costume shop, the day he grinned as Penny turned pale as chicken fat laid open by a knife as he walked in. President Trump. SAD. Not sad. He put it on. He smiled. It was time.

67

J. P. roused himself and looked at the girl. "You said we were going to stop someplace and call."

"I lied," Penny said.

"This is insane."

"You've got that right."

"Then stop. We can't do this alone."

"No. We're almost there."

Helpless, aching from his injuries, J. P. sat in the passenger seat of the red Honda Pilot as the pale green Darbytown water tower grew closer and closer. He couldn't quite make out the town motto wrapped around the base of the tank, despite the fact it was painted in letters three feet high. It didn't matter. Everyone knew it. "The Little Town with The Big Heart." He thought of Marks's version, unerringly uttered with a boyish guffaw that was old the first time J. P. heard it: "The Little Town with The Big *Fart*!"

He was having trouble focusing, was the problem. Shapes went hazy, then clear, then hazy, as though he couldn't quite blink away water in his eyes after a shower. Guessing it was the final blow to the head that did it, the one he received after clocking Pryor on the chin in his fruitless attempt to delay them, to steal a few seconds from their plan. Just a few seconds: that's all he wanted. But it could have been from any number of his injuries, come to think of it. There were plenty to choose from.

"Are you okay?"

He turned and looked at the girl. She had a thin face, her chin strong and her brow high, and she wore her brown hair in a tight ponytail. Fit, but not like a jock. Like she lived on a farm, though he sensed she was from the city, from Columbus maybe. Her eyes dark with exhaustion. He considered further arguing the point about the phone. Insisting they stop and signal the rescue vehicles and cruisers flying past. But he just didn't have the energy. It was easier at this point just drifting along as she drove. Falling in and out of consciousness. And she was right—they were almost there anyway.

Now she glanced at him, saw him staring, and repeated her question: "Are you okay?"

"I don't know."

"What's that supposed to mean?"

"Everything hurts. But I don't think anything's broken."

"That's good, I guess."

They traveled for another minute, the van straddling the middle of the road when traffic was clear, the girl pushing the speed on the straightaways. J. P. watched the fields of corn rush past like waves carved open by a boat's prow.

"What's your name?"

"Penny."

"I'm J. P."

"Nice to meet you, J. P."

"Nice to meet you too." He cleared his throat. "That guy. Pryor."

She didn't say anything, just kept her eyes on the road. Between them, a pile of burnt yarn, something that might have been a piece of clothing once. Two knitting needles jutting out of the smoky mess like meat skewers.

"What about him?"

"Who is he?"

"What do you mean?"

"Just that," J. P. said. "Who is he?"

"He's a bad guy."

"I think I figured that part out." He grinned, even though it hurt his face to move those particular muscles. She looked at him and smiled herself.

"How do you know him?"

She shrugged. "Everybody knows him."

"Is he a friend?"

"No."

"But you know him."

"I just said that."

"But he's not a friend."

"Dogs know if another dog is vicious. Doesn't mean they're friends."

"How did you find me? How did you know where to look?"

"It's a long story."

"You saved my life."

She didn't reply, but after a moment nodded, as if it were a point in an argument about religion or sports teams she'd never considered before.

"Take a right," J. P. said, as they approached a stop sign.

"Thanks."

As she turned onto the London–Darbytown Road, Penny started talking. Quietly at first, a few words at a time, then louder and in longer and longer sentences. Pouring out words, as though she'd bottled things up for years that suddenly needed to be told. About her boyfriend, Myles, and how Pryor shot him. About a girl named Mae, and a guy named Lem, and about someone called Robby. She told J. P. something about a motel he wasn't quite sure he believed but he kept listening anyway, not interrupting.

They passed the sign welcoming them to Darbytown, and a minute later drove past the Dutch House Inn. The parking lot was full, which was not surprising on a Saturday morning on such a beautiful fall day.

"That's pretty amazing," he said when she finished.

"I guess. I'm sorry I didn't do more. I'm sorry I missed."

"You didn't miss. You hit him. I'm pretty sure you took off his ear."

"But I didn't kill him."

"You did your best."

"Like that means shit."

"It does to me," J. P. said.

She didn't respond. But what she was thinking was: maybe it was true. Maybe you couldn't really kill Pryor.

A few seconds passed, and then she said: "How did your father die?"

"What?"

"Your father. Back at the farm. You said he died. How?"

J. P. swallowed. He thought about the story she just told him. He thought about his realization in the barn. *So. Fire and fuel. Just like my father.*

"He burned to death."

She glanced over at him, nodding once before looking back down the road.

"It was right around this time of year," J. P. said. Starting slowly, but warming up as he went. "Five years ago. Late at night. He pulled over a guy from Columbus two blocks from the station. White Blazer, pretty beat up. Expired tags and the right rear brake light out. The guy was wanted on a minor warrant. For some reason, after my dad had him stopped and got out of his cruiser, the guy took off. Nobody's ever understood that part. Why run, *after* he was stopped? My dad went back to his cruiser and chased him."

Not, as the reports later read, *initiated a pursuit of the vehicle.* He had chased him, plain and simple.

"So, what happened?"

"They were on the old Marysville Road, which kind of winds around the deeper it goes into the country. There's a curve about two miles out of Darbytown where it bends around a little creek. You have to be careful, especially at night if the mist rises and the road gets slick. Been a lot of accidents there over the years. My dad was already braking two hundred yards back, knowing it was coming, but this guy took it at seventy or eighty. Never had a chance. Overcorrected, went airborne, hit a tree head-on. My dad pulled up twenty seconds later. He got out and you could see the smoke pouring from the car's engine. On the dash cam video, I mean. He radioed for help and ran into the field and up to the tree and pried the front door open and tried to pull the guy free. He almost did it too. He almost had him. From the video it looks like the guy's foot was stuck under something and that's what delayed him. Exactly five seconds too long. Then the van exploded. It turned out the guy had three plastic gas containers in the back and one of them hadn't been closed right and spilled after the crash. They were both gone when the ambulance showed up. He never had a chance. My dad, I mean."

Finished, he looked shyly at Penny. She drove, not meeting his gaze. He realized he had never told the story like that before. The whole thing. There had never been any reason to. Everyone he knew already knew what happened. Had heard it from someone else or read it in the papers or saw it on TV or on the computer. Even June, the day they met at church, her very first week in town as one of the new schoolteachers, had known about it thanks to the girlfriend she came with. Though of course she didn't mention it at the time.

They took a left onto Main and headed toward the square. Trees just beginning to turn—patches of red and yellow leaves standing out against the brilliant blue sky. J. P.'s heart sank as he saw how crowded the little downtown was. In his fog he forgot about the farmer's market and the Amish baked goods sale. So many people.

Penny pulled the Pilot into a parking spot two blocks down on the other side of the street from the bank.

"Let's go."

"What?"

"I said let's go."

"Go?"

"Into the bank," Penny said. "We need to get in there—right now."

"No," J. P. heard himself say.

"No?"

"I can't."

"What are you talking about?"

"I can't do it."

68

"Can't do it?" Penny said. "Are you fucking serious?"

"I," the deputy said, haltingly. "I just don't—"

"Don't what?"

"I don't know if I can. I don't know if I can go in there."

"Why not?"

"I can't explain it. My father. What happened. Everything. What they—"

"What they what?"

"What they did to me, back there. In the barn. And what I saw inside the farmhouse. I haven't told you that part."

"He killed the aunt and uncle, didn't he?"

He stared at her. "How did you know?"

"I know Pryor. I know how he is."

"Then you can understand what I'm saying."

"No. I can't. I don't get it."

"Don't get what?"

"You." She looked in frustration at the bank entrance. "Why are you being like this?"

"Like what?"

"Why are you so scared?"

"Why am I scared? What about you? Why are you so angry?"

They glared at each other for a long moment.

Penny said, "I'm angry because Myles betrayed me. He was home one day, one single fucking day, and then went and got himself shot. Trying to go after Pryor himself, alone, instead of talking to me about it, telling me what he was going to do. And look what happened. He's in the hospital. I lost my job. I stole this car"—no point in lying to herself any further—"I let a guy . . ." She trailed off, thinking of Mae's pimp, the guy Pryor sold her to, slumped on the parking lot asphalt, struggling for breath that wouldn't come. That would never come.

"You saved that girl."

"What girl?"

"The prostitute. You saved her."

"Who cares? Who gives a shit? This is all Myles's fault."

"It was Myles's fault that Pryor shot him?"

"No," she said. "Yes. I don't know. Why did he do that?"

"Maybe he was trying to protect you. You and your boy."

"You don't do that kind of shit with Pryor. You just don't—"

"Don't what? Don't be brave?"

"You don't know what you're talking about."

"Maybe not. But you can't blame Myles for what happened. Maybe it wasn't the smartest thing to go after Pryor like that. But you just said you know him, what kind of guy he is. Blaming Myles for getting shot is like, I don't know, blaming a tree for letting a tornado suck it up."

Penny stared out the van window, feeling her heart race. She thought about what she told Robby, in the AFD. *You told Pryor where they lived. . . . That's like pushing wood into a buzz saw.*

She said, "You didn't answer my question."

"What?"

"Why are you so scared?"

"Scared?"

"You heard me."

He swallowed. "Because of my father."

"Your father?"

"I'm scared because all I ever wanted to do was to be as good as him. And I'll never get that chance now. I tried, back in the barn, but I couldn't do it."

"That's not true."

"Yes it is. I couldn't stop them."

"Stop Pryor? Did you hear yourself, just now? What you told me?"

"That's different."

"Bullshit. And the fact is, you're sitting here with me. You know what that means? You're not as good as your father. You've got that part right. You're *better*. Do you know why? Because you're alive. You're alive and he's not."

"Stop—"

"You may not like that fact. You may hate it the rest of your life. But it's the truth. And you know it. You just won't admit it."

"How dare you."

She opened the car door.

"What are you doing?" the deputy said.

"I'm going in there."

"By yourself? Alone?"

"Why not? Myles did."

"No."

"I'm not stopping now. Not after coming this far."

"You can't—"

Penny reached into Brandi's purse, pulled out the Glock, and showed it to J. P., butt end first. "See this?"

"Where did you get that?"

"Yes or no, goddamn it."

"Yes. I see it."

“Okay, then,” she said, shifting the gun to her left hand as she grabbed the pile of knitting and the two needles between them, climbed out of the car, and slammed the door.

He caught up with her halfway down the street. He held her eyes as he reached out and took the gun from her. He shifted it in his own hands and took her left hand with his right. And held it. She glanced at him but didn’t let go. She realized she couldn’t see the gun; he put it away some place. His hand was warm, and a little sweaty, but also strong. It had been a while since she held a strong hand. He was limping, badly. His shirt was torn and his pants were ripped with burn marks in four different places. They walked that way, hand in hand, all the way down the street to the bank.

69

At first, Pryor thought he'd go for the woman with the kid in her arms. Two hostages in one. Except the stroller complicated things, not that he gave a shit about babies. What changed his mind was seeing the lady in the lobby through the glass doors. Alone, chatting with someone in line. A bank employee, to judge by her blue blouse.

He opened the door, walked inside, pointed his gun at the ceiling and fired once. He lowered the gun, reached out with his left arm and jerked it around the employee's neck.

"Everybody down," he yelled through the mask, not screaming but so everyone could hear him. When nobody moved, he put the gun to the woman's head. "Everybody down or I'm painting the walls with this lady's brains."

Everybody lay down.

He stayed where he was, not approaching the counter. A common, though understandable mistake. One he'd made himself, once. They could hear him from where he was, plenty good. And the camera angles were worse, if anything went south with the mask.

He shouted the demands. Money, no dye packs, no secret alarms or he'd shoot the woman standing frozen beside him, the stench of fear rising through her blouse. It was also possible, Pryor thought with secret pleasure, that she'd soiled herself.

He figured he bought himself five, maybe ten minutes with the fire. The town emptied of law enforcement. Not a great margin, but tons more than he usually had. So much more. He'd be on the highway by the time sirens started screaming.

He watched the tellers moving swiftly, their actions accompanied by quiet sobs and sniffing from people on the floor. A child at the far side of the lobby was crying. He was just about to tell the kid to shut it or else when he heard a sound behind him. The door was opening. He turned and squinted through the mask. A heavy-set man in a torn brown shirt and pants limped into the lobby toward him, his hands raised high over his head. No, he thought to himself. No. It wasn't possible. The deputy. The deputy?

Behind him came a girl holding something in her right hand. A girl he knew. No. Doubly not possible.

"Penny," Pryor said.

70

"You shot Myles."

"What are you doing here?"

"You fucking shot Myles," Penny said.

She watched as he hesitated. Even with his face hidden by the Trump mask, she could tell he was taken aback. Something had happened he hadn't counted on.

"Get down," Pryor said.

"No."

Pryor yanked hard on the neck of the woman he was holding. She gurgled in pain and distress. Her face was red, like she was having a hard time breathing or about to have a heart attack. Or both.

"Get down or I'm going to fucking kill her. You know I will."

"No," Penny said.

"Yes."

She started. The deputy had spoken. J. P.

"I'm not getting down," she said to him.

"Yes," he said. "It's too late."

"You're goddamn right it's too late," Pryor said.

"You said—"

"I didn't say anything," the deputy said. "Lie down. It's over."

"You coward," Penny said, defiantly.

"I'm sorry," the deputy said.

"No."

"Now, I said," he yelled.

71

J. P. didn't want to. He could see the pain in Penny's face. But he had to do it. It was clear to him what had to happen. He was only surprised he hadn't thought of it before. Because it was all a question of time, in the end. Time you had and time you didn't. What his father discovered at the last moment, when it was too late. You never knew when time was up and when another few seconds would have mattered, until it's too late. Until the time you need isn't there anymore.

He took a step back until he was even with Penny, groaning at the effort, but kept his eyes on Pryor. Keeping his right arm in the air, he put his left hand on her shoulder.

"I told you to get down."

"And I told you I'm not going to."

"He's going to kill that lady."

Jan. *Lucky man, J. P.*

"I thought you said you were going to help me," Penny said.

"And I told you it's too late."

"No it's—"

"Jesus Christ," Pryor yelled at Penny. "Would you just listen for one second in your life, you stupid fucking loudmouth—"

That was it. That was all J. P. needed. Just a couple seconds. Just a little more time. It was what he'd been going for in the barn with the upthrust of his head a few hours earlier, cracking Pryor on the chin in defiance of death. A pause just long enough to slow things down. All he wanted since his father's death. He lowered his right hand in a quick, smooth motion and pulled the Glock through the gap in his torn shirt, the weight of the gun familiar, the grip warm from his body heat. He pushed Penny down, hard, raised his hand and fired three quick shots.

Jan screamed and twisted away and fell to the floor as Pryor jerked backward like something flailing on a string. Momentarily deafened, J. P. limped toward Pryor, his gun arm extended. Pryor lay on the floor on his back, blood welling from his right shoulder, but still alive to judge by his movements. J. P. breathed through his nose in dissatisfaction. The red-hot fork tines had taken their toll. His aim off by just that much. Pryor raised himself to his knees and used his feet to inch back, a foot at a time, away from the advancing deputy. At first J. P. thought he was trying to avoid being shot again. Then he saw Pryor's right hand start to rise, his own gun still in it. J. P. sighted the Glock but felt his left knee buckle and knew he was too late.

72

Penny ran. Ran as fast as she could. Ran not as if her life depended on it—which it did, of course—but because Myles's did. Myles, and so many others.

Funny, because Myles had always been the sprinter, no matter how the coaches treated him. Somehow they always focused on his name, like that meant anything. She's the one who could run the miles, after all, who could take the long journey and not be bothered by it. He was always the one with the speed. The gun and the go. Avoid the molasses of hesitation. Why couldn't they see that?

She didn't bother with the gun in J. P.'s hand, the deputy on his knees, struggling to stand. She wasn't running the risk of a near-miss again. She plucked a needle from the ruined mess of a sweater. The stupid fucking sweater she'd been dragging all over town. Destroyed now, thanks to the fire at the barn. The needle in her hand feeling far more natural than the Glock ever had. It seemed so stupid to bring the knitting along on her search for Myles, on her journey. But it made sense now, at last, why she'd done so, and she was glad. There had been a purpose, after all.

"Penny," Pryor said, gun rising in his hand.

She had to guess a little, with the mask still over his head. No time to pull it off. But she had a pretty good idea, having stared at Pryor—and been stared at—so many times. *Nice tits.* She fell to her knees and used both hands, fingers grasping the needle near the top. The metal felt cool and a little slippery in her grip. She thought about the way Ma-Maw taught her to hold it, firmly but not too tight.

"Penny," Pryor repeated. "All this for Baby?"

"His name is Myles," she said, plunging the point through the eyehole of the mask and into Pryor's good eye. She felt a crunch as she applied her full weight and drove down, hard. Pryor screeched and jerked and twisted as though he'd been hit with several volts of electric current. She recoiled as Pryor somehow managed to raise his left hand and grasp her wrist, but then his fingers loosened as blood poured through the mask like water from a spring uncovered by a farmer's shovel. The hand fell away a second later and settled on the carpet where it shook a moment, then went still.

Trembling, Penny heard what sounded like a siren far, far in the distance.

73

"There's something wrong with your hair."

"It's fine."

"Come here, Deputy."

J. P. walked to his wife, his arms by his sides.

"It's the cowlick," June said, reaching out and smoothing it with her right hand. "It has a mind of its own. Your mom is right. And the patch where it got burned isn't helping."

"I probably need to go."

"Just give me a minute."

She worked diligently, moistening her fingers, smoothing and tugging, finally producing a comb from someplace. Changed into the sweat clothes she liked to put on after school. The sweat clothes she put on after she came home and took her school clothes off and they had a moment in bed. Their first since everything happened. Not babymaking anymore, he supposed, now that he'd seen the blue strip on the test. He told her he was afraid of hurting her or the baby or something, and maybe they should be careful.

"Oh, so maybe just do it on your birthday?" she tut-tutted.

"I'm just saying," J. P. said, pushing away the thought of Jan and Hank Rittmaier. It had not gone well for the bank manager when he confessed that Pryor knew about the bank and its operations because Hank had been visiting one of Pryor's prostitutes when everyone thought he was on business in Columbus.

All those thoughts evaporated as June reached for him in bed. "And I'm saying, that's not the way it works, Deputy," she said.

Now, as June worked on the cowlick he breathed in the smell of her perfume and shut his eyes so she wouldn't be able to tell what he was thinking. At last she stood back to examine him.

"Perfect. Now you're one hundred percent handsome."

He blushed. She was always saying things like that. Her—so beautiful, yet she was the one finding compliments for him.

"Okay. Now you can go. I've got church tonight. We'll probably go out afterward. Can I bring you anything?"

"If they have pie."

"Apple?"

"Or pecan. Or shoofly. That sounds good."

She laughed. "All of them?"

"Why not? I'm eating for three now."

"Ha ha. That's my line."

"Then we both are, I guess."

"If you say so, Deputy. All right. Goodbye. Good luck."

"Goodbye," J. P. said, reaching out and giving her a hug. "I'll see you tonight."

"Wake me when you get home."

"I will."

◆

Joyce stood up from behind the glass lobby window and waved when J. P. walked into the station. He smiled and waved back, distractedly, trying to gauge whether his left leg was in danger of buckling. It hurt a little when he climbed out of the car in the parking lot, as it sometimes did if he moved a funny way or put too much weight on it too fast. It had only been ten days, and the doctor said he was ready, but he didn't want to be at anything less than full strength.

The roster room was full even though he was five minutes early. Vick was there, of course, and the entire afternoon shift—Dalton, Livingston, Jenks—but Sheriff Waters came by too. He was the first to shake J. P.'s hand when the round of applause died down. A light round.

"It's good to have you back, Deputy."

"It's good to be back, sir."

The sheriff cleared his throat and said a few words, and J. P. blushed for the second time in an hour. When the sheriff was done he shook J. P.'s hand again and told him how proud he was of him and left the room. It was four o'clock on the nose. When the sheriff went home each day. The rest of them stood and stared at J. P. It was Marks who broke the silence.

"Pretty good shooting."

"Thanks."

"Almost killed the sonofabitch."

"Almost."

"But the girl finished him off."

"That's right."

"Good thing she was there."

"I guess."

"I mean, because you didn't kill him."

J. P. didn't say anything.

Marks looked around the room, taking in his audience. J. P. watched out of the corner of his eye to see who met Marks's glance and who turned away.

"Had a rule, in Iraq. You start something, you finish it. Period."

"In Iraq," J. P. said.

"Damn straight."

J. P. shifted from foot to foot. There was no question about it. His left leg ached a bit more than his right, from absorbing his full weight after they dropped him during the fight before the photo in front of the van. Whatever that was about. His leg and his hip and his knees. He was doing exercises with the physical therapist each day, squats and knee lifts and that one that made him feel like a goose as he balanced on one foot with his arms stretched wide, self-conscious thanks to the full-length mirrors that encircled the therapist's exercise room. He had also begun walking around the block once he was awake for real in the morning to work out the stiffness. He was up to almost a mile and a half. It felt good to be out in the cool fall air so early. He saw a deer today, in the fields across from the school. He thought about June inside, already hard at work with her class.

"You weren't in Iraq," J. P. said.

Marks looked hard at him. "What did you say?"

"I said you weren't in Iraq."

The room went as quiet as the bank the day of the robbery.

"The hell—"

"June's brother checked you out. He served three tours. He has a Purple Heart. He has a way of looking that kind of thing up. You were in Kuwait. Doing requisitions or something. Paperwork. Like a clerk, he said, except not even that high up. Like an assistant, assistant clerk."

"June's brother?"

"He said none of that stuff would ever happen. Ripping off a lady's burqa? No way. He said they drilled on proper behavior all the time."

"So he's some kind of expert?"

"He is. Served three tours, like I said."

"That fat little bitch. *Junebug.* You put her up to that? Or was that her idea?"

"I would appreciate you not talking about June like that."

"Go to hell. I'll talk about her any way I want. Stupid cow. Let me tell you something, J. P.—"

He didn't finish the sentence. J. P. walked up to him, looked him in the eye, and punched him in the nose. Just once, but hard, very hard, like his father taught him. No need to show off. Most men, they take a fist to the nose, it's Good Night, Irene. No exception today.

"The fuck," Marks said, stumbling back, shock in his eyes like someone was at the door he hadn't expected to see for a long, long time. He raised his hands to his face. Blood bloomed through his fingers. J. P. braced for what might come next. It wasn't what he thought. Marks took his hands away from his face, looked at the blood, and fell to the floor as his eyes rolled into the back of his head.

J. P. dropped onto one knee to see if Marks was all right. As he did, Marks's eyes opened and he saw J. P. and his right arm involuntarily flinched, hitting the bottom of the lockers, and J. P. felt something sharp hit him and fall to his side with a loud splintering sound. He reached up and rubbed the top of his head. That hurt a bit, whatever it was. As he lowered his hands Marks flinched again and he let out a long, high squeal of fear. The squeal filled the roster room like a smoke alarm. It seemed to last forever. Everyone in the building must have heard it. You couldn't help yourself. J. P. thought it might have been the loudest, longest squeal he ever heard, and he spent a lot of time as a boy around his grandfather's hogs."Okay, now," he heard Vick say from behind him. He felt the lieutenant's hand on his shoulder.

"Sorry, Vick," J. P said. "But if you don't take your hand off me in two seconds flat I'm going to put you through the wall."

When he heard the lieutenant scuttle backward, he cleared his throat.

"What I said," J. P. said, directing his comments to Marks, "Was that I would appreciate you not talking about June like that."

"June like that," Marks croaked.

With the ache in his left leg and all, it took J. P. two attempts to stand. It was only when he was upright that he saw what hit him on the head. His father's framed photo, the one hanging above the lockers. The vibration of Marks's arm smacking the locker must have caused it to drop. It lay on the ground beside Marks, the glass shattered in a spider web emanating from a point by his father's chin. J. P. reached down and picked the picture up and set it carefully on the table. He didn't want any of the glass pieces falling on the floor where someone might accidentally cut himself. He straightened up and keyed his radio.

"Joyce? It's J. P."

"Unit 12?"

"Just J. P. There's a change in the shift roster. Deputy Marks isn't feeling well. Let's send Livingston out to Route 31 instead, and I'll take his warrants and then go on patrol. Dalton and Jenks are fine the way they are. But be sure those wellness checks get done out at Darby Lane Estates. A couple people have already gone to Florida for the season and those houses are sitting empty."

Static crackled over the radio during almost ten seconds of silence. J. P. knew if he just ducked his head out the door he could have practically seen Joyce down the hall, sitting at the console, working things out in her head.

"Unit 38 knows about this?" she said at last.

"Vick knows, yes."

"Okay. Ten-four."

"Ten-four," J. P. said. What the heck.

He turned and looked at Vick, who was staring at him as if J. P. had gone and died and then sat up at his own calling hours. J. P. waited until Vick dropped his gaze before stepping back toward the lockers, avoiding Marks and the blood on the floor around him. "There's a mop in the utility closet down the hall," J. P. said. "It'd be good to clean all that up before it dries."

"I didn't—" Marks said.

"Thank you," J. P. said, and left the room to begin his shift.

74

Penny squinted through the windshield of Randy's Pilot as she made a right off Sullivant onto Hilltonia, trying to find the garden. It had been a while since she was last over here, even though the neighborhood was barely a mile from Mama's house. She drove two blocks, looking this way and that, until at last she spied it. The grounds were bigger than she expected. Nearly half an acre if you counted the flowers planted on the outside edge of the fence. One of the houses that once made up the property burned a couple of years ago and the second was a boarded-up drug den. Just little cottages in this neighborhood. Both demolished under some city program and turned into a community vegetable garden. Volunteers hauled in topsoil and manure to work the earth. It was only after everything happened that someone told Penny the manure came from a farm out in Darby County. That sounded about right.

"There he is." Penny pointed at the man on his knees on the far side of the plot.

"Yeah," Myles said.

Penny helped him out of the car. It took him a while. He still had to use the cane. She hadn't been thrilled about the idea, a trip like this, but Myles said it was time. She let him go ahead of her. She tried taking Mack's hand but he skipped past her until he was side by side with

Myles. Slowly, they walked to the gate into the garden. Gus trotted after them, tail wagging as if it were the first time he'd ever been outside. Penny looked back at the SUV. She wasn't sure how much longer they would have it. Brandi told her just to hang on to it and not worry about the insurance for now. She had more important things to worry about, starting with the divorce.

Slowly, flinching a little, Myles lifted the latch on the garden gate and let Mack go in first and then Penny, Gus right behind her. He followed and latched the gate behind them. The garden was laid out in a tic-tac-toe design with paths running between the raised beds and the tomato cages and the stakes for the beans. The ten rows of corn ridiculously tiny to Penny after being in the country, like a drainage pond after you've seen the ocean. She wondered how in the world they survived the neighborhood raccoons. Yet several ears extended from the tall stalks, so fat and ripe it seemed they might pop off at any moment.

"Larry," she called, hoping to catch his attention before they marched right up on him.

"He looks good," Myles said.

"He looks tired."

"I know how he feels."

The man turned at the sound of his name and shielded his eyes from the late afternoon sun. He was wearing a Mid-Ohio Vintage Days T-shirt and cut-off blue jeans and red sneakers. He had on work gloves and beside him lay a pile of weeds. Trying to make out who it was, his face uncertain. He rose stiffly and brushed dirt off his knees and removed the gloves and stuck them in a rear pocket.

"You found me."

"It wasn't hard," Penny said.

Myles stepped forward—step, cane, step, cane—stopped, and looked as if he might say something. Instead he took another step and reached out his right hand. His father took it and they stood like that for a moment, joined together but not moving. Not exactly a shake, Penny thought. More like a dance invitation stopped short in its tracks.

"You're okay?" Larry said, dropping his hand.

"Yeah," Myles said.

"I came to see you. In the hospital."

"I heard. I'm sorry I don't remember."

"You should be," Larry said with a grin.

"Thanks for coming."

"I'm glad you're okay."

"So am I."

"How about you?" The question directed at Penny.

"I'm fine."

"And you?" Larry said to Mack. The boy turned and buried his head in Penny's waist.

"He's good," Penny and Myles said at the same time.

"You did all this?" Myles said, pointing at the garden.

"Me and a few others," his father said. "Couple Mexican ladies and one Black family and one little guy I'm not sure what he is. Kind of share the duties."

"It's good," Myles said.

"What will you do?"

Myles stood without answering, looking past his father, over his shoulder at something in the distance.

"I'm not sure yet. May be a while before I can work again. Can't lift anything much, right now."

"What about you?" Larry said to Penny. "Still at that costume shop?"

"Not likely. But the lady found me a different job anyway."

"Lady?"

"The deputy's wife. Their church runs a daycare over here. For poor people. But they pay pretty good. I start Monday. Mack can go for free. We were sort of hoping—"

Myles raised his hand before she could finish. Penny felt her face warm. But then she saw how nervous he was. The fingers on the hand he'd lifted were trembling like reeds waving underwater.

"I was going to ask if you had anything at the garage," Myles said.

"The garage?"

"I learned some things, up at Mansfield. They had an auto-body shop. I was just thinking."

"Were you now?"

Myles's father looked at him, and sort of smiled. After a moment, he reached out and poked Mack in the neck and grinned as the boy giggled. To Penny, he said, "Can you grab one of those?" Gestured at a pair of straw bales at the edge of the fence. "We've got some pretty good pumpkins going over here and I want to mulch them one last time before it rains. Otherwise they may rot."

"Sure."

Myles and Mack helped Larry tear fist-sized clumps off and working together they scattered the loose straw under the pumpkin vines. Penny took the opportunity to pull out her phone and check the time. A real phone, finally, thanks also to the deputy's wife. She saw she had a text from Lessner. The detective. *Just checking in. You OK?* She almost didn't reply but then shot him a thumbs-up emoji at the last second. Probably paid to stay on his good side. With Pryor dead—and Archie, and Michigan—there wasn't much to investigate at this point, though Lessner continued to ask both her and Myles about the gun. Penny told him she had no idea and Myles said he couldn't remember anything about that day. Which might have been true.

She looked at her phone again. Almost four o'clock. She might have time for a workout before dinner. She'd run the past two afternoons, just circling the block, Myles sitting on the porch with Mack and Mama, watching, applauding each time she passed; her grinning as she ran and him threatening to lace up his own shoes soon and beat her by a mile.

"You wish," she said. But she didn't doubt it. He'd always been the faster of the two, after all. The gun and the go. Whereas Penny was the one with endurance, with perseverance, the person who could step out there and stretch her legs a little and then run and run forever.

ACKNOWLEDGEMENTS

I'm grateful to Jen Del Carmen, Bill Parker, and Dawn Stock, who read early versions of *The End of The Road* and offered valuable suggestions and insights. I'm also appreciative of several people who encouraged my fiction writing before and during the book's drafting, including Kristopher Armstrong, Rusty Barnes, Nancy Basmajian, Gillian Berchowitz, Michael Bracken, Kerry Carter, Ehsan Ehsani, Lori Lewis Ham, Rick Huard, Janet Hutchings, Jeff Kallet, Linda Kass, Linda Landrigan, Andrea Murray, Johnny Temple, and David Weaver, among many others. Special thanks to Otto Penzler at Mysterious Press and my agent, Victoria Skurnick, for believing in this project and taking it on. Lyrics from *Ohio* used courtesy of Karin Bergquist, *Over the Rhine*. This book is dedicated to William McCulloh, Kenyon College Classics professor emeritus, who taught me Homeric Greek, corrected my errors with wit and grace, and bent rules to allow me to write a historical novel for my senior thesis, which sent me down all sorts of welcome paths. As always, I reserve my greatest thanks for my wife, Pam, who makes sure I never look back but always keep my eyes on the road ahead.